# Blonde Faith

## Walter Mosley

W F HOWES LTD

This large print edition published in 2008 by
W F Howes Ltd
Unit 4, Rearsby Business Park, Gaddesby Lane,
Rearsby, Leicester LE7 4YH

1  3  5  7  9  10  8  6  4  2

First published in the United Kingdom in 2008
by Weidenfeld and Nicolson. An Hachette Livre.
UK Company

A CIP catalogue record for this book is available
from the British Library

ISBN 978 1 40741 342 6

Typeset by Palimpsest Book Production Limited,
Grangemouth, Stirlingshire
Printed and bound in Great Britain
by Antony Rowe Ltd, Chippenham, Wilts.

In memory of August Wilson

# CHAPTER 1

It's hard to get lost when you're coming home from work.

When you have a job, and a paycheck, the road is set right out in front of you: a paved highway with no exits except yours. There's the parking lot, the grocery store, the kids' school, the cleaner's, the gas station, and then your front door.

But I hadn't had a regular job in a year and here it was two in the afternoon and I was pulling into my driveway wondering what I was doing there. I cut off the engine and then shuddered, trying to fit inside the sudden stillness.

All morning I had been thinking about Bonnie and what I'd lost when I sent her away. She'd saved my adopted daughter's life, and I had repaid her by making her leave our home.

In order to get little Feather into a Swiss clinic, Bonnie had reacquainted herself with Joguye Cham, a West African prince she had met in her work as a flight attendant for Air France. He made a temporary home for Feather, and Bonnie stayed there with her – and him.

I threw open the car door but didn't get out.

1

Part of my lethargy was exhaustion from being up for the past twenty-four hours.

I didn't have a regular job, but I worked like a dog.

Martel Johnson had hired me to find his runaway sixteen-year-old daughter, Chevette. He'd gone to the police and they had taken down her information, but two weeks had gone by and they hadn't turned up a thing. I told Martel that I'd do the footwork for three hundred dollars. On any other transaction he would have tried to dicker with me, giving me a down payment and promising the balance when and if I did the job. But when a man loves his child he will do anything to have her safely home.

I pocketed the money, spoke to a dozen of Chevette's high school friends, and then made the rounds of various alleys in the general vicinity of Watts.

Most of that time I was thinking about Bonnie, about calling her and asking her to come home to me. I missed her milky breath and the spiced teas she brewed. I missed her mild Guyanese accent and our long talks about freedom. I missed everything about her and me, but I couldn't make myself stop at a pay phone.

Where I came from – Fifth Ward, Houston, Texas – another man sleeping with your woman was more than reason enough for justifiable double homicide. Every time I thought of her in his arms my vision sputtered and I had to close my eyes.

My adoptive daughter still saw Bonnie at least once a week. The boy I raised as my son, Jesus, and his common-law wife, Benita Flagg, treated Bonnie as the grandmother of their newborn daughter, Essie.

I loved them all and in turning my back on Bonnie I had lost them.

And so, at 1:30 in the morning, at the mouth of an alley off Avalon, when a buxom young thing in a miniskirt and halter top had come up to my window, I rolled down the glass and asked, 'How much to suck my dick?'

'Fifteen dollars, daddy,' she said in a voice both sweet and high.

'Um,' I stalled. 'Up front or after?'

She sucked a tooth and stuck out a hand. I put three new five-dollar bills across her palm, and she hurried around to the passenger side of my late-model Ford. She had dark skin and full cheeks ready to smile for the man with the money.

When I turned toward her I detected a momentary shyness in her eyes, but then she put on a brazen look and said, 'Let's see what you got.'

'Can I ask you somethin' first?'

'You paid for ten minutes; you can do whatever you want with it.'

'Are you happy doing this, Chevette?'

Her years went from thirty to sixteen in one second flat. She reached for the door, but I grabbed her wrist.

'I'm not tryin' to stop you, girl,' I said.

3

'Then let me go.'

'You got my money. All I'm askin' is my ten minutes,' I said, letting her wrist go.

Chevette settled down after looking at my other hand and around the front seat for signs of danger.

'Okay,' she said, staring into the darkness of the floor. 'But we stay right here.'

I lifted her chin with one finger and gazed into her big eyes until she turned away.

'Martel hired me to find you,' I said. 'He's all broken up. I told him I'd ask you to come home but I wouldn't drag you there.'

The woman-child glanced at me then.

'But I have to tell him where you are . . . and about Porky.'

'You cain't tell Daddy 'bout him,' she pleaded. 'One'a them get killed sure.'

Porky the Pimp had recruited Chevette three blocks away from Jordan High. He was a pock-faced fat man with a penchant for razors, diamond rings, and women.

'Martel's your father,' I reasoned. 'He deserves to know what happened with you.'

'Porky'll cut him. He'll kill him.'

'Or the other way around,' I said. 'Martel hired me to find you and tell him where you are. That's how I pay my mortgage, girl.'

'I could pay you,' she suggested, placing a hand on my thigh. 'I got seventy-fi'e dollars in my purse. And, and you said you wanted some company.'

'No,' I said. 'I mean . . . you are a fine young thing, but I'm honest and a father too.'

The teenager's face went blank, but I could see that her mind was racing. My appearance had been a possibility that she'd already considered. Not me exactly but some man who either knew her or wanted to save her. After twenty blow jobs a night for two weeks, she'd have to be thinking about rescue – and about the perils that came along with such an act of desperation. Porky could find her anywhere in Southern California.

'Porky ain't gonna let me go,' she said. 'He cut up one girl that tried to leave him. Cassandra. He cut up her face.'

She put a hand to her cheek. It wasn't a pretty face.

'Oh,' I said, 'I'm almost sure the pig man will listen to reason.'

It was my smile that gave Chevette Johnson hope.

'Where is he?' I asked.

'At the back of the barbershop.'

I took the dull gray .38 from the glove compartment and the keys from the ignition.

Cupping my hand around the girl's chin, I said, 'You wait right here. I don't wanna have to look for you again.'

She nodded into my palm and I went off down the alley.

★   ★   ★

Tall and lanky LaTerry Klegg stood in the doorway of the back porch of Masters and Broad Barber Shop. He looked like a deep brown praying mantis standing in a pool of yellow cream. Klegg had a reputation for being fast and deadly, so I came up on him quickly, slamming the side of my pistol against his jaw.

He went down and I thought of Bonnie for a moment. I wondered, as I looked into the startled face of Porky the Pimp, why she had not called me.

Porky was seated in an old barber's chair that had been moved out on the porch to make room for a newer model, no doubt.

'Who the fuck are you?' the pimp said in a frightened alto voice. He was the color of a pig too, a sickly pinkish brown.

I answered by pressing the barrel of my pistol against his left cheekbone.

'What?' he squeaked.

'Chevette Johnson,' I said. 'Either you let up or I lay you down right here and now.'

I meant it. I was ready to kill him. I wanted to kill him. But even while I stood there on the verge of murder, it came to me that Bonnie would never call. She was too proud and hurt.

'Take her,' Porky said.

My finger was constricting on the trigger.

'Take her!'

I moved my hand three inches to the right and fired. The bullet only nicked the outer earlobe, but his hearing on that side would never be the same. Porky went down to the floor, holding his head and crying out. I kicked him in his gut and walked back down the way I'd come.

On the way to my car, I passed three women in short skirts and high heels that had come running. They gave me a wide berth, seeing the pistol in my hand.

'So why'd you leave home like that?' I asked Chevette at the all-night hamburger stand on Beverly.

She'd ordered a chili burger and fries. I nursed a cream soda.

'They wouldn't let me do nuthin',' she whined. 'Daddy want me to wear long skirts and pony-tails. He wouldn't even let me talk to a boy on the phone.'

Even in a potato sack you could have seen that Chevette was a woman. It had been a long time since she had been a member of the Mickey Mouse Clubhouse.

I drove her to my office and let her sleep on my new blue sofa while I napped, dreaming of Bonnie, in my office chair.

In the morning I called Martel and told him everything – except that Chevette was listening in.

'What you mean, walkin' the streets?' he asked.

'You know what I mean.'

'A prostitute?'

'You still want her back?' I asked.

7

'Of course I want my baby back.'

'No, Marty. I can bring her back, but what you gonna get is a full-grown woman, not no child, not no baby. She gonna need you to let her grow up. She gonna need you to see what she is. 'Cause it won't make a difference her bein' back home if you don't change.'

'She my child, Easy,' he said with deadly certainty.

'The child is gone, Marty. Woman's all that's left.'

He broke down then and so did Chevette. She buried her face in a blue cushion and cried.

I told Martel I'd call him back. We talked three more times before I got all the way through to him. I told him that it wasn't worth it for me to bring her back if he couldn't see her for what she was, if he couldn't love her for what she was.

And all the time, I was thinking about Bonnie. I was thinking that I should call her and beg her to come home.

# CHAPTER 2

It only me ten minutes or so to climb out of
the car.

Walking across the lawn, I heard the little
yellow dog barking. Frenchie hated me and loved
Feather. We had something in common there. I
was happy to hear his canine curses through the
front door. It was the only welcome I deserved.

When I came into the house the seven-pound
dog began screaming and snapping at my shoes.
I squatted down to say hello. This gesture of truce
always made Frenchie run away.

When I looked up to watch him scamper down
the hall toward Feather's room, I saw the little
Vietnamese child Easter Dawn.

'Hello, Mr Rawlins,' the petite eight-year-old
said.

'E.D. Where'd you come from, girl?' I looked
around the room for her village-killing father.

'Vietnam, originally,' the cogent child replied.

'Hi, Daddy,' Feather said, coming from around
the corner.

She was only eleven but seemed much older.
She'd grown a foot and a half in little more than

a year and she had a lean, intelligent face. Feather and Jesus spoke to each other in fluent English, French, and Spanish, which somehow made her conversation seem more sophisticated.

'Where's Juice?' I asked, using Jesus's nickname.

'He and Benny went to get Essie from Benny's mom.' She hesitated a moment and then added, 'I stayed home with E.D. today because I didn't know what else to do.'

I was trying to figure it all out while standing there.

My son had agreed to stay with Feather while I was out looking for Chevette. He and Benita didn't make much money and had only a one-room studio apartment in Venice. When they babysat they could sleep in my big bed, watch TV, and cook on a real stove.

But Jesus had a life, and Feather was supposed to be in school. Easter Dawn Black had no business in my house at all.

The child wore black cotton pants and an unadorned red silk jacket cut in an Asian style. Her long black hair was tied with an orange bow and hung down the front, over her right shoulder.

'Daddy brought me,' Easter said, answering the question in my eyes.

'Why?'

'He told me to tell you that I had to stay here for a while visiting with Feather . . .'

My daughter knelt down then and hugged the smaller child from behind.

10

'. . . He said that you would know how long I had to stay. Do you?'

'You want some coffee, Daddy?' Feather asked.

My adopted daughter had a creamy brown complexion that reflected her complicated racial heritage. Staring into her generous face, I realized for the twentieth time that I could no longer predict the caprice or depth of her heart.

It was with the sadness of this growing separation that I said, 'Sure, baby. Sure.'

I picked up Easter and followed Feather into the kitchen. There I sat in a dinette chair with the doll-size child on my lap.

'You been having a good time with Feather?' I asked.

Easter nodded vehemently.

'Did she make you lunch?'

'Tuna fish and sweet potato pie.'

Looking up into my eyes, Easter relaxed and leaned against my chest. I hadn't known her and her father, Christmas Black, for long, but the confidence he had in me had influenced the child's trust.

'So you and your daddy drove here?' I asked.

'Uh-huh.'

'And was it just you and him in the car?'

'No,' she said. 'There was a lady with yellow hair.'

'What was her name?'

'Miss . . . something. I don't remember.'

'And was this lady up in your house in Riverside?'

11

'We moved away from there,' Easter said, a little wistfully.

'Moved where?'

'Behind a big blue house across the street from the building with a real big tire on the roof.'

'A tire as big as a house?'

'Uh-huh.'

By then the coffee was beginning to percolate.

'Mr Black dropped by this morning,' Feather said. 'He asked me if Easter Dawn could stay for a while and I said okay. Was that okay, Daddy?'

Feather always called me Daddy when she didn't want me to get angry.

'Is my daddy okay, Mr Rawlins?' Easter Dawn asked.

'Your father is the strongest man in the world,' I told her with only the least bit of hyperbole. 'Whatever he's doin', he'll be just fine. I'm sure he's gonna call me and tell me what's going on before the night is through.'

Feather made hot chocolate for her and E.D. We sat around the dinette table like adults having an afternoon visit. Feather talked about what she'd learned concerning American history, and little Easter Dawn listened as if she were a student in class. When we'd visited enough to make Easter feel at home, I suggested that they go in the backyard to play.

★   ★   ★

12

I called Saul Lynx, the man who had introduced me to Easter's father, but his answering service told me that my fellow private detective was out of town for a few weeks. I could have called his home, but if he was on a case he wouldn't have known anything about Christmas.

'Alexander residence,' a white man answered on the first ring of my next call.

'Peter?'

'Mr Rawlins. How are you, sir?'

The transformation of Peter Rhone from salesman to personal manservant to EttaMae Harris would always be astonishing to me. He lost the love of his life in the Watts riots, a lovely young black woman named Nola Payne, and pretty much gave up on the white race. He moved onto the side porch of EttaMae's house and did chores for her and her husband, Raymond 'Mouse' Alexander.

Rhone worked part-time as a mechanic for my old friend Primo in a garage in East LA. He was learning a trade and contributing to the general pot for the upkeep of Etta's home. Peter was paying penance for the death of Nola Payne because in some way he saw himself as the cause of her demise.

'Okay,' I said. 'All right. How's the garage workin' out?'

'I'm cleaning spark plugs now. Pretty soon Jorge is going to show me how to work with an automatic transmission.'

'Huh,' I grunted. 'Raymond around there?'

'I better get Etta for you,' he said, and I knew there was a problem.

'Easy?' Etta said into the phone a moment later.

'Yeah, babe.'

'I need your help.'

'Yes, ma'am,' I said, because I loved Etta as a friend and I had once loved her as I did Bonnie. If she hadn't been mad for my best friend, we'd've had a whole house full of children by that time.

'The police lookin' for Raymond,' she said.

'For what?' I asked.

'Murder.'

'Murder?'

'Some fool name's Pericles Tarr went missin', an' the cops here ev'ry day askin' me what I know about it. If it wasn't for Pete I think they might'a drug me off to jail just for bein' married to Ray.'

None of this was a surprise to me. Raymond lived a life of crime. The diminutive killer was connected to a whole network of heist men that operated from coast to coast, and maybe beyond that. But for all that, I couldn't imagine him involved in a petty murder. It wasn't that Mouse had somehow moved beyond killing; just the opposite was true. But in recent years his blood had cooled, and he rarely lost his temper. If he was to kill somebody nowadays, it would have been in the dead of night, with no witnesses or clues left behind to incriminate him.

'Where is Mouse?' I asked.

'That's what I need to find out,' Etta said. 'He went missin' the day before this Tarr man did. Now he ain't around and the law's all ovah me.'

'So you want me to find him?' I asked, regretting that I had called.

'Yes.'

'What do I do then?'

'I'm worried, Easy,' Etta said. 'These cops is serious. They want my baby under the jailhouse.'

I hadn't heard Etta call Ray *my baby* in many years.

'All right,' I said. 'I'll find him and I'll do what I have to to make sure he's okay.'

'I know this ain't for free, Easy,' Etta told me. 'I'm'a pay you for it.'

'Uh-huh. You know anything about this Tarr?'

'Not too much. He's married and got a whole house full'a chirren.'

'Where does he live?'

'On Sixty-third Street.' She recited the address, and I wrote it down, thinking that I had found more trouble in one day than most men come across in a decade.

I had called Mouse because he and Christmas Black were friends. I had hoped to find help, not give it. But when you live a life among desperate men and women, any door you open might have *Pandora* written all over the other side.

# CHAPTER 3

I hadn't imbibed any alcohol whatsoever in years. But since Bonnie left I thought about sour mash whiskey every day. I was sitting in the living room in front of a dark TV, thinking about drinking, when the phone rang.

Another symptom of my loneliness was that my heart thrilled with fear every time someone called or knocked on the door. I knew it wasn't her. I knew it, but still I worried about what I could say.

'Hello?'

'Mr Rawlins?' a girl asked.

'Yes.'

'Is something wrong? You sound funny.'

'Who is this?'

'Chevette.'

It hadn't been a full day since I'd almost murdered a man over the woman-child, and already I had to reach for her in my memory.

'Hi. Something wrong? Is pig man botherin' you?'

'No,' she said. 'My daddy told me that I should call and say thank you. I would have anyway, though. He says that we gonna move to

Philadelphia to live with my uncle. He says that way we can have a new start back there.'

'That sounds like a great idea,' I said with poorly manufactured enthusiasm.

Chevette sighed.

I got lost in that sigh.

Chevette saw me as her savior. First I took her away from her pimp and then I allowed her to see her father in a way he could never show himself.

I got lost trying to imagine how I could see myself as that child saw me: a hero filled with power and certainty. I would have given anything to be the man she had called.

'If you have any problems, just tell me,' that man said to Chevette.

The front door swung open, and Jesus came in with Benita Flagg and Essie.

'Okay, Mr Rawlins,' Chevette said. 'My daddy wanna say hi.'

I waved at my little broken family.

'Mr Rawlins?'

'Yeah, Martel. She sounds good.'

'I'm movin' us all out to Pennsylvania,' he said. 'Brother says there's good work at the train yards out there.'

'That sounds great. Chevette could use a new start; maybe you and your wife could too.'

'Yeah, yeah,' Martel said, treading water.

'Is there something else?' I asked.

Essie started crying then.

'You, um, you said that, uh, that the three

hundred dollars was for the week you was gonna spend lookin' for Chevy.'

'Yeah?' I said with the question in my voice, but I knew what was coming next.

'Well, it only took a day, not even that.'

'So?'

'I figure that's about fifty dollars a day, excludin' Sunday,' Martel argued. 'You could get another job to make up the difference.'

'Is Chevette still there?' I asked.

'Yeh. Why?'

'I tell you what, Martel. I'll give you two hundred and fifty dollars if Chevy could come spend the next five days with me.'

'Say what?'

I hung up then. Martel couldn't help it. He was a working-man and had the logic of the paycheck wedged in his soul. I'd saved his daughter from a life of prostitution, but that didn't mean I'd earned his three hundred dollars. He'd go to his grave feeling that he'd been cheated by me.

'Hey, boy,' I said, rising to meet my son.

'Dad.'

He hugged me and I kissed his forehead. Benita got in on it, kissing my cheek while Essie wailed in her arms.

I took the baby in my hands and heaved her around in a circle. She looked at my face in wonder, reached up to my scratchy cheek, and then smiled.

For a moment I felt nothing but love for that

infant. She had Benita's medium-brown skin and Juice's straight black hair. There wasn't one drop of my blood in her veins, but she was my granddaughter. It was because of my love for her that I had been ready to kill Porky.

Looking at her trusting face, I thought of the child that my first wife took away with her to Texas. That shadow of loss brought on the memory of Bonnie, and I handed Essie back to her mother.

'Are you okay, Mr Rawlins?' Benny asked me.

Hadn't she just asked me that? No.

'Fine, baby.'

'You need us tonight, Dad?' Jesus asked. He knew that I was hurting and so tried to save me from Benita's concern. He was always saving me – ever since I first brought him home from the streets.

'No. I found who I was looking for. But you guys could stay anyway. I'll sleep in your room, Juice.'

Jesus knew that I wanted him to stay, to keep my house filled with movement and sound. He nodded ever so slightly and looked into my eyes.

I couldn't tell what he was thinking. Maybe it was that he could watch TV or sleep in a big bed. But the way I felt then, I was sure that he could see right through me. That he knew I was way off course, lost in my own home, my own skin.

'Juice!' Feather and Easter Dawn shouted.

They ran in to hug the boy who took them on

boat rides and taught them how to catch crabs in a net. All the commotion caused Essie to cry again, and Benita brought out her bottle.

I drifted into the kitchen and started dinner. Before long I had three pots and the oven going. Fried chicken with leftover macaroni and cheese, and cauliflower with a white sauce spiced by Tabasco. Easter and Feather joined me after a while and made a Bisquick peach crisp under my supervision.

The whole dinner took forty-seven minutes from start to the table. While the pastry cooled on the sink, Feather and Easter Dawn helped me serve the meal.

Dinner was boisterous. Every now and then Easter got a little sad, but Jesus sat next to her and told her little jokes that made her grin.

Everyone but me was in bed by nine.

I sat in front of the dark TV, thinking about whiskey and how good it once tasted.

After a while I forced myself to consider the Vietnamese child who had been taken from her war-torn homeland, whose parents (and all their relatives and everyone they knew) had been murdered by the man who had adopted her – Christmas Black.

The professional soldier's patriotism had soured when he realized what America's war had cost him. He was a killer on a par with Mouse. But Christmas was also a man of honor. This made him more dangerous and unpredictable than the homicidal friend of my youth.

If Christmas had left E.D. with me, then he must have been at war somewhere. What he wanted was for me to look after his little girl, but he wasn't my client. Easter had asked me to assure her that her father was okay. The only way I could do that was to go out and find him.

After that, or maybe blended up in it, I would have to find Mouse and see what was what in those murder allegations. Raymond had once spent five years in the can for manslaughter. He had made it known that he would never go into prison again. That meant if the cops found him first, a goodly number of them were likely to get killed. Even if Etta hadn't hired me, I'd still try to save the lives that Mouse would take – that was one of my self-appointed duties in life.

# CHAPTER 4

I was jarred out of a deep sleep by something
– a sound. It was very late. The first thing I
saw when I opened my eyes was the little
yellow dog glaring at me from between the drapes
that covered the front window. I wasn't quite sure
that the phone had rung. But then it jangled again.
There was an extension in my bedroom, and I
was worried about disturbing the baby, so I
answered quickly, thinking that it was either
Christmas or Mouse calling in from some
hazardous position in the street.

'Yeah?' I said in a husky tone.

'Easy?'

The room disappeared for a moment. I was
floating or falling into a dark night.

'Bonnie?'

'I'm sorry it's so late,' she said in that sweet
accent. 'I could call you tomorrow . . . Easy?'

'Yeah. Hey, babe. It's been a long time.'

'A year, almost.'

'It's great to hear you, your voice,' I said. 'How
are you?'

'Fine.' Her tone was reserved. But why not?

I thought. She was taking a big chance calling me. The last time we spoke, I had kicked her out of my house.

'I was just sittin' here in front of the TV,' I said. 'Jesus and Benita sleepin' in my bed. Easter Dawn is here. You don't know her, but she's the daughter of a friend's mine.'

Bonnie didn't reply to all that. I remember thinking that Feather had probably told Bonnie about Easter. She and Christmas had been by a few times. The ex-soldier thought that his little girl needed to have friends, and because he home-schooled her he was worried about her being too influenced by his being a man.

'It's funny that you should call,' I said in the voice and demeanor of a man alien to me. 'I've been thinking about you. Not all the time, I mean, but thinking about what happened . . .'

'I'm going to be married to Joguye in September,' she said.

My spine felt like a xylophone being played by a dissonant bebop master. I actually stood up and gasped as the discordant vibrations ripped through me. The spasms came on suddenly, like a downpour or an explosion, but Bonnie was still talking as if the world had not come to an end.

'. . . I wanted to tell you,' she said, 'because Jesus and Feather will be part of the wedding and I . . .'

Was that what I had seen in Juice's eyes? Did he know that Bonnie planned this, this betrayal?

Betrayal? What betrayal? I had sent her away. It wasn't her fault.

'I waited for you to call . . .'

I should have called. I knew that I should. I knew that I would, one day. But not soon enough.

'Easy?' she said.

I opened my mouth, trying to answer her. The tremors subsided and I eased back onto the sofa.

'Easy?'

I cradled the phone, hanging up on a life that might have been, if I had only picked up a telephone and spoken my heart.

# CHAPTER 5

You can't wake up from a nightmare if you never fall asleep.

I was out of the house by 4:30 that morning. I had showered and shaved, trimmed my nails, and brushed my teeth. I drank the rest of the pot that Feather had brewed the afternoon before and spent every other minute trying not to think about Bonnie Shay and suicide.

The only big tire on a roof in South Los Angeles at that time was a Goodyear advertisement atop Falcon's Nest Bakery on Centinela.

The sky was lightening at the edges and traffic was only just picking up. I could feel my teeth and fingertips and not much else.

I wasn't angry, but if Porky the Pimp had walked by me then, I would have pulled out my licensed .38 and shot him six times. I might have even reloaded and shot him again.

The big blue building across from Falcon's Nest Bakery was the Pride of Bethlehem Negro People's Congregational Church. There was a bright red cross on the roof and a yellow double door for the entrance.

These colors seemed hopeful in the dawning light.

I tried for the first time since I was a child to imagine what God was like. I remembered men and women going into apoplectic convulsions in church when *the Spirit entered them.* That sounded good to me. I'd let the Spirit in if he promised to drive away my pain.

I lit a Camel, thought about the taste of sour mash, tried and failed to push Bonnie out of my mind, and climbed out of the car like Bela Lugosi from his coffin.

The long white bungalows behind the Pride of Bethlehem were on church property. They looked like the downscale military barracks of an army that had lost the war. There had once been a patch of lawn between the two long buildings, but now there was only hard yellow earth and a few weeds. The white plank walls were dirty and lusterless, and the green tar paper on the roofs had begun to curl as the cheap glue that once held them lost adhesive strength.

The forty-foot-long structures faced each other and were perpendicular to the back of the church.

At the center of each long wall was a plain door. I went up to the door on the right. There were labels on either side that had inked names on them that had faded in the sun.

26

Shellman was on the left and Purvis on the right. The opposite door was Black and Alcorn.

I opened this door to the slender entrance chamber.

Alcorn was a regular family. In the dim light of the utility hall, I could see that they had left a broken hobbyhorse, a filthy mop, and three pairs of worn-down shoes outside their door. There was dust and dirt on the black rubber doormat and a child's jelly fingerprints under the doorknob.

The Black residence was a whole different experience. Christmas had a stiff push broom leaned up against the wall like a soldier standing at attention. There was a mop in a lime green plastic bucket that exuded the odor of harsh cleanliness. The concrete floor before this entrance had been washed, and the white door was newly painted.

I smiled for the first time that morning, thinking about how Christmas and Easter formed the world around them just as surely as the holidays they were named for.

I knocked and waited and then knocked again. You didn't just walk in unannounced on Christmas Black.

After a few more attempts, I tried the doorknob. It gave easily. The studio apartment was cleaner than a new hospital wing.

There was a tan couch against the center wall across from a long window that looked out on two lonely pines. On the left side of the far end of the room was an army cot and on the right was a child's bed with pink sheets and covers. Both were immaculately neat. The floor was swept, the dishes washed and stacked away, the small coffee table in front of the couch didn't have one ring on it from a water glass or a coffee cup.

The trash can was empty – and even washed.

Not a hair was to be seen on the white porcelain sink in the bathroom. There was a tiny bar of pink soap in the shape of a smiling fish in the dish next to the tub. I was wrapping the soap in a few sheets of toilet paper when I had an inspiration.

I went back into the main room and pulled the couch away from the wall. I remembered that when Jesus was a child he often hid his treasures and mistakes behind the couch, figuring that only he was small enough to fit in that crawl space.

There were a few candy wrappers, a headless doll, and a framed photograph back there. It was the picture of a maybe-beautiful white woman wearing a black skirt, a pink sweater, a red scarf that completely covered her head, and dark, dark sunglasses. The woman was leaning against the rail of a good-sized yacht, looking out over the side. The name of the boat was below her: *New Pair of Shoes*.

The glass had been cracked as if from a fall. Maybe, I thought, Easter had set it up on top of the cushions to study the woman who was a friend of her father's, a woman who looked like a movie star and had also earned the right to be framed and set up in their home. After a while, Easter began horsing around and the couch came away from the wall, allowing the picture to fall and the glass to break.

All of this was very important to me. Christmas Black was an immaculate and obsessive man. All other things being equal, he would have checked behind the sofa before decamping. This meant that he was in a hurry when he left. That hidden picture told me that the placid and clean apartment had been the scene of fear and maybe even violence.

I removed the picture from its broken frame and put it in my pocket. I put the frame back where I found it and pressed the sofa against the wall in keeping with the order of the Black home.

I looked around again, hoping that there was something else that might help me discover more about Christmas and his sudden disappearance. It was hard to concentrate because there was a sense of delight that kept interfering. I was almost unconsciously overjoyed at being distracted from Bonnie and her upcoming marriage.

Thinking about Christmas demanded that I keep focused, because if he got spooked there was definitely death somewhere in the vicinity.

# CHAPTER 6

I was sitting on that tan couch, wavering between giddiness and the heavy sense of impending violence, when the door came open. Three uniformed men entered. Soldiers. A captain followed by two MPs. The military policemen wore holsters that carried .45-caliber pistols. They were white and massive. The captain was smaller, black, and, after a moment of surprise, smiling. It wasn't a friendly smile, but it seemed to be a natural expression for this man.

I thought about grabbing my gun, but I couldn't find an excuse for such an action. In my heart I was desperate and confused, but it was my mind that I chose to follow.

'Hello,' the black captain said. 'Who are you?'

'Is this your house, man?' I asked as I stood up.

The captain's empty grin grew larger.

'Is it yours?' he asked.

'I'm a private detective,' I said. It always gave me a little thrill to say that; made me feel like I was on a movie set and Humphrey Bogart was about to make an entrance. 'I've been hired to find a man named Christmas Black.'

I wondered if there were women who were fooled by that officer's smile. He was dark skinned like me and deadly handsome. But his bright eyes, I was sure, had never seen into another human being's heart. He hoarded the coldness of a natural predator behind those deep brown eyes.

'And have you found him?'

'Who's askin'?'

The MPs fanned out on either side of their commanding officer. I wasn't going to get out of there by force of arms.

'Excuse my rudeness,' the smiling predator said. 'Clarence Miles. Captain Clarence Miles.'

'And what are you doing here, Captain?' I asked, wondering what Mouse or Christmas might have done if they were in my situation.

'I asked you a question first,' he said.

'I'm on the job, Captain, and my military years are far behind me. I don't have to answer to you and I sure don't have to tell you my client's business.'

'Once a soldier, always a soldier,' he said, glancing at the man to his right.

I noticed that this MP had three medals over his left breast. They were red, red, and bronze. He was a younger white man with shocking gray eyes.

'They say that about niggers too,' I said, to see if I could get a rise.

But Captain Miles had only smiles for me.

'What's your name, Detective?'

'Easy Rawlins. I work out of an office down on Central. A woman hired me to find Mr Black. Paid me three hundred dollars for a week's worth of walking.'

'What woman?'

I hesitated then, but not from uncertainty. I knew what I wanted from the captain and I also had a notion of how I could get it.

'Ginny Tooms,' I said. 'She told me that Black was the father of her seventeen-year-old sister's child. They want him to come back and do the right thing.'

'Sounds like they want to put him in prison,' Miles speculated.

I shrugged, saying without words that it wasn't my business what a man with a foolish dick got himself into. I just needed the three hundred dollars, that's why I was there.

'What's this Miss Tooms look like?' he asked.

'Why you wanna know? I mean, you said you was lookin' for Black.' My dialect deepened as I talked. I knew from experience that Negro career soldiers looked down on their uneducated brothers. And in underestimating me, Miles might slip up and tell me something he didn't think I would understand.

'I am,' Miles said. 'But anybody that knows anything about him might help us.'

'What do you want with him, Captain?' I asked.

The MPs were moving closer. Bonnie entered my mind for a second. I thought that no beating

32

could hurt me more than the announcement of her upcoming marriage.

Miles pretended to waver then. We were made for each other, him and me, like the Tyrannosaurus rex and triceratops dinosaur figurines that Jesus loved to play with when he was a boy.

'Have you come across the name of General Thaddeus King in your investigation, Mr Private Detective?'

I pretended to ponder this question and then shook my head.

'He's our boss,' Miles confided. 'Black's too. Lately he'd sent Christmas out on a delicate assignment. That was three weeks ago, and nobody's heard from him since.'

'What kind of assignment?'

'I don't know.'

I made a face that said I didn't believe him.

He made a face that replied, *But it's true.*

'Mr Rawlins.'

'Captain.'

'Tell me about this Ginny Tooms.' The smile was gone and the MPs were in position. He might as well have said, *Either you talk now or after we kick the shit out of you.*

I could take the punishment, but I saw no reason that I should.

'White woman,' I said. 'Twenties, maybe thirty. Pretty, I think.'

'You think?'

'She wore sunglasses and had a blue bandanna

wrapped around her head Might'a been scarred up under all that for all I know.'

'Blond?'

'I couldn't tell. Maybe she was bald. Nice figure, though. She couldn't hide that.'

The smile returned. Clarence was beginning to enjoy our conversation.

'Her address?'

I shook my head. 'She paid with fifteen twenty-dollar bills and promised to call me every other day. The perfect woman as far as I'm concerned.'

That was the standoff. I'd told my lies and he had told his. His men were in position, but there was no real reason to punish me. Everything I'd said was plausible.

I looked around the room and saw what looked like a bumblebee hanging upside down on the ceiling over the decorated soldier's head.

'Can I see some identification, Mr Rawlins?' Captain Miles asked.

I kept my PI's license in my shirt pocket for easy access. I took this out and handed it over like a good soldier. The officer studied it. The black-and-white photo of my smiling face and the signature of the deputy police commissioner, my nemesis, Gerald Jordan, were enough to prove everything I'd said.

'Not too many Negro detectives in Los Angeles,' he said to the card. Then he looked at me and grinned.

'Is that all, Captain?'

'No. No, it's not.'

'What else do you want? You know I got a job too.'

The bumblebee was in the same position. I found myself hoping that the creature would come to life and startle the soldiers. I only needed a moment to get to my gun, which was nestled at the belt line at the back of my pants. I was feeling the need for an equalizer.

'General King is in charge of some very sensitive operations, both in this country and abroad. He reports to the White House. More than once I've answered his phone and the president was on the other end of the line.'

'What that got to do with a niggah like me or Christmas Black for that matter?'

'We need to find Black,' Miles said with a reluctantly straight face. 'We must find him.'

'I'm not standin' in your way, brother.'

'How did you locate this apartment?'

'Tooms had been here,' I said.

'Then why didn't she come here herself?'

'She told me she had only been to his place once, at night. The only thing she remembered was that there was a building across the street with a giant tire on the roof. The minute she said that, I knew the address.'

'So why not just tell her that?' Miles asked.

'You see, man,' I replied airily, 'you a niggah like me, but you been in the army too long. They buy your clothes, your food, give you a bed, a car, and a gun. You think you all bad 'cause you in the biggest gang in the world, so you don't understand when a man be runnin' aftah a dollar.

'If I had just said to Ginny that I knew where the address was, she'd a parted with twenty dollars, not three hundred. You got to milk a client just like you would a cow. Ain't no PX with bottles'a cream out here, just us workin' niggahs is all.'

If I tied it any tighter someone might have strangled on that lie. My only problem was keeping the smug satisfaction off my face so that Clarence wouldn't know how good I thought I was.

'Stand down,' Miles said to his men.

The MPs relaxed and took a step back.

'What have you found here, Mr Rawlins?'

'A cleaner house than I could imagine and one busted picture frame.'

'What was in that?'

'Nuthin'.'

I couldn't have looked into a woman's eyes as deeply as Miles stared into mine – not without passion growing out of it.

'We need to find Christmas Black,' he said with a smirk.

'You said that.'

For a minute there the four men in that room might have been manikins we were so still.

'Are you committed to this woman?'

'I ain't give her no ring or nuthin'.'

'Will you take on the job of finding Christmas

Black for the United States government?' he asked.

Life doesn't travel in a straight line like we think it does. I was positive that these men were the reason Christmas had left his adopted daughter with me. My intention was to lead them on in hopes of finding out what had happened to my friend. But my mind took that information and imagined me coming home over a year ago and telling Bonnie about my adventure. She had been the first person I could share my thoughts with.

The pain that came with the reverie almost sank me. I couldn't speak because I knew the sob in my chest would come out with whatever words I spoke.

'Mr Rawlins,' Miles prodded.

I held on to my silence ten seconds more and then said, 'You got anything against Miss Tooms gettin' a line on him?'

'Do you care?'

'I like it when people tell their friends that I did the job they paid me for, yeah.'

'No problem,' the black captain said. 'Matter of fact, I'd like to meet this Ginny Tooms.'

'How come?'

'Maybe she knows something about what Black's been doing.'

'Stickin' his black dick in her white underage sister is what,' I said, and Miles actually laughed.

'I'll give you seventy-five dollars,' he said, 'as a retainer.'

'You'll give me three hundred dollars for a week's worth of lookin',' I said. 'That's my fee. That's what everybody else pays. Uncle Sam ain't no exception.'

'You already been paid for this.'

'Three hunnert dollars or you an' General King could go jump in a lake.'

I was absolutely sure that Clarence Miles had murdered men with that mirthless grin on his face. He reached into his back pocket and came out with a large secretary-type wallet. He counted out three crisp new one-hundred-dollar bills and handed them to me. It was then I knew that whatever he was into, it was illegal.

Honest government men on official business wouldn't hand out hundred-dollar bills. Since the day it was founded, the army hadn't given out that high a denomination without a raft of accompanying paperwork.

I took the money, though, and put it in the pocket with the picture of the woman I had christened Ginny Tooms.

'How do I get in touch?' I asked my bent employer.

'What's your phone number?'

I told him. He wrote it down on a slip of paper in his big wallet.

'We'll call you tomorrow morning at nine hundred hours,' he said. Then he did an about-face and walked between his sentries. They executed somewhat less precise turns and followed him out.

It took them less than ten seconds to vacate the premises completely.

They might have been criminals, but they had been soldiers at some point along the way.

# CHAPTER 7

I had been distracted from my inspection of the neat little household but not derailed. Those soldiers hadn't come for the kind of search I was mounting. They had come to either find Black or not. There was no subtley to their intrusion.

It would have taken a dead body or a spilled bucket of blood to satisfy their curiosity. Also, they obviously didn't know Christmas all that well; otherwise they would have come at him from three different directions, with their guns drawn and cocked. Christmas Black was a government-trained killer, one of the best of his kind in the world.

I went back to my seat on the little tan couch and looked around. After a while I spied that bumblebee again. It hadn't moved in quite some time.

There was a wall that meant to be a kitchen toward the back of the studio apartment. The stovetop was empty and the sink too. There was nothing in the little refrigerator, and all the two-person dining table had to offer was a pair of sturdy maple chairs.

I carried one of these to the corner where the decorated soldier had stood. I climbed up and looked into the depths of a smallish black hole that had masqueraded as a bee. Only a bullet could have created that perfect little cavity.

Along with the PI's license, I carried a yellow number two pencil in my shirt pocket. This I poked into the hole. The pink eraser pointed me back to the the little sofa.

I got down on my hands and knees next to the foam rubber settee. I was about to inspect the wall and the floor when a wave of fear went through me.

What if Clarence Miles was smarter than I gave him credit for? Maybe he had gone out to wait for me to look around a bit more. His plan might have been to come back in on me, take whatever I'd found, and then have one of his soldiers execute me for good measure.

Grunting, I got to my feet, walked to the door, and locked it. Then I returned to the sofa, placing my pistol on the floor nearby for easy access.

Moving the sofa away from the white wall, I spied a faint red smudge. Not a droplet or a spatter but something that had been washed away as well as possible in the time allowed.

If Christmas had had ninety minutes, he would have gone to the hardware store and then painted over the blood he'd spilled.

The couch was now facing the front door. I sat

on it again and tried to imagine what had happened.

Whoever it was that got shot was in the middle of the room when he was surprised by his assailant. The victim was armed and probably had his gun out. He turned quickly but was shot while pulling the trigger of his own piece. He was falling backward, so the shot hit the ceiling.

There were other possibilities. The victim could have been unfamiliar with the use of firearms so the shot went wild. Christmas might still have shot this novice; he (or she) was obviously armed. But I doubted it was a chance burglar or a devious neighbor who broke in; not with Clarence Miles and his boys in the landscape. The assailant, I believed, was someone who intended to do harm to Christmas. That someone was armed and trained in the use of his weapon.

Whoever it was, he was now dead. His killer was Christmas Black; there wasn't a doubt in my mind about that. Only Christmas would have cleaned up so scrupulously after a killing of that sort.

Christmas had been expecting an attack, or maybe he had a warning system that told him when his enemy was approaching. He went out through the side door and then back around to the front. He came in fast and shot the invader, then cleaned up everything, somehow disposed of the body, and decamped to another hideout.

I was pretty confident about my hypothesis.

Christmas had killed for a living most of his life. He was raised by a whole family of government killers. He would have heard the outer door to the building open. In the time it took the assassin to make it into the apartment, Christmas could have been away.

But what happened to the body?

Outside again, I walked around both shabby buildings. This was 1967, and LA hadn't filled out. The area behind the church had been a big empty lot before the prefabricated bungalows were dropped in.

The back of the property was accessible by an unpaved alley that led to a small street that had no name that I knew of. The lot was strewn with beer cans, condom wrappers, and empty packs of cigarettes. By the side of Christmas's apartment there was a wheelbarrow. It had been scrupulously cleaned.

There was no trail through the grasses and weeds from the side of the house to the alley, but Christmas had learned to hide his comings and goings from eyes as sharp as those of the Vietcong. He would've been able to go back and forth leaving no evidence of his passage.

I walked out under the dawning sky into the alleyway. There were willows on either side of the packed-dirt lane but no houses. Halfway to the nameless street, I came upon a decrepit shed made from cheap pine, tar paper, and tin.

No wheelbarrow track there either, but Christmas was that good too.

Inside the shed was an accumulation of items left by construction workmen, drunks, lovers, prostitutes and their johns, and inquisitive children. There were animal droppings, piles of useless tools, tarps, and metal and plastic containers of all sorts.

In one corner there was a big crate that had been piled high with all kinds of rags, metal casings, and broken furniture. This crate had been calling to me ever since I'd realized that the bumblebee was not moving.

After I'd received my investigator's license, Saul Lynx, the Jewish PI, had given me lessons in what tools a shamus needed.

'You need things that can't be seen as criminal,' he'd told me one day as his half-black children played around us in their View Park home. 'No lock-picking tools but a long slender metal ruler with a nick on one side that happened from an accident. That will get you into most doors and cars. You should also always have a pair of cotton gloves in your back pocket . . .'

I donned my gloves and inspected the crate.

Along an unobstructed side there were the heads of eight brand-new nails that had been recently driven home. I found an old screwdriver and pried that side of the crate away.

The corpse didn't surprise me in the least. Neither did it bother me – much. I had seen a whole mountain of dead people in my life, most of them murdered because of their race or nationality. All the way from New Iberia, Louisiana, to Dachau I had seen them shot and hanged, blown up and lynched, gassed, burned, tortured, and starved. One more dead man couldn't rattle me.

He was young and wore dark clothes. There was a neat little bullet hole over his left eye and a blank stare on his ant-covered face. The colony of the queen had claimed him. Thousands of the little black socialists swarmed over his pale skin and dark clothes. I was sure that he'd been relieved of anything that could identify him. But I didn't need a name. His blond hair was cut in the military style and his shoes were black combat boots of military issue. This was a scout for the good captain and his brave men.

I reattached the side of the crate and left the funerary shed. I walked down into the nameless street and around the neighborhood.

It was still quite early.

As I wended my way back toward Centinela and my car, my mind drifted to Bonnie again. She was the love of my life, then and now. She loved another man, maybe not as much as she loved me but enough to be swayed by him.

I tried to think of some way that I could have stayed in a life with her. It was a dialogue I'd had in my head almost every day since I showed her the door. And every day I came to the same

45

conclusion: I couldn't bear lying there next to her with him in her mind.

Mountains of dead bodies and criminal soldiers meant nothing compared to the loss of Bonnie Shay.

# CHAPTER 8

On the drive away from Christmas Black's pied-à-terre, his killing ground, I wondered about my new friend. He wasn't like most black people I knew. His family had been members of the American military since before there was a United States. Many of his ancestors had lived through slavery without being slaves. For all I knew, some of them might have owned slaves. They had all studied the arts of war and violence, had passed down that knowledge in a great hand-bound book that Christmas had relinquished to his first cousin Hannibal Orr after he, Christmas, decided that the America his forebears fought for had lost its way.

Christmas and Hannibal's family was more American than most white people's. They had been at every important moment in America's tumultuous attempt at creating democracy. They had been at every victory and every massacre, their heads wreathed in glory and their hands drenched with blood.

I would have gone home and looked for Hannibal to take Easter Dawn off my hands if I believed that Christmas had gone completely crazy and was on a killing spree. But Clarence Miles, and that buzzless bumblebee, told a different story. Christmas was in trouble, and I owed him.

When I was wounded by a sadistic assassin named after a Roman statesman, Christmas and Easter had nursed me back to health. They had saved my life, and even though my life wasn't worth very much to me at that moment, a debt was still a debt.

All I had to do was wait until the next morning at nine and I could string Clarence a little further along. But the long span of hours between this morning and the next was too much for me.

Thinking about Bonnie's departure was like staring into the sun. I needed to get my mind off her, to distract myself. Bonnie was in the seat next to me, on the street walking to some store. She was smiling at me when I got mad over some small mistake I'd made.

'Life goes on,' she'd told me at least once a week.

Not anymore.

Life had stopped for me just as surely as it had for that foolish soldier who had dared to invade Christmas Black's personal, portable sovereignty.

The din coming from behind the pink, dented, and smudged front door was reminiscent of a riot. No, not a riot, a war. And it wasn't just the broken wagons, splintered wood, and scorched-earth lawn, but a full-pitched battle being waged inside the home. I could have sworn that there was machine gun fire, airplanes dive-bombing, a whole army on the march behind that portal.

I pressed the doorbell and knocked loudly, but I could not imagine that anyone would hear me over the racket that emanated from that small domicile. For some reason my intelligence failed in the presence of such tumult. I didn't know how I could make them hear me. Anyway, who would want such a ruckus to turn its attention to him?

I was ready to walk away when the front door opened. The sentry was a slack-shouldered, bone-thin brown woman with half-straightened hair. She wore a dress that had faded to such a degree that the pattern on its bluish fabric had become indistinct. The repeated images might have been fleeing birds, dying flowers, or once solid and specific forms driven to madness by the dozen leaping, screaming, fighting, and very, very ugly children that inhabited the Tarr household.

'Yes?' the poor woman whined. Her shoulders sagged so far down that she most resembled a building that was in the process of collapse.

'Mrs Tarr?'

For some reason the sound of my voice brought complete silence to the war-torn household.

The beady-eyed brood of unsightly children peered at me as if I was to be their next target, one war over and another about to begin.

I felt the beginnings of panic in my diaphragm.

49

There were at least two sets of unattractive twins in the litter. Not one was under two or over the age of eleven.

'Yes,' the careworn medium-brown woman said. 'I'm Meredith Tarr.'

I felt sorry for her. A dozen children and a husband murdered. As low as I was, I couldn't imagine being in Meredith's place. Just the thought of that many hearts beating under my roof at night, looking to me for health and succor, love, was beyond my comprehension.

The silence extended into a long moment, thirteen pairs of hungry eyes boring into me.

'My name is Easy Rawlins,' I said. 'I'm a private detective hired to find out what has become of your husband.'

Too many syllables for her mottled brown brood. One child screamed and the rest followed her into chaos.

'Who hired you?' she asked. Her voice was strained and tired, but still she had to yell if she wanted to be heard.

'A woman named Ginny Tooms,' I said to keep my fabrications simple. 'She's one of Raymond Alexander's cousins and is absolutely sure that he didn't kill Pericles.'

'No, Mr Rawlins,' Meredith Tarr assured me. 'Ray Alexander done killed Perry. I know that for a fact.'

It was hard for me to plumb the depths of this haggard woman's heart. Maybe she was exhibiting hatred for my friend. But she was so exhausted that there was little meat left on her bone of contention.

From the chaos of children a small eight- or nine-year-old emerged. This girl, though as ugly as her brothers and sisters, had a different look about her. Her yellow dress was unsoiled and her hair was combed. She wore red shoes of cheap but shiny leather.

The child moved close to her mother, watching her.

There's a bright spot in every shadow, my aunt Rinn used to say.

'What's your name?' I yelled at the girl.

She took her mother's hand and said, 'Leafa.'

Leafa was Meredith Tarr's little islet of light.

'I don't know who did what,' I said to Meredith. 'I don't owe Alexander a thing. All I know is I got paid three hundred dollars to spend a week lookin' to find your husband. If he's dead like you say, I intend to prove it. If he's alive—'

'He ain't,' Meredith said, interrupting my lie.

'If he is, I will prove that too. All I need is to ask you some questions, if you don't mind.'

My certainty set up against Meredith's conviction that her husband was dead brought the sagging woman to tears. At first no one but Leafa and I noticed. The child hugged her mother's thigh and I put a hand on her shoulder.

'It's my fault,' she sobbed. 'It's my fault. I kept on complainin' that there wasn't enough money to feed and clothe all these kids we got. He had two jobs and got another one on weekends. He was hardly evah home, he worked so hard. And then he borrowed money from that man they named aftah a rodent.'

'Did Pericles tell you that?' I asked.

'He didn't have to. Raymond Alexander came here to this house to give it to him,' Meredith said as if she were a preacher quoting from the Bible. 'He sat in this very livin' room.'

I looked at the couch, which six children had set up as the Alamo or Custer's last stand. They were shooting and jumping and cutting one another's throats.

'Ray Alexander sat there?'

'In the presence of his own chirren, Perry took the blood money from that evil man. He said he was gonna start a doughnut cart out in front of the Goodyear gate, but the man he gave his money to cheated him and he didn't have nuthin' to pay back his debt.'

'Raymond Alexander came to your house and handed over a loan to Pericles Tarr?' I asked, just to be sure that I heard her right.

'I swear by God,' she said, raising her left hand because her right was held by Leafa.

'What happened when Perry couldn't pay?'

'He told me that Mouse told him that he had three weeks to come up with the money or he would have to work off the debt. For about two months he spent every night doin' bad things for the loan shark. And then he come home one night and say that if somethin' happened to him, he had paid for our security with his life.'

By this time all of the children had gathered around their mother, blubbering along with her. Everyone but Leafa was crying. The good child kept her calm for the whole family. In my eyes, her ugliness was transforming into beauty.

'Perry loved us, Mr Rawlins!' Meredith wailed. 'He loved his kids and this house. He haven't called or written in eight days. I know he's dead. And I know who killed him too.'

On cue the little Tarr tribe stopped crying, their eyes now holding a glare of hatred for their father's killer.

'Where did he work?' I asked, straining a little from a dry throat.

'Down at Portman's Department Store on Central. He was a salesman there.'

I nodded and tried to smile but failed. Then I thanked Meredith and turned away. The door closed behind me and I took a few steps toward the street. I was surprised when a small hand grabbed my baby finger.

It was Leafa. She pulled on my hand and I crouched down to hear what she had to say.

'My daddy's too smart to be dead, mister. One time he was in a war and the Koreans ambushed him an' his friends. An' aftah that they came down to make sure that they was all dead. But my daddy took his friend's blood and put it on his head, and when the endemy soldiers come to look at him they didn't shoot him 'cause they thought he was already dead.'

'So you don't think that this man Ray killed him?' I asked.

She shook her head solemnly, and I found it hard to imagine that such intelligence could be wrong.

# CHAPTER 9

I also found it hard to believe that Mouse would have sat on that ratty sofa amid the screams of all those ugly kids. Raymond didn't have patience for more than one child at a time, and then he would be the center of attention, not the child. And Ray wasn't a loan shark either. He might decide that he wanted his money back at any time, even before it was due, and the borrower had better beware.

Mouse was not a businessman in the conventional sense. He was a special agent, an enforcer, a boss man. Ray Alexander was a force of nature, not a bank.

But neither could I believe that Leafa's mother was lying. She had gone to the police to accuse Mouse of a crime. There was not one in a thousand people in Watts brave or stupid enough to do something like that.

And Mouse had disappeared at the same time Pericles had gone missing. It was a real mystery; almost enough to divert me from Bonnie.

Almost.

I was all alone in a car full of phantoms. Bonnie

was there next to me with Easter Dawn on her lap. Mouse and Pericles Tarr sat in the backseat, muttering about money and blood. Next to them were Christmas and a white woman swathed in a polka-dotted scarf; maybe they were making love.

Behind us was a jeep filled with armed military men, rogues.

I had to choose between Bonnie and the suicide soldiers, the ones who thought they could come up on a man like Christmas and win.

The main branch of the LA library had a librarian named Gara Lemmon. She was a black woman from Illinois named for her father and educated by her mom. She was a heavy woman with big, well-defined features. Her hands were larger than mine, and her broad nose seemed to go all the way up to her forehead.

Gara liked me and my friend Jackson Blue because we were well-read and willing to talk about ideas. Sometimes the three of us would go back to her little office to argue the finer points of philosophy and politics. Jackson and Gara were better read and smarter than I was, but they also took a few nips from Jackson's flask, so we were on pretty much even footing when the talks got heavy.

'Easy Rawlins,' Gara said when I entered the librarians' lounge.

She was sitting in a big green chair in the cavernous sitting room.

'How'd you get in here?' Gara asked.

'Mr Bill knows me by now,' I said. 'He told me I could just come on back.'

'Jackson with you?'

'Since he got that computer job, Jackson don't do a thing but work,' I said.

'Oh, well. I know you didn't come here all by yourself to talk.' She put down the book she was reading and arranged her mass in the huge chair.

'What you reading?' I asked.

'*The Catcher in the Rye*,' she said, a little frown at the corner of her pillow lips.

'You don't like it?'

'It's okay. I mean, it's good. But I just think about a little black child or Mexican kid readin' this in school. They look at Caulfield's life an' think, Damn, this kid got it good. What's he so upset about?'

I laughed. 'Yeah,' I said. 'So much we know that they never even think about, and so much they think about without a thought about us.'

I didn't have to tell Gara who *they* and *us* were. We lived in a they-and-us world while they lived, to all appearances, alone.

'You got any books in here tell me who's who in the army?' I asked, sitting down on a three-legged stool across from her.

'You know we do. I told you about the grant the government gave us to house their special publications. We got a whole locked room filled with that stuff.'

'I'm lookin' for a General Thaddeus King and a Captain Clarence Miles.'

Gara pursed those big lips. I had met her husband. He was a small man who looked like a rooster. I couldn't imagine him kissing that woman, but I supposed he couldn't think of anything else.

'It's a special-access stack,' she said.

'Yeah, I figured. But there's a little girl missing her father, and this is the only way home for her.'

'Write down the names,' Gara said.

I scribbled the names on the top leaf of a pad of paper sitting on the table between her grand inquisitor's chair and my supplicant's stool.

'You wait here,' she said. 'I'll look 'em up.'

At any other time I would have picked a book off one of the shelving carts and started reading. I'm a reader. As a rule I love books, but not that day. The only things I was interested in then breathed and bled or cried.

I sat there trying to come up with a plan for approaching General Thaddeus King. I couldn't get to him on a military base, and even Gara's precise records wouldn't have a home address. That meant I had to use the phone. I'd have to find his number somewhere and call him.

But what would I say? That I knew about the scam he and Miles were up to? An approach like that might work on a street punk but not a soldier, certainly not a general. No. A general in this army had seen combat. He'd faced death and done things that would sicken any normal man.

And who was I to say that King knew anything about Miles's criminal activities? Maybe I should tell King about Miles and see what he'd have to say about that.

But for subtle investigation, I'd have to meet him eye to eye. He wouldn't give up his heart over the phone like some teenage girl.

Love over the phone was the wrong avenue of conjecture. It brought Bonnie to mind, curled up in the living-room chair, talking on the phone and laughing. Her voice got very deep when she laughed. Her head tilted back, and that long brown throat offered itself to me.

That image shattered any ability I had to resist the hurt. All I could do was stare at the buff-colored wall of the librarians' lounge. I imagined my mind as that inarticulate, meaningless flat plane. It was a kind of temporary intellectual suicide.

'Was that a trick question?' Gara asked as she entered the room.

I looked up, and the mirth in her eyes died.

'What's wrong with you, baby?'

'I . . .'

Gara pulled a chair up next to me and took my hands in hers. Gara had never touched me in all the time we'd been acquainted. She was a proper woman who didn't want to give the wrong impression.

'It's okay,' I said. 'Just a problem at home. It's all right. Nobody's sick. Nobody's dying.'

I took a deep breath and pulled away. 'What you talkin' about a trick?'

'There ain't no General, Colonel, or Major Thaddeus King anywhere in the army, and the only Clarence Miles is a master sergeant in Berlin.'

'Can I smoke in here?' I asked.

'No, but I'll allow it anyway. You look like you need somethin'.'

The inhalation of cancer-causing smoke felt like the first breath I'd taken in a long time. It reminded me of what a man, I'd forgotten his name, that was friends with my maternal grand-father used to say: 'We born dyin', boy,' he'd opine. 'If it wasn't for death, we'd nevah draw a breath.'

Everything Miles had said was a lie. What he'd said but not what I'd seen. They'd come armed and in force. They all had at least been in the mili-tary. They were killers and soldiers inasmuch as they were willing to put their lives, and others' lives, on the line.

60

# CHAPTER 10

I always had a pretty good memory in times of stress. When I felt that my life was threatened or someone I loved was in danger, I began to pay very close attention to detail. It was like that when the liar Captain Miles and his men came in on me. Many of those details, including the decorated MP's medals, had stuck in my mind.

One medal had red and yellow stripes with a bronze leaf across it and an ornate bronze circle dangling underneath; another had a yellow background with green and yellow stripes on it with a medal like a coin; the last ribbon was green, yellow, red, yellow, and green, holding up a bright red star.

Gara let me go into the small military library after seeing my haunted expression. She probably thought I was upset because someone I loved was dying or near death. If I had told her about Bonnie, she would probably have laughed and sent me packing. A broke heart was no reason to put her job in jeopardy.

The medals on my soldier's chest were all earned in Vietnam: the Republic of Vietnam Gallantry

Cross, the Vietnam Service Medal, and a medal given specifically for wounds.

I wrote down the names and came out to the lounge to see Gara once again in her big green chair. She'd finished Salinger's masterpiece and moved on to some fat tome. She was drinking from a sixteen-ounce soda bottle, smirking at the text.

'I have a need,' I said, all the sadness and remorse gone from my face and my voice.

'We all do,' she replied, continuing her reading and drinking.

'I need to know what soldiers have received these three medals in the last five years.'

I placed the list on the table next to her.

'Here at the library we lead the horse to water, Mr Rawlins,' she said. 'We don't get down on our knees and drink for him.'

I placed one of Miles's hundred-dollar bills on top of the list. That was just another example of my emotional distress. If I had been in a normal state, I would have put a twenty down. Twenty dollars was enough for what I was asking. But there was something poetic, something that resonated with justice, about paying for my information with the very money the liar had given me.

Gara put down her sparkling sugar water and her book. Then she took up the hundred-dollar bill and the short list.

'I'll have it by three o'clock tomorrow,' she said. 'If it's earlier than that, I'll call you.'

I smiled and made a mock salute.

I was about to leave when she asked, 'How's the kids?'

'Fine. Great. Jesus and his girl had a baby.'

'They gettin' married?'

'We'll see.'

'How's Bonnie?'

'We'll see,' I said again.

I headed for the door before she could question my answers.

The little yellow dog must have been chasing gophers in the backyard, because he wasn't barking as I came up on the porch. Frenchie knew the sound of my car. Bonnie had told me that she knew I was coming from a block away just because of his angry bark.

But that day I made it all the way to the front door undetected. The door was open and so only the screen separated me from the sounds of the house. I could hear Essie crying a few rooms away and Feather speaking in French. Her time in Switzerland in the clinic and then later with Bonnie and Jesus had taught Feather to converse easily in that tongue. But the only person she spoke French to on the phone was Bonnie. Now that my daughter was becoming a woman, they chattered like girlfriends.

I reached for the door handle and stopped. Feather laughed out loud and said something that was both a question and an exultation. I spoke some French, Creole mostly from my childhood in Louisiana, but the fast-paced Parisian that Bonnie had taught Feather was too much for me.

I pulled the screen door open but didn't walk right in.

'He's here,' Feather said in a voice she tried to muffle. 'I gotta go.'

She'd hung up by the time I came in.

'Daddy!' she cried, and ran up to hug me.

I held her harder than I should have. But I needed to hold on to someone who loved me.

'Hi, baby.'

Feather leaned back and looked into my eyes. She knew that I'd heard her. She wanted to help me feel better.

'It's okay,' I said. 'Don't worry.'

'Hi, Dad,' Jesus said.

He was standing at the door to the kitchen wearing a brown apron and yellow rubber gloves.

'Hey, boy.'

'Hello, Mr Rawlins,' Easter Dawn said. She was standing by Jesus's leg, flour on her hands and cheeks.

'You guys cookin', huh?' I said.

'I'm making pound cake,' the little doll said. 'And Juice is washing the dishes and helping.'

'You want to help me with lunch?' I asked her.

The child's black eyes glittered and her mouth opened into a perfect circle. Domesticity was her bastion of power in her father's house. He never made a decision about household matters without first consulting her. And Easter almost always had the last word.

I had oxtails in the refrigerator. We dredged them in flour and seared them in lard with green peppers, diced onions, and minced garlic. While they simmered, we took out the pound cake, set rice boiling, and chopped up some brussels sprouts, which we sautéed in butter and then laced with soy sauce.

While we did all this cooking, the child and I discussed our adventures.

Feather was spending another day at home taking care of her. They had gone to the art museum, then read Feather's history book and done her lessons for school. I realized that I had to enroll Easter in school or Feather's education would suffer.

I tried not to think about how Bonnie would have taken care of all that when she was there.

Bonnie had made the house run smoothly, even when she was away on international flights for Air France. She hired people and had friends do chores that made my life easier.

How could I have thrown that concern away?

'Did you find my father?' Easter asked, and I was drawn back into the world.

'Gettin' close. How long did you live in that house across the street from the big tire?'

'I don't know . . . a week, maybe.'

'Hm. I found some people who might know

where he is,' I said. 'They're supposed to call me tomorrow morning with what they know.'

'Who did you talk to?' she asked.

'A man named Captain Miles. Black guy in the army. Have you ever met him?'

Easter was standing on a chair next to me at the stove. It was her job to drop in the vegetables while I stirred them in the hot butter.

She thought for a moment and then shook her head.

'No. No Captain Miles has ever been to our house. Not when I was awake.'

'Do people come over in the night when you're asleep?' I asked.

'Sometimes.'

'Have you ever seen any of them? I mean, maybe you woke up and looked downstairs.'

'No,' she said very seriously. 'That would be spying and spying is bad. But . . .'

'Yeah?'

'But one time that lady with yellow hair came at night, and she was still there in the morning.'

'What was she like?'

'Very sad.' Easter nodded to assure me of what she was saying.

'About what?'

'Her husband was in trouble. His friends were mad at him and they were mad at her too.'

'Did she say anything else about those men?'

'No. Can we have strawberries on our pound cake?'

'I'll send Jesus to the store to get some.'

Our conversation went back and forth about cooking and the people her father knew. There wasn't much useful to me. But when E.D. was making the rice, I remembered the bar of soap wrapped in paper.

'Mr Fishy,' she cried, unwrapping the bar. 'I thought I lost you.'

'I found it at the place across the street from the big tire.'

'Was my daddy there?' Easter Dawn asked.

'No. No, he wasn't. But I wondered . . . Did you drive down to LA in your father's Jeep?'

'No. The lady had a green car. Daddy drove that.'

'And did she let him keep it?'

'No. He borrowed a blue car from a friend of his, but then he said he was going to buy a red truck with a camper on it from that funny man.'

'What funny man?'

'The one on the TV who has the animals and the pretty girls around him all the time.'

# CHAPTER 11

Mel Marvel's Used Cars was an institution in Compton. Every car on his lot was good as new; at least that's what his late-night TV ads said. He was a rotund white Texan who kept himself surrounded by pretty white girls in bathing suits, smiling for the cameras. Very often he had caged lions and trained elephants on the lot. Marvel was a con man who knew that most people wanted to be fooled.

A few years before, I'd bought a car from one of Mel's salesmen, Charles Mung. It was a sky blue Falcon. My Ford was in the shop for a couple of weeks, and I thought I'd drive the Falcon around until mine was fixed. Then I'd give it to Jesus.

The trouble was that a back tire broke off on the way home from Compton. It popped right off the axle and rolled down the street.

I hired a tow truck and brought the car back to the lot.

Charles Mung was a tall white guy with freckles and corn-flower blue eyes.

'Tire broke right off,' I told him under a blazing

sun on the five-acre lot. It was only three hours into my thirty-day guarantee.

'We don't cover accidents,' he replied as he turned to walk away.

I grabbed his arm, and three very big men came out of nowhere. They crowded me, freeing the salesman from my grip as they did so.

'You owe me four hundred dollars,' I said over an ugly car thug's shoulder.

'Show Mr Rawlins off the lot, will you, Thunder?' Mung replied.

They didn't hurt me. Just deposited me on the curb.

'Come back here again,' Thunder, a polar bear of a man, told me, 'and me and my friends will break all your fingers.'

It's funny the things that stay with you. I was so humiliated by that treatment that all the way home on the bus I planned my revenge. I was going to get my gun and go back there. If they didn't return my money, I was going to kill Mung and Thunder.

I was in the bedroom loading my third pistol when Mouse called.

'What's wrong, man?' he asked after I'd only said hello.

I told him my problem and my intentions.

'Hold tight, Easy,' he said to me. 'I got friends down there. Why'on't you let me call 'em first?'

'They humiliated me, Ray. I ain't gonna stand for that.'

69

'Do me a favor, Easy,' he said. 'Let me call my friend first. If it don't work, I'll go down there with ya.'

I agreed, and later on, after Feather and Jesus got home from school, I came to my senses. I was about to go on a killing spree over four hundred dollars and four fools.

I made dinner and put the kids to bed.

I was sitting in the living room, watching the ten o'clock news, when there was a knock on my door. It was Charles Mung. He wore a thick white bandage that completely covered his left eye, and his right hand was swollen, obviously the source of great pain.

'Here,' he said, handing me a big manila envelope.

Before I could ask him what it was, he rushed away.

The envelope contained automobile registration papers and four hundred and twenty dollars. The car, which was parked in front of my house, was Mung's own '62 Cadillac.

I used the money to buy another car and gave the Caddy to my old friend Primo, who made travel money by selling American cars down in Mexico.

I left before eating but promised Feather and Easter that I'd be back for dinner.

The huge car lot was twice the size it had been the last time I was there. Mel had bought out the property across the street and built a three-story showroom. The showroom was surrounded by huge columns of red and blue balloons and topped with a forty-foot American flag.

The place was so big now that it seemed like a military installation.

I parked in the customers' lot and walked toward the glittering steel-and-glass headquarters. When I reached the doorway, a skinny man in a bright green suit approached me.

'May I help you?' the gray-colored black man asked. This was also a new addition, a Negro salesman.

His eyes were fevered. His smile twisted like an earthworm in the sun.

'I need to speak to somebody in records,' I said, showing him my PI's license.

He held the card between quivering fingers. He was a pill popper, no doubt. I was sure that he couldn't concentrate on my identification.

He winked, blinked, and grimaced at the card for a few seconds and then handed it back.

'Brad Knowles,' he told me. 'Out on the lot somewhere.'

'What does he look like?' I asked.

'Knowles,' the hopped-up salesman said. 'Out on the lot.'

I wandered around for a while looking for somebody named Knowles. Most of the people walking around were customers pretending that they knew something about cars. But there was security too.

After the Watts riots of '65 everybody had security: convenience and liquor stores, supermarkets, gas stations . . . everyplace but schools; our most precious possession, our children, were left to fend for themselves.

I went up to this one big brawny white guy and asked, 'Brad Knowles?'

He pointed over my left shoulder. When I gazed in that direction I spied a white guy wearing a cherry red blazer. He was gabbing with a young white woman. If somebody looked at me the way he was gawking at her, I would have run or pulled out a gun. But the woman seemed to be enjoying the attention.

'Thanks,' I said to the white museleman, and made my way across baking asphalt, past a hundred dying automobiles, toward the wolf and his willing prey.

'Mr Knowles?' I said in my friendliest voice.

Even in that awful coat, Knowles was a handsome devil. The woman, who was plain faced and well built, frowned at me.

'Excuse me a moment, ma'am,' I said through the rising heat. 'I just need to ask Mr Knowles a quick question.'

'What is it?' he asked.

I wondered if I was a white man would he have put a *sir* on the end of that sentence.

'I bought a car from a man named Black,' I said as affably as I could. 'He left his power tools behind the front seat. The only things I know for sure about him are that his first name is Christmas and he bought the car, truck actually, on this lot.'

Power tools, honest citizen – I had all the bases covered. Not only would I get the information, I might also receive a medal.

'Get the fuck off my lot,' Brad Knowles said to me.

I was actually speechless, so surprised that for a moment I forgot my deep sorrow. My mouth hung open.

'Do I have to call security and have you removed?' Brad added.

Despite my shock I could still shake my head and did so.

The plain white woman smiled at me, at my humiliation.

I turned and walked away, wondering what had happened.

Was it my interruption of his line on that woman? Was it racism? Or maybe they'd cheated Christmas on his truck. His complaint might have raised some hackles.

I opened my car door and waited a minute for the interior to cool down a little before I climbed in. I drove out of the lot and around the back of the big glass showroom, where a sign said there was overflow parking. I parked again and made my way into the building.

A young Asian woman, Korean I thought at the time, came up to me with a big smile on her face.

'May I help you, sir?'

'Yeah, yeah,' I said as I looked through the glass walls, hoping I hadn't been seen by the indelicate lot boss. 'Brad Knowles told me that I could find out something I need to know from somebody in records.'

'Miss Goss?' the woman asked.

'Yes. That's who it is.'

'Third floor. The stairs are behind you.'

The stairway was next to the glass wall. As I made my way up, I felt like a hornet in a clear plastic bag. Just a glance at the building would have shown Knowles that I was there. All he had to do was put down his foot to get rid of me.

I'd hoped that the records office had solid walls to hide behind, but it didn't. All that separated me from the outside world was a wall of colorless glass. I was the best man trying to take the groom's place at the top of a three-tiered wedding cake.

'May I help you?' another woman asked me.

I had expected a face to go along with the name Goss. So when I saw the lovely young black woman sitting in the dark red chair, I was surprised. I guess it showed on my face.

'I'm not what you expected?' she asked.

I tried to speak, but I didn't want to call her name ugly.

She smiled and cocked her head to the side.

Miss Goss was not pretty. Her features were too pronounced and insolent to be pretty. Her high

74

checkbones and ready-to-be-angry eyes made her beautiful. For the first time in a year, without the aid of sleep or stress, Bonnie completely slipped away from me. But as soon as I realized Bonnie was gone from my mind, she was back again.

'Do you want something?' Miss Goss asked.

'No . . . I mean, yes. Brad Knowles said that you could give me some information.'

Speaking his name, I glanced out at the lot. As if by magic, he looked up at the same time and saw me seeing him.

The hourglass was set. I smiled, putting love on the back burner for a moment.

'That's a lie,' Miss Goss said.

'What is?'

'Brad sendin' you up here. He wouldn't send anybody up here and certainly not a big black man like you. I'm surprised he didn't call security.'

'The man I need to find is named Christmas Black. He bought a red truck from you within the last three weeks.' Pretending to scratch my neck, I got a glimpse of Knowles looking around – for security, no doubt.

'What's your name?' she asked.

'Easy. What's yours?'

'Tourmaline.'

That made me happy. I laughed and decided that the .38 in my pocket would equalize any situation that security might raise.

'My name is funny?'

'Quite the contrary,' I said. 'It's a beautiful name. A gem.'

'I like your name too,' she said.

I could almost hear the heavy breathing of overweight guards climbing the stairs.

'Why's that?' I asked as if I had all the time in the world.

'It's got two syllables. I hate one-syllable names. Mel and Brad and all the rest of them: Bill, Max, Tom, Dick – I especially hate Dick – and Harv.'

'Christmas has two syllables,' I said.

Tourmaline admired my ability to think for a moment that seemed to last minutes.

'What's it worth to you?' she asked.

'A hundred dollars or dinner at Brentan's,' I said. 'Both.'

Tourmaline smiled and I saw a light somewhere.

That's when my old friend Thunder and a black security guard just as big as he was came out from the entrance to the stairs.

'Hey, you,' Thunder said.

I swiveled my head to regard him and his minion.

Instead of snarling, he gave me a quizzical look.

But I wasn't worried about what was on the big man's mind. I wondered if I could take him down. I decided that it was possible. I'd get hurt in the process, but I was a man trying to impress a woman. I could maybe take him . . . It didn't matter, though. With his helper, Thunder would have torn me in two.

The big white security guard was looking at me,

still pondering. I turned my head to see that Tourmaline was frozen, probably holding her breath.

'Mr Rawlins,' Thunder said, and I knew that Mouse had had a talk with him too.

'Hey, Thunder. Listen, I know you gotta kick me out. Just give me one word with the lady here.'

'Come on, Joe,' Thunder said to his partner.

Joe showed no emotion, just followed his supervisor down the stairs.

I turned to Tourmaline, and she said, 'I'll meet you there at eight, Mr Rawlins.'

# CHAPTER 12

Raymond Alexander had always been a fixture in my life. He was a ladies' man, a philanderer, a fabulous raconteur, a stone-cold killer, and probably the best friend I ever had; not a friend, really, but a comrade. He was the kind of man who stood there beside you through blood and fire, death and torture. No one would ever choose to live in a world where they'd need a friend like Mouse, but you don't choose the world you live in or the skin you inhabit.

There were times that Mouse had stood up for me when I wasn't in the room or even the neighborhood. That's why, sometimes, men like Thunder backed away from me, seeing the ghostly image of Ray at my shoulder.

I lived in a world where many people believed that laws dealt with all citizens equally, but that belief wasn't held by my people. The law we faced was most often at odds with itself. When the sun went down or the cell door slammed, the law no longer applied to our citizenry.

In that world a man like Raymond 'Mouse'

Alexander was Achilles, Beowulf, and Gilgamesh all rolled into one.

I stopped at a phone booth and dialed a number.

'Library,' a man's voice answered.

'Gara, please.' I knew she'd told me to wait for a day, but I also knew my hundred-dollar incentive would get her to move quickly.

I waited there, smoking a low-tar cigarette. Usually when I smoked I thought about quitting. I knew that my breath had been shortened and that my life would suffer the same fate if I continued. At the end of most smokes I crushed out the ember planning for it to be my last – but not that day. That day Death held no sway over me. She could come and take me; I didn't care.

'Hello?' Gara said in a rich tone that I associated only with black women.

'Any headway?'

She laughed at my knowledge and said, 'Come on by.'

Whenever I saw Gara she brought to mind deities. She was in that green chair again, fat as Buddha and wise as Ganesh. There was no gender to her divinity, no mortality to her time here on Earth.

'I got somethin' for you here, Easy,' she said, indicating a buff-colored folder on the table.

There were eight sheets of paper inside. The first

listed seven names, neatly typed in the top left-hand corner, single-spaced.

Bruce Richard Morton
William T. Heatherton
Glen Albert Thorn
Xian Lo
Tomas Hight
Charles Maxwell Bob
François Lamieux

After that, each page gave all the information that Gara had been able to find on the various heroes.

I scanned the pages. There were lots of abbreviations and acronyms. I didn't understand most of them, but that didn't bother me.

'No photos?' I asked.

Gara frowned and sucked a tooth.

'Yeah,' I said. 'I didn't think so.'

'Don't show those papers to anybody. Easy. And burn 'em up when you're through.'

'Either I'll burn them or they'll burn me.'

On the way home I stopped by the Pugg, Harmon, and Dart Insurance building. It was the newest and tallest glass-and-steel skyscraper to grace the downtown LA skyline. On the top floor was Brentan's, one of LA's finest restaurants.

As I headed for the red elevator whose sole purpose was to bring fine diners to Brentan's, a guard in a tan short-sleeved shirt and black pants approached me. The pale-faced, slender-armed guard had a holster on his left hip. The leather pouch contained what looked to be a .25-caliber pistol.

Most white people at that time wouldn't have given that guard a second thought. I, on the other hand, saw him as potentially life threatening.

'Sorry,' he said. 'No one goes up without a reservation.'

He was a small white man with eyes of no certain color and bones that would have worked for a hummingbird.

'This is nineteen sixty-seven,' I reminded him.

The guard didn't understand what I meant; his perplexed expression told me that.

'What I mean,' I said, 'is that in this day and age even Negroes can have reservations at nice places. You can't just look at a man and tell by his suntan whether or not he has a right to be somewhere.'

My tone was light, which made the words even more threatening.

'Um,' he said in a voice that hovered somewhere between scratchy alto and tentative tenor. 'I mean, yes, the restaurant is closed.'

'You mean to say that the restaurant is not open for business. It isn't closed. I have an appointment with Hans Green in seven minutes. That's because the restaurant employees are working.'

I smiled into the crooked little face that represented every rejection, expulsion, and exclusion I had ever experienced.

Most of my days went like that. Maybe 15 or 20 percent of the white people I met tried to get a leg up over me. It wasn't the majority of folks – but it sure felt like it.

I pressed the button on the elevator while the guard stood there behind me, trying to figure a way around my reasoning. The bell rang and the doors slid open. I got in and the guard joined me.

I didn't say a word to him and neither did he speak to me. We rode up those twenty-three floors silently wasting our energies over a feud that should have been done with a hundred years before.

When the doors came open, the guard scuttled around me, making a beeline for the podium where a young woman was writing in a big reservations log. She was white, with long blond hair and a horsey face. Her high heels made her taller than the guard; her teal gown put her in a completely different class from him.

The guard talked quickly, and I took my time approaching them. When I finally got there, she was saying, 'I'll go speak to Mr Green.'

The guard smirked at me, and again I wondered at all the minutes and hours and days that I'd spent on meaningless encounters like this one.

I wanted to say to the little white man, 'Listen, brother, we're not enemies. I just want to go up in an elevator like anybody else. You don't need to worry about me. It's the men that own this building that are making you poor and uneducated and angry.'

But I didn't say anything. He wouldn't have heard me. I couldn't free either one of us from our bonds of hatred.

The young woman returned with another white man behind her. This man was tall, ugly, and impeccably dressed in a dark green suit. He glanced at me and then turned to the guard.

'Yes?'

'This man says that he has an appointment with you, Mr Green.'

'What is your name?' Green asked the guard.

'Michaels, sir. But this guy—'

'Mr Michaels, how many times a day do I receive people who have made appointments?'

'I don't know . . . a few.'

'And how often do you ride up the elevator humiliating those people?'

'Um . . .'

'If a man or woman or child tells you that they have an appointment with me, I'd appreciate it if you would allow them to come here and discharge their business.'

'I just thought—'

'No,' Green said, interrupting the excuse, 'you did not think. You saw this man, this Negro man, and decided that you would play the hero, protecting a restaurant where you couldn't afford even a lunch from a person you don't know a thing about.'

I felt bad for Michaels, I really did. Green didn't say another word. Michaels knew enough not to argue. The horsey woman watched her boss with inquisitive eyes. We all stood there for more moments than we should have. I don't know about them, but I felt that I had somehow lost my way in life, ending up on that high floor embroiled in a conflict that made no sense.

Michaels finally got the message and went back toward the elevator.

'Mr Rawlins,' Hans Green said, 'it's so nice to see you.'

We shook hands as the young woman watched, trying to understand what was happening.

'Come back to my office,' Green was saying.

As I followed him, I smiled and nodded at the hostess.

How could she know that eighteen months before, Hans Green was being framed for embezzling money from the last restaurant he worked for, Canelli's. Melvin Suggs, an LAPD detective, was a friend of his and he passed my card along. I took a job as a dishwasher at the restaurant and discovered that the chef and Green's wife were cooking the books, and each other, at Hans's expense.

The big window of the restaurant manager's office looked all the way from downtown to the Pacific. I liked sitting there. The only thing I would have liked better was Bonnie back in my arms.

Green's ears and nose were way too big for his face. Red and blue veins had risen to the surface of his cheeks. His teeth were too small, and his thin lips were loose and flaccid. He was a caricature of a man.

'What can I do for you, Easy?' he asked when we were both seated and I had turned down a drink.

'I'm coming tonight with a very special woman. I'd like a good seat and perfect service.'

'What time?'

'Eight.'

'Done. On the house.'

'I can pay for it.'

'If Michaels is any indication, you pay for it every day of your life.'

# CHAPTER 13

By the time I got home, I had plotted and abandoned six different ways to get to Bonnie and convince her to come back to me. I considered everything from just apologizing to buying her a house in Baldwin Hills where we could start life anew. I even flirted with the notion of killing Joguye Cham . . . That was when I understood that I was truly, madly in love.

Frenchie was waiting on the other side of the door this time, growling and baring his teeth. He snapped at me when I crossed the threshold into my own home.

'Hi, Dad,' Feather said, coming out of her room. Easter Dawn came after her, wearing a pink kimono and carrying an ornately crocheted purse that looked something like a briefcase with a red silken shoulder strap.

'Hey,' I said to the children, the crush of melancholy just below the surface of my greeting.

Feather stared at me a moment and then turned to the tiny child.

'E.D., go into my room and set up all the dolls the way you did for me so Dad can see them.'

The child's eyes glittered. 'Okay,' she said excitedly, and then she ran for the back of the house, the shoulder-strap briefcase flapping at her side.

It was the first time I'd seen Feather manipulate a situation with a third person in order to get her way. She looked intently at my face and came up to me, putting her hands on either side of my head.

This gesture made me very uncomfortable. It wasn't the father-and-daughter relationship I'd had with Feather for close to a dozen years. She was almost a woman and I was nearly a man.

'We have to talk,' she said.

I wanted to find the child in her, to tell her a joke or tickle her. I wanted to dismiss her serious stare, but I could not.

I sat down on the love seat in the small room that divided the living room from the kitchen, and she sat there beside me.

'Juice and I are going to Bonnie's wedding,' she said.

'So I've heard.'

'We have to do it,' Feather continued. 'Bonnie is as much our mother as you are our father.'

*Did she find you two in the street like I did? Would she have brought you to live with her with no father to help her? Would she have risked her life to save you?* I thought these things, but I did not say them. Bonnie was a wonderful woman and of strong mind. She might have done more than I could have imagined. As far as I knew, her affair with

Joguye was to ensure that Feather had the medical treatment that saved her life.

'I know you love her,' I said. 'And I would never stand in the way of that.'

'And you should come too,' Feather said. 'She needs you to tell her it's all right.'

I don't think that the experience of losing my mother at the tender age of seven hurt as much as Feather's request. I looked up with a blank expression on my face and absolutely nothing in my mind.

'She has to move on, Daddy. She can't wait forever for a man who doesn't have forgiveness in his heart.'

I'd been called a nigger many times in my life. It was always a painful, enraging experience. But it was nothing compared to the simple truths that Feather was speaking. I wanted her to be quiet. I wanted to stand up and go into my bedroom, take out my .38, and just start shooting: the mirror, the wall, the floor under my feet.

'She waited for you to call,' Feather continued. 'She told me that she loved you more than any other man. She knew what happened with her and Uncle Joguye was wrong, but she got all confused when she was watching him make those doctors work on me. She wanted to come back home, Daddy, but you wouldn't let her.'

Maybe, I thought, there was a God. He wasn't some gigantic and powerful deity but just the vessel of all knowledge and therefore a judge of

88

truth. Now and then he inhabited some person and made them say the words that had gone unsaid. At this moment Feather was the expression of that God. He was using her to condemn me for my wrongdoing.

'You can't expect us to choose between you,' Feather was saying. 'We can't help what happened.'

I wanted to say that I understood what she was telling me and that it was true. I opened my mouth and a sound came out, but it was not words. It was a small mewling utterance, something that had never before come from me or anyone else I'd heard.

When Feather heard this muted cry, a look of shock crossed her face. She was my daughter again. I could see in her alarm all the things she was feeling.

Feather had been mad at me for making Bonnie leave our house. She identified with Bonnie's broken heart and her need for love in her life. Now she felt guilty about going to the wedding and angrier still that. I would feel betrayed about her going.

I was her father. I never felt pain or weakness. I never got tired or brokenhearted. I was invulnerable and could therefore hear her anger without danger of being hurt.

But the moment that sound came from me, Feather understood the pain that had been festering inside me, the pain I had never shared with her.

She put her arms around me and said, 'I'm sorry, Daddy. I'm so sorry.'

'It's okay, honey,' I said in constricted little words. 'I know you love both of us. I know I was wrong. You do whatever you feel is right, and I will love you no matter what.'

'Mr Rawlins,' Easter Dawn said, running from Feather's room. 'I have all the dolls set up for you to see.'

It took me almost an hour to get dressed for dinner. I closed my door and sat on the bed, trying to will myself into normalcy. Feather's words had cut so deeply that I couldn't even think of a place that wasn't filled with hurt.

Deciding on a pair of socks took me five minutes; putting them on took ten.

Feather and E.D. kissed me good-bye at the door. My daughter looked at me, feeling for the first time what it was like to be in my mind. It was a curse I wouldn't have wished on my worst enemy.

# CHAPTER 14

On the drive to Brentan's, I tried to imagine myself at Bonnie's wedding. I got stuck on what color and kind of suit to wear. I knew that I would never be able to go, but I wanted to *imagine* being there at the ceremony, watching them kiss after promising each other forever. If I could see it in my mind, maybe I could get past it.

I parked on the street and climbed out of my car. It was 7:48 by the gold-and-copper Grumbacher watch on my wrist.

A police car was passing by. The cops slowed down and stared out their window at me. Me: dark as the approaching night, tall, in shape enough for one good round with a journey-man light heavyweight, dressed in a deep gray suit that fit me at least as well as the English language.

The car slowed down to three miles an hour, and the pale faces wondered if they should roust me.

I stood up straight and stared back at them.

They hesitated, exchanged a few words, and then sped off. Maybe it was close to the end of the shift for them, or maybe they realized that I was a citizen of the United States of America. Probably, though, some real crime had come in over the radio and they didn't have the leisure to bring me under their control.

In the first-floor lobby, another white guard, this one tall and lanky, came up to me.

'May I help you, sir?' he asked.

Manners before insults. Little blessings.

'Goin' up to the twenty-third floor to grab a bite,' I replied.

'Do you have a reservation?'

'Is the pope Catholic?'

'What?'

I walked past him to the express elevator door. I pressed the button, conflicted about whether I wanted the guard to come over to me so that I could break his jaw, or just to be left alone.

The car came and the doors slid open. The guard was nowhere in my vicinity.

Another white woman in a lovely gown adorned the podium. The dress was scarlet, and her face contained the beauty of youth. It was full, with green eyes and a nose that stood out like a petite lever on a whole world of laughter.

When the woman-child saw me, the potential for laughter dimmed a little.

'Yes?' she asked, giving me only her insincere smile.

'Rawlins for dinner for two at eight,' I said.

Without looking at the log in front of her, she asked, 'Do you have a reservation?'

'Why don't you tell me?'

The pretty thing looked down and moved her finger around.

'Excuse me a moment,' she said very politely.

As she walked away, I lit up a cigarette. Jackson Blue had once told me that cigarette smoke constricts the veins and raises the blood pressure to a dangerous degree. But all I felt was calm. The smoke took off the sharp edge that I'd honed on the way to that restaurant.

A white couple came up behind me.

'Excuse me,' the tall white man said. He wore a tuxedo and had a white cashmere scarf around his neck. He was my age. She was twenty years younger, platinum from head to toe.

'It's a line, man,' I said, no longer wanting to placate a world seemingly filled with my adversaries.

Hans Green arrived a minute or two after that. He was attended by the young scarlet-clad beauty. The man in the tuxedo went around me and said, 'We're here for our reservation.'

Hans turned to the hostess, saying, 'Go change your clothes, Melinda.'

Tears appeared in her eyes and she hurried away.

The man in the tuxedo said, 'Excuse me, sir, but we'd like to be seated.'

'Don't you see this man standing in front of you?' Green asked. 'Are you blind or simply an ass?'

The Tux backed up and Hans said, 'Come on, Mr Rawlins, let me show you to your table.'

On our way, Hans touched a waitress on her shoulder and whispered something to her.

'Right away, Mr Green,' she said, and then made her way to the podium.

The table Hans had for me was perfect. Removed from the other tables, we were still in sight of everyone. The western view looked down upon an LA that was coming alive with electric light.

I sat and so did Hans.

'How do you do it?' he asked me.

'What?'

'I'm a white man,' he said. 'An Aryan. I golf, belong to a men's club. My parents came to America in order to be free and to share in democracy, but ten minutes with you and I've had arguments with four people about their bigotry. If that's what I face in ten minutes, what must life be like for you twenty-four hours a day?'

'Ten years ago I didn't have it so bad,' I said.

'Things have gotten worse?'

'In a way. Ten years ago you wouldn't have been able to seat me. Ten years ago I wouldn't have been in this neighborhood. Slavery and what came after are deep wounds, Hans. And, you know, healing hurts like hell.'

The ugly restaurateur sat back and stared at me. He shook his head and frowned. 'How can you be so calm about it?' he asked.

'Because the other choice would kill me and a dozen other folks don't know the difference between a fellow citizen and an imminent threat.'

'Hello,' a woman said. 'I didn't know it was going to be a party.'

Tourmaline was wearing a very tight fitting knee-length white dress. There was a blue hat shaped like a delicate seashell on the side of her head. The white high heels did not impede her grace.

Hans and I got to our feet.

I noticed that it was the woman Hans had whispered to who had brought Tourmaline to our table.

'Hi,' I said. 'This is Hans Green, the manager here. Hans, this is Miss . . .'

'Goss,' she said, just in case I had forgotten her last name. It's always nice when your date wants to keep you from being embarrassed.

Hans bowed and kissed her hand. 'Easy is a lucky man.'

He held out a chair for Tourmaline, and she sat with exceptional grace. 'Is there anything you don't eat or drink, Miss Goss?' he asked, as I regained my seat.

'I don't like veal very much,' she said.

'Then leave the rest to me.'

Hans and the new hostess walked off.

'I'm glad we didn't go to some little place down on Central,' I said.

'Why's that?'

'Because I'd have to fight the men off down

there. Hans had his eyes poppin' outta his head and he just told me that he was an Aryan.'

Tourmaline smiled. 'Who are you?' she asked.

'Easy Rawlins at your service.'

'I mean, how can you get into a place like this and have the manager visiting at your table? You a gangster or something?'

My blood was thrumming. I smiled and hunched my shoulders.

'Every once in a while I get together with my friends Ray and Jackson,' I said. 'We shoot the shit and joke around. Jackson is what he calls an autodidact. That means—'

'Self-educated,' Tourmaline said.

'Yeah. Anyway, Jackson calls the three of us the vanguard, the people up front blazing new trails. We make inroads to all kinds of places. From this restaurant on.'

Tourmaline was impressed, but it hardly showed.

'Where'd you learn all those big words, Mr Rawlins?'

'Reading and talking. What about you?'

Before Tourmaline could answer, Melinda, the demoted hostess, came over to our table. She was wearing a green-and-white waitress's uniform and had her long red hair tied back.

She put glasses of water in front of us.

'Mr Green and the chef are planning your meal, but is there anything special you want?'

I shook my head without speaking.

'No, thank you,' Tourmaline said graciously.

96

After Melinda walked away, Tourmaline observed, 'She looks sad.'

'Yeah,' I agreed. 'I wonder why.'

The evening was the best I'd had in a year. Tourmaline was only working at the used-car lot for a few months. She was a student at UCLA full-time, getting her master's in economics.

'Marxist economics or the kind that makes money?' I asked.

'The science,' she said with a smirk. 'I'm political but not a revolutionary; interested in a good living, but I have no need to be rich.'

'Yeah,' I said, 'but you got to admit that the science meets man on the front page of the paper. I just glanced at the headlines today and I saw articles on Vietnam, the USSR, and the Chinese Cultural Revolution.'

'But what about that boy and his brother?' Tourmaline asked.

'I didn't see that one.'

'It was on the lower left,' she said. 'A sixteen-year-old boy carried his dying brother through the snow for ten hours in the San Gabriel Mountains. When the rescuers found them, the younger boy was dead.'

'Yeah,' I said. 'There's a lotta good strong hearts out there. Problem is they get lost when they wander too far from home.'

I had made up my mind not to mention the red truck until she did. There was a dance to our date.

It was something we both needed. I didn't know a thing about her as a person, and I was a mystery myself at that table.

Melinda served us duck with cherry sauce, ramps, and potatoes roasted with garlic and parsley. For dessert Hans brought us fresh strawberries in whipped cream with champagne for Tourmaline and Squirt grapefruit soda in a glass for me.

'You don't drink?' Tourmaline asked.

'No.'

'You sound sad about it.' The way she let her head tilt to the side told me she cared. For the first time in a long time, I felt physically drawn to a woman.

'Whiskey for me is like having an allergy to aspirin along with the worst headache you could imagine.'

Tourmaline didn't respond to that, not with words. She sipped from her flute and looked at me.

'I have the information you wanted,' she said. 'And I'll give it to you if you promise not to try and pay me.'

'I can't even try?'

'No.'

# CHAPTER 15

I was further impressed by Tourmaline because she had taken the bus to make our date. I drove her home with hardly a thought about Christmas Black and the hard men after him, or about Mouse and his war with the LAPD.

It was after eleven when I walked the beautiful young black woman to her door. She lived in an apartment that had been added on to the side of a garage at the back of a home on Hooper.

While she fumbled in her purse for the key, I said, 'This has been a really wonderful evening, Miss Goss.'

Almost as an afterthought she took an envelope out of her bag and handed it to me.

'This is what you asked me for,' she said.

'Thank you.'

She looked up at me, waited for more words, and when those words didn't come, she said, 'Is that it?'

'What?'

'I expect a man to at least try and kiss me. You know it took me two and a half hours to look like this.'

Time didn't exactly stop for me right then. It was more like it slowed down to an excruciatingly sluggish ooze. I could feel my lips wondering what to say – or do.

'Hello,' Tourmaline prodded when I didn't answer.

And then suddenly everything became normal again. I knew exactly who I was and what I needed to say.

'If I were to kiss you right now, with everything that I'm feelin', neither one of us would make it through the door. We'd be right out here on the concrete, under the palm trees, making babies.'

Tourmaline gazed at me, deciding how to react to my declaration.

'That's better,' she said at last.

She opened the door and went in. Before the door closed, she put her head out and kissed the air.

I got to Cox Bar a few minutes shy of midnight. Most places in LA were already closed, but Ginny Wright's bar was just getting started. It was a tin-and-tar-paper structure that would have been condemned on the day it was erected, but Cox was hidden in an alley and no health inspector, no building inspector even knew it was there.

Somewhere around fifteen men and women sat in the dark room, leaning on mismatched tables, perched on chairs, stools, benches, and even a crate or two. The room stank of sour beer and cigarette smoke, but I can't say that it didn't feel like home. The dark despair contained within the walls of Cox Bar was the memory and sensibility that were contained within the confines of my skull. The darkness was a place to hide and plot and grieve.

I took a deep breath and walked toward the pine plank set upon two sawhorses that stood for the bar. I expected to see big black Ginny come around the closet that held the liquor bottles, but instead it was my old friend John from Fifth Ward, Houston, Texas. John – one of my oldest friends in California. Tall and broad and brown as the mud oozing up between an alligator's claws.

John was born to be a bartender. For a few years he had tried to make it in the construction business. He bought lots and built houses. At night he'd go home pretending that he was just a regular guy, a businessman who never thought about straight liquor and prostitutes, payoffs and gangsters.

'Easy.'

'Alva's gone for good, huh, John?'

Alva had been John's wife for a few years. He had helped raise her son, hired me to save the brooding boy's life one time there.

'Yeah,' John replied. 'She wanted a daytime man, and you know I can't even talk straight 'fore four in the afternoon.'

I sat on the bar's one high stool, and he served me a glass of water with three ice cubes in it.

'Where's Ginny?' I asked. 'I don't think I've ever been here when she wasn't workin' the bar.'

'Lupus.'

It was only a word, but we both knew that it might well be a death sentence for our old friend from Houston.

After an appropriate span of reverent silence, John asked, 'Mouse in trouble?'

I laughed; I had to. Black folk of my generation and before had to be able to see around the corner to ensure their safety. We couldn't afford to suffer surprise. I had a card that told anyone who was interested that I was a detective, but I was no more a private eye than John or Jackson or Gara or any soul sitting in that dark, dark room. Each and every one of us was examining and evaluating clues all the time, day and night.

'Why you ask?' I asked John's question.

'He ain't been in here in eight, nine days, an' you don't drink.'

'That's a big jump.'

'Only if you fall,' John said with certainty.

I laughed again. 'Yeah. Cops seem to think that Raymond killed somebody, an' Etta wants me to check it out.' There was no reason to lie to John. He knew more secrets than a whole monastery of retired confessors.

'Cops just now thinkin' that Ray killed somebody?' John said, his humor as deep as our history.

'Not just anybody, man.'

'Oh. You mean Pericles.'

'You know Tarr?'

'For three weeks before Raymond stopped comin', him an' Pericles was thick as thieves.'

'Friends?'

'Oh, yeah. Ray buy one drink an' Perry buy the next. Women come up to 'em, an' they sent 'em away. They was friends, but they was serious too.'

'How well you know this Pericles?'

'He come in here now and then for a long time, tryin' to get away for a few minutes,' John said.

'Away from what?'

'All them ugly kids. He had a dozen of 'em an' said that there was only one he could stand.'

'Leafa?'

It was John's turn to smile.

'Yeah, that's what he called her. He said that them kids even made a ruckus in their sleep. His wife always askin' him for more money, and the kids screamin' like they was in Bedlam.

'Perry sit down at the end of the bar and nurse two beers all night long. He'd tell his wife he had a second job, but you know he just couldn't stand them chirren.'

I was thinking that maybe Perry had deserted his family. But why would Mouse be involved with that?

'Then, about three months ago, he hooked up with this woman,' John continued.

'What was her name?'

'Never said. You know how secretive a niggah

103

can be, Ease. Pericles moved to a table when he was with his girl and he always got the drinks at the bar and brought them back to her. She liked scotch – neat.'

# CHAPTER 16

I got home not long after one. The dog grinned his hatred for me at the door. I could tell by the jumble of cushions on the love seat that Jesus and Benita were still in the house; that made me feel good. Easter and Feather were in Feather's bed. Essie murmured somewhere in her sleep.

I went to Juice's old room and undressed. He was a short boy who had grown into a small young man, so I never got him a big bed. The lumpy little mattress was good enough for me, though.

Jesus's room smelled like the desert. I often thought that he was an ancient soul who found his way back to the land of his people after it had been sundered by the white man – and the white man's slaves.

As a rule, thinking calmed me. I wasn't afraid of blood or pain. I wasn't protected as a child and so I knew that I'd die one day. Danger and life were synonyms in my personal thesaurus; dancing and boxing were too.

This thought came to me as I rested on the bed of the son of my heart. The words I knew had only the slightest relationship to the same words in the white American lexicon. It's not that I felt more or deeper, it was that I thought differently. I had another knowledge.

Following this esoteric line of thinking, I came upon Leafa: little, brown, ugly, loving child of a man with too much of a good thing.

Leafa had told me that her father was a survivor, that he would be able to stay safe among men bent upon his demolition.

I had another knowledge, and most children did too. Adults liked to think that they knew the world better because children didn't have the words to express their visions and because they were fearless. But I knew that young people always saw the world more clearly and closely than I. They smelled things and saw the tiniest variations. They thought without preformed conclusions and listened with their hearts.

Pericles Tarr was not in debt to Mouse, not in the ordinary way. Raymond took on friends now and again, hung out with them, made clandestine plans with them. Mouse was a criminal, a master criminal. He was also an active member of an outcast community. Whatever it was that made Tarr disappear, it had something to do with Mouse's business. Pericles might have been dead, but it wasn't because Mouse had lent him money.

And where was Raymond? He wasn't the type to kill a man and run. Mouse ran after things, not away from them.

The effort of thought was making me tired. I was falling asleep when I remembered the bill of sale that Tourmaline had stolen for me. Why had she done that? Was it because she was a poor college student who could use the money for books? But then she just handed it over, refusing the money.

As I got older, my profession began to take center stage in my life. I wanted to know why things happened, but not like when I was a young man. In my early life, I wanted money and women, success and respect, not for what I did but for who I was. Now I was interested in Tourmaline because I couldn't quite understand her motivations; I didn't know what she saw in me, and that was very unusual.

It was also beside the point.

Easter Dawn was sleeping in Feather's room, dreaming about the man she called father. One day he would hand her a pistol and tell her that he'd murdered her parents, aunts, uncles, cousins, and all their friends – but until that day her love for him would be bigger than the sky.

These thoughts comforted me. In the morning I'd go looking for Christmas again. Maybe I could help him. Maybe he would help me find Ray.

Ray: the closest friend in my life before Bonnie came on the scene.

Thinking of Bonnie was the turn that guaranteed me another sleepless night. Once Bonnie entered my mind, there was no possibility for repose. She was the book I couldn't put down, the life savings I had lost, the question I could not answer.

And it wasn't only her. I had a blood daughter somewhere, lost to me, and parents who had died before I was eight.

I remembered a woman – Celestine. She was a distant cousin of my mother's who took me in when I was orphaned. Her house was so clean that I was afraid to walk across the floor. Because no matter where I went, there was dust and lint, crusts and detritus of all kinds cascading off me. Celestine's life was perfectly ordered and spotless. I didn't belong in her world, though I longed for it.

At the age of nine I ran away after breaking a jar of strawberry jam that clotted her perfect kitchen floor. I didn't know how to clean up the sticky red disaster and so I ran away and never returned.

I grew up and went to war. The red stains there were taken away by explosions, flies, and dogs getting a taste of their onetime masters. Cleaning up in Europe was killing. I could do that.

I kept a list in my head of every human being I had slaughtered. The roll was far too long. And even though I had never actually murdered anyone, there were many innocents who died by my hand: white men and blacks, young and old. I once shot a German sniper who turned out to be a nine-year-old boy chained to his post by a teenage superior.

★   ★   ★

The long dark morning passed like that, an interminable chain of associations among the things lost to me or the crimes I'd committed. Just before the sun began to rise, I came to understand that my mind was a deep chasm, a fault of culpability. Before I threw her out, Bonnie would call to me when I began that inevitable fall into myself.

I had other realizations, but they didn't mean anything. I was like a pothead solving the problems of the world with a hash pipe and too much time on my hands.

After some time had passed, the sun came up and I climbed out of Jesus's lumpy bed. I showered and shaved, put on the same charcoal suit I'd worn on my date.

I tried for a moment to think about what I'd feel like if I'd had sex with Tourmaline, but I couldn't wrap my mind around the notion.

I took out the folder Gara had given me from her research on the medals and started going through the names and their sketchy descriptions.

I rejected Xian Lo first off. The man I had met wasn't Asian, and though it was possible for an Occidental to have an Asian name, the probability just wasn't there. Morton, Heatherton, and Lamieux were all too short for my guy.

It also wasn't Charles Maxwell Bob because he was a Negro. It said so at the bottom of his sheet: *Rc. Neg.* It was the only indication of race in any of the files. This didn't surprise me; it wouldn't have surprised two people out of two million in

America at that time. I noted the bias, but that was just another case.

It was a good morning's work. I'd cut down my suspects from eight to two.

Either Glen Thorn or Tomas Hight was my man. Tourmaline wouldn't have liked the first one: not enough syllables for her.

I went through my Southern California phone books and found addresses for both men. Life wasn't good, but at least it kept moving forward.

# CHAPTER 17

I was sitting at the kitchenette table a few minutes shy of 6:30 when the baby cried. I was considering which problem I should tackle first. I had Christmas's most recent address from the bill of sale that Tourmaline had provided and two soldiers I could look up. I knew that Pericles Tarr had a girlfriend somewhere. Each of these potential paths had equal weight in my mind.

If I had had a clue about the whereabouts of Mouse, that's the direction I would have taken.

I was missing Ray, not because he could help me through this violent period but for his sense of humor. He liked to laugh and tell a good story. Added to that, Mouse didn't understand guilt or broken hearts – that was just the kind of ignorance I craved.

'Hi, Dad.'

Jesus was standing in the kitchen with Essie in his arms. I reached out for her without thinking about it. She cried and then cooed. After getting used to my smell, she practiced kicking and turning her head from side to side.

111

Jesus went about making coffee.

I had had almost fifteen years of that boy brewing me coffee and bringing me the gifts of life. He'd been brutally abused when he was little older than his daughter, but somehow that had not twisted him. I would have liked to say that it was my firm hand and loving home that saved the boy, but he was the one who saved me more often than not. It was Jesus that emptied all my liquor bottles when my first wife left. It was Jesus made me coffee and dinner more times than I could count.

And now he had brought me a granddaughter. Here we couldn't have a gene in common going back more than twenty thousand years, but that boy was my blood.

He brought two mugs to the table and took Essie from me. The way he cradled that baby made me think of the few years he spent with my friend Primo before coming to me. Maybe the Mexican and his Panamanian wife, Flower, had saved Jesus's soul.

'Feather said that you're mad at her,' my son said.

'I'm not.'

'She said that she gave you a hard time about the wedding and that, and that you got mad.'

Essie grabbed his lip and pulled, just a little.

'You remember when you were a boy?' I asked.

'Yes.'

'You remember when you didn't talk those first years, never spoke a word?'

Jesus looked at me, mute as he was back in those days.

'Why?' I asked. 'Why didn't you talk for all that time?'

'I did,' he said in a voice reminiscent of his first whispering years of conversation. 'I did with my mind. I was thinking answers and I thought you could hear me. And you did, Dad. You knew everything I wanted to say.'

'So why ever talk, then?' I asked.

'One day when Feather was little and you were at work, she was about to knock over a hot pot, and I wasn't close enough so I told her no.'

The look on my son's face was one of fascination. He was remembering that word.

'It surprised both of us,' he said. 'Feather's jaw dropped and her eyes got real big. It felt like I opened my mouth and a bird, a big bird flew out. I wondered if there were any more inside of me, and then Feather ran up and hugged me and told me to read her a story.'

I had never asked about Juice's first word. I was afraid that to question his speech would have returned him to silence.

'Are you mad at Feather?' he asked.

'No. I just can't understand when she stopped being a child and started bein' a woman. That's what's got me.'

'I don't think Bonnie wants to marry him,' Jesus said, as if it were the logical extension of our talk.

'No? She don't love him?'

'No,' the boy-sage replied. 'She loves him. He loves her and needs her, and so she can see them together. But if you had ever called her, she would have come back here to us.'

'So then let me ask you, Juice,' I said. 'Are you mad at me?'

Essie made a sound akin to a laugh. Jesus stared at me like the man he'd always been.

'No,' he said, shaking his head. 'I'm with Benita and off on my boat half the time. Feather talks to Bonnie every other day. Bonnie has Joguye, and even though she wants you, that's something.'

It felt as if each declarative phrase was a nail driven into my coffin. I wanted to tell him to stop talking, but I had asked the question.

'Mr Rawlins?'

Easter Dawn was my savior. She wore a plaid skirt that Feather had outgrown years before and a white silk T-shirt. Her black hair was tied back with a yellow ribbon, also of silk. Her shoes were black, her socks white, and there was a pink Cracker Jack plastic ring on the forefinger of her right hand. On her shoulder was hung the fancy briefcase-like satchel.

'Aren't we dressed up,' I said, lifting the tiny eight-year-old and putting her on my lap.

'Feather said I could wear her old clothes,' Easter confessed, the hint of guilt in her voice.

'And you look beautiful in them.'

The child smiled at me and clasped her hands.

'I want to go to school,' she said.

'You do? Don't you like being on vacation?'

'No. And I want to be in school. My daddy says that school is bad, that it makes people bad, but Feather and Juice are nice and they went to school. And anyway, Feather has to stay home every day to take care of me and she's missing her tests.'

'Hm. Yeah. I guess you're right. Okay. Go get your sister, and I'll take you off to school at about eight.'

As E.D. ran toward the back of the house, I thought about calling Feather her sister. I suppose I was preparing for the worst. I had been training for disaster as far back as I could remember.

I drove the girls to school. Feather went off to the library to study, and I brought E.D. to the office. There I encountered Mrs Canfield.

She had a decade on me, all of it traveled on a rutted, hardscrabble road. She was a white woman, but her coloring had some liver to it. Her mouth hadn't known mirth, maybe ever, and her eyes gave you the impression that you were the most worthless person in the world.

After I told her my name and she told me hers, I said, 'I'm Feather's father.'

'Oh,' she said haughtily. 'Feather called in days ago. She said that there was a family emergency an that you would call. But my records show no such call.'

'I was dealing with the emergency,' I said.

115

'Education is the most important part of a child's life, Mr Rawlins. If you cannot take that seriously, how can your children hope to make it in this world?'

It was the wrong morning for us to meet. I was an American Negro. And while not being a Rochester stereotype or a white-lipped minstrel clown, I was quite aware of how to deal with people like Mrs Canfield. Don't get me wrong: she wasn't looking down on me because of race. She was in her seat of power and would have lectured Lyndon Baines Johnson had he wandered into her court. And Lyndon could have learned something from my long experience. I could have told him that the way to deal with Canfield was to say, *Yes, ma'am. I'm sorry, ma'am. You are right, ma'am.*

That's what I should have said, but it wasn't the day for it.

'Really?' I replied. 'It seems to me that health, food on the table, love, and shelter would come before a child could ever think about reading a book. I mean, how could you expect an ailing, hungry child to come in here and take your tests? Do you serve free lunches here, Mrs Canfield?'

The edge on her gaze could have cut diamonds.

'What is it that you want of me, Mr Rawlins?'

'I want to enroll this child in school.'

'She doesn't look like your child.'

After speaking, the school administrator sat back

116

a little. Her sharp eyes had caught a hint of the violence in my posture.

Before I could come up with the appropriate lie, Mrs Canfield added. 'In order to enroll a child in this school, you will need her birth certificate, inoculation history, and proof of guardianship.'

'I can have all that by next week.'

'Bring her back then.'

Easter Dawn pulled on the sleeve of my dark gray jacket.

'I thought you wanted all kids in school all the time?' I said.

'This is not your child.'

Easter pulled on my sleeve again.

'We're talking, honey,' I said.

'Look in here, Mr Rawlins.' She was handing me the ornate satchel.

I took the crocheted case and flipped it open. In there was a paper file, among other things. The manila folder held the information that Canfield had asked for. Christmas had made me Easter's legal guardian and he had the Riverside Board of Education's homeschooling certification of her first- and second-grade evaluation exams. She'd had her smallpox, polio, and tetanus vaccines.

I handed the papers over to Mrs Canfield, and she studied them like a poker player in the biggest game of her life. Three minutes went by while Easter and I sat silently.

117

'Everything seems to be in order,' the ogre said at last. 'I'll take Miss Black to her classroom.'

'Have Feather walk her home, please,' I said, happy to be mannered and victorious with a single word.

# CHAPTER 18

I took Easter's shoulder bag with me because it seemed a better idea than leaving it with her or taking out the two bound stacks of thousand-dollar bills inside.

Thousand-dollar bills. Two hundred of them.

Christmas was a soldier and he planned for almost every exigency. He knew that I would have to put Easter in school. He knew better than I did what the school would demand for her admittance. There was a sealed envelope in the satchel that had a list of names and addresses: his lawyer, Thelda Kim; Easter's doctor, Martin Lewis; a bank officer in Riverside oddly named Bertrand Bill; and his parents. Each name had a phone number and an address beside it. The parents must have been separated. Christmas had told me that almost all the marriages in his family dissolved; something to do with military rigor among professional soldiers.

In his mind Christmas was ready for everything – even what he'd left out of his typewritten catalog proved this.

There was no letter or even a note to me. Not one detail about why he had gone to ground, passing his most precious possession into my hands. This negative space, this silence, was a clear message that I should work with what I was given – and sit tight.

Christmas Black, despite his civilian status, thought of himself as my superior. He was the tactical commander, and I was just a grunt with a stripe or two.

That's what Christmas thought, but he didn't know me all that well. I was a dog that got cut from the pack at an early age. I was no man's soldier, no leader's peon. The president of the United States stood on two feet and so did I.

And so I drove out to Venice Beach to look up Glen Thorn on Orchard Lane, the first of the names I'd narrowed down from Gara's list.

It was a small cottagelike house behind three crab apple trees. There was a porch and a green front door that was solid and locked. I knocked with the butt of my pistol and called out in a raspy voice, hoping that would conceal my identity. No one attacked or answered me.

The window was locked too, but the wood had become rather punky. I just pulled hard, ripping off a piece of the sill with the lock, and climbed in.

I was sure that Glen Thorn was not my man from the state of that one-room hut. The sink was overflowing with dishes, and the floor was cluttered with clothes, fast-food bags and boxes, girlie magazines, and sensationalist rags. BABY WITH TWO HEADS BORN TO SECRET KENNEDY COUSIN. ALIENS CONTROL LADY BIRD'S MIND. BROKENHEARTED LOVER EMASCULATES SELF IN TIJUANA TOILET.

There were no weapons or pictures of him in evidence or secreted away in any drawer or the closet. The war hero I had seen had nothing in common with this mess. Mentally I crossed him off my list, then went through the front door and out to my car.

I wanted my quarry to be Glen Thorn because Tomas Hight lived all the way out in Bellflower; that was a long drive through enemy territory.

It was very, very white out in Bellflower. Many of the people around those parts had southern accents, and even though I knew racists came in all dialects, I had experienced my worst bigotry accompanied by sneers and southern drawls.

But I was an American citizen and I had a right to drive into danger if I wanted to.

Tomas hight lived in a six-story lavender apartment building on Northern Boulevard, a kind of main drag. There were a lot of people out on his block and almost all of them were very interested in me: white women pushing baby carriages and white men having loud arguments on the corner, white teenagers who when they saw me saw glimmers of something that their parents could never comprehend, and of course the police – the white police.

A cruiser slowed down a little to study my profile but then moved on.

Being alone in the late-morning sun was the only thing that saved me from an immediate rousting. More than one Negro at a time in a white neighborhood in 1967 was an invitation to a rumble or a roust.

I came to the front door of the apartment building, wondering if the series of lies I'd constructed would get me over the hump I'd been riding since the age of eight.

I'd tell Hight that I noticed his medals and looked them up, finding his address. I'd tell him that I'd found Christmas but that the man nearly killed me. I was afraid to go to my office and so I didn't know how to get in touch with his captain. I'd lull the former MP and then, when he began to trust me, I'd pistol-whip him and get the lowdown on what he was doing.

It wasn't a perfect plan, but it fit my state of mind and my need for an outlet for all that anger.

A big, powerful-looking white man with long, long dirty blond hair flowing from his head and jaw stood up from the stairs to bar my way into the building.

There were crumbs and naps in his beard. He smelled of sweat and incense oils. The mild vapors of alcohol wafted around him and so did a big, lazy fly.

'Can I help you?' he asked in a Texas drawl that I felt all the way down to the soles of my feet. Then my right testicle began aching, and I knew that the dark side of my mind was preparing to go to war.

'Looking for Tomas,' I said, as if I weren't preparing to kill this big aberration of the hippie movement.

'And who the fuck are you?'

'Why don't we ask Tomas?' I said airily.

'You messin' with me, nigger?'

'If I was to mess with you, brother,' I said in the same light tone, 'you would never even know it.'

'Say what?'

I put my right hand in my pocket, trying to imagine that I was Mouse, and said, 'Stand the fuck outta my way or I'll kill you where you stand.'

Somewhere inside the machinery of my mind I found the will and the recklessness to kill the man who had commandeered my people's reformation of his language to threaten me.

His china blue eyes faltered. He was used to being the top dog, but he also knew what I had in my pocket. He knew it and I knew it, and so he moved to the side and went past me down the stairs.

After that performance I knew that I didn't have much time. I went to the bank of mailboxes, homed in on THIGHT, and ran up the three flights of stairs to apartment 4C.

The door was an impossible combination of pink and lime, with a lacquered but rusty-looking doorknob. I imagined the long-haired sentry gathering his tribe to teach all my people a lesson through me.

I knocked and, before there was time to answer, knocked again.

There came a sound from down the stairs. I knocked one more time.

Men's voices, angry men's voices, were making their way up the stairs.

I tried the doorknob; it wouldn't budge.

I tried knocking again while looking around for a good defensive position.

I was desperate, but the irony of the situation was not lost on me even then. Here I was after Hight, wanting to bring him down in order to help my friend, but at the same time I was knocking on his door hoping that he might save me from the strangers I could hear saying the word *nigger* as they mounted the stairs.

Across the way from Hight's door was an inset doorway with no apartment number on it, a storage room or maybe the super's hopper. It was only a few inches of protection, but I crossed the way.

My pursuers were half a flight down when I took out my pistol and molded myself into the unmarked doorway.

I was ready to go down protecting myself when a thought came into my mind.

It occurred to me that I was the victim not only of those men but of the conditioning that made me wait for them to come before I acted. I was sure that a group of four or five men was coming up those stairs to cause me serious bodily harm. I was innocent of any crime warranting this attack. Why should I cower in a corner, giving them the upper hand, rather than run down among them, pistol blazing?

I was acting like a guilty man even though I knew I wasn't. I was being defensive when I should have been on the offense. I had six bullets and all the training I'd ever need.

The decision to slaughter those men came with no fear of law or prison or death.

I was about to run down shooting. The war cry was in my throat.

When the door to 4C came open, my gears changed so fast that I was a little confused. I put the pistol in my pocket before the dark-haired white man came out into the hall. Half a second after that, the long-haired man I had threatened appeared at the top of the stairway.

'There he is.' Long-Hair pointed a gnarly, cigarette-stained finger at me.

There were sounds of rage and indignity issuing from the throats of men I had never met.

'Tomas Hight!' I shouted.

The white man who came from the apartment was tall and well built. His dark brown hair was short but not military. His black eyes studied me briefly and then turned to the five men after me.

'What's up. Roger?' the man asked my blond, and until then nameless, archenemy.

'Nigger insulted me, threatened me,' Roger replied.

A few of his friends agreed, though they had not witnessed the encounter.

'And you had to get a whole mob for just one nigger?' Hight asked, putting an odd emphasis on the last word.

'He said he was after you,' Roger said, trying to enlist the new player.

'Are you after me?' Tomas Hight asked me.

'I wanted to talk to you about another MP,' I said. 'Glen Thorn.'

Tomas squinted as if in pain, then turned to Roger and the suddenly docile pack.

'This man and I have business,' Tomas said. 'So get outta here and leave us alone.'

'He's got a gun,' Roger said in a last-ditch attempt to turn the tide of his potential revenge.

'Then I probably just saved your life,' Tomas said.

It was true. Even Roger seemed to understand

that chasing an armed man into a corner was a stupid thing to do.

'Come on in,' Tomas said to me.

I was glad that he wasn't the man I was looking for. I was elated that he was the man I'd found.

# CHAPTER 19

Tomas Hight lived in a one-room studio. The walls were pale fuchsia and the furniture mostly forest green and dark wood. There was no bed in evidence, so I figured that the couch folded out. A yellow hard hat sat upright on the oak table with two newspapers under it.

Hight wore a white T-shirt and black jeans. He was barefoot and my hero.

'You have a gun?' he asked me.

I handed him my PI's license.

He scanned it, handed it back, and asked again, 'You have a gun?'

I nodded. 'But I didn't come here looking for trouble.'

It's worth the time to explain the complexity of my feelings at that moment. Tomas Hight was the quintessential white man, the white man that all other white men wanted to be. He was tall and good-looking, strong and restrained but willing to act. He had saved my butt from a beating or the gas chamber and even brought me into his home, such as it was, even though I may have been armed, dangerous, and depraved. I felt gratitude toward him while at the same time feeling that he was everything that stood in the way of my freedom, my manhood, and my people's ultimate deliverance. If these conflicting sentiments were meteorological, they would have conjured a tornado in that small apartment.

Added to my already ambivalent feelings was the deep desire in me to respect and admire this man, not because of who Tomas Hight was or what he had done but because he was the hero of all the movies, books, TV shows, newspapers, classes, and elections I had witnessed in my forty-seven years. I had been conditioned to esteem this man and I hated that fact. At the same time, the man standing before me had actually done me a great service without coercion. I owed him respect and admiration. It was a bitter debt.

My two minds slammed against each other, and I was stunned. This, and the adrenaline from my recent near-death experience, explains my candor in the conversation we shared.

'What do I have to do with Glen Thorn?' Tomas Hight asked.

'Can I sit?'

He gestured at the couch and took an oak chair from under his all-purpose table.

I sat down, hoping that taking the strain off my legs would clear my thinking, but it didn't.

'Glen Thorn?' Hight prodded.

'I've been hired to find a man named Christmas Black,' I said. 'He was a Green Beret, a major, but left the armed services for political reasons. I was looking for him when three soldiers, or men dressed like soldiers, blindsided me and tried to force me to find Black for them.'

'One of these men was Thorn?'

'I think so.'

'You say that they were pretending to be soldiers?' Hight said. 'Why would you question the uniform?'

If he hadn't just saved me, I could have given him a whole list of unrelated reasons, but instead I said, 'When they said I had to look for Black for them, I said that I charge three hundred dollars for a week's work—'

'Three hundred!'

'Detectives don't work every week, but the bills still want paying,' I said. 'Anyway, they paid right up, gave me three crisp new one-hundred-dollar bills.'

Hight was smart too. He nodded, showing me that he knew that no soldier, not even a general, rolled out that denomination.

'How did you get to me?' he asked.

I explained about the medals and the library.

'You really are a detective,' he said with admiration in his tone.

I didn't want his approbation, and yet at the same time it was the most important thing in the world to me.

'Did you serve with Thorn?' I asked, to keep from shooting either Hight or myself.

Hight leaned back in his chair, scowling at me. Something was going on in him, something that had been simmering long before I ever came to his door.

'I worked with a unit of MPs that guarded a warehouse where we stored shipments of supplies coming in from the States and elsewhere. We were guards, you know. We made sure that the black marketeers didn't get their hands on our goods.'

Where I was at odds with myself over everything, Tomas Hight was absolutely sure of his purpose and his place in the world. He had been doing the right thing in Vietnam, even if Vietnam was wrong. He had done the right thing in the hall, even if I turned out not to be worthy of his actions.

'Thorn work with you?' I asked.

I noticed that there was a small picture frame standing on the coffee table. It was an old pewter frame with the photograph of a five- or six-year-old boy standing up straight and smiling. He stood in front of a pink cinder-block wall. The sun was in his eyes, but he still smiled.

'He was a malingerer,' Hight said with the barest hint of a snarl. 'Always disappearing. He was seen removing a bag from a large crate of crockery that came in from Austin one day, and they arrested him for smuggling.'

'What was in the bag?'

'I don't know,' the Hero said. 'The CO confiscated it.'

'What happened to Thorn?'

'Nothing. Not a thing. They transferred him to another unit, and he was stateside in six weeks. I heard he even got an honorable discharge. Can you believe that?'

'I've been believin' nuthin' but that for four hundred years,' I said.

'What?'

I stood up on steady legs. I knew something more about my *employers*, and I, even though he didn't understand me, had shared a common confusion with Tomas Hight.

The boy in the picture looked just like Hight, only smaller. His son? His brother? Him? Why not a girlfriend or parent?

'Where are you going?' he asked me.

'Down to my car.'

'I was just getting ready to go to work. I'll walk down with you.'

I realized then that I couldn't escape the kindness of Tomas Hight. He was going down the stairs alongside me with a hard hat under his arm because he knew that Roger and his friends might be waiting down there. He gave me his protection without a thought to race or even if I deserved it. He would have protected a malingerer on the same principle.

At my car, we shook hands.

'Be careful around Thorn,' he advised. 'A couple of his friends in the MPs were killed right after he left. And it wasn't Charlie that did it either.'

# CHAPTER 20

Tomas Hight stayed on my mind all the way back to the city. He'd saved a life in that hall, but not necessarily my life; it was just as likely that one or more of his acquaintances would have been shot.

I thought about his one-room apartment. I owned two houses and three apartment buildings but still felt that he had more than I did. I thought he was more heroic too, but hadn't I been the one to stand up first against those men?

It's strange how you can know something and still not feel it, how you can covet the assets of others though you would never think of trading places with them.

The address Tourmaline had given me for Christmas Black was on a street named Gray. It was a single block in the area between the black neighborhood and downtown. There were warehouses and small wholesale businesses all over that unzoned neighborhood. The building across the street from Christmas's house was Cairo Cane Distributors.

There wasn't a soul anywhere to be seen.

I had waited till midmorning to go to Christmas's door because he was not the kind of man you wanted to take unawares. Black was at least as proficient a killer as Mouse. Added to that, he was crazy and paranoid; added to that, there really were people after him.

I parked in front of Cairo Cane but didn't get out immediately. Black's address was another cottage. The small yard was laid with green concrete. There was an attempt at a porch, though I doubted that there was enough room for a stool on that thin band of wood.

Flowerless flowerpots hung on either side of the front door.

I watched the house for five minutes and no one passed by.

The debacle at Tomas Hight's house had made me temporarily cautious. I didn't want to run out into another dangerous situation, and I needed to put the words together that I would say to Christmas when and if I found him.

The minutes went by, and my confidence returned.

For a while there I had forgotten the answer to the unasked question framed by fearful caution. *Will I die?* the mortal asks from the fear shared by all his kin. *Yes, you will die,* the answer comes from the infinite experience of our race. I might get hurt, be hungry, get old, contract some fatal disease. When my children uttered these fears, I

135

told them not to worry, that nothing was going to happen. But in my life I knew better. The only way to end fear was to stop breathing, to stop moving forward . . . and there I was on a street named Gray under a bright sun with no one else in sight.

The front door had been broken down and put back in place hastily. This was not a good omen. I clasped my hands and prepared to back away. I swayed, but my feet stayed planted on that faux porch.

There was nowhere else to go. If I didn't want to be a detective, I should have gone back to the LAUSD and asked them to reinstate me as a school custodian. Medical insurance, retirement program, two weeks vacation . . .

Gripping the doorknob with a gloved hand, I levered the half-unhinged door open. This brought me to an entry chamber. The uncharacteristic foyer was probably why Christmas had taken the place. Anyone trying to come in on him would have been stymied by the second door, and at the same time the occupant would have been warned of his attacker.

I wrenched the front door back in place and strode through a short passageway into the living room, as the second door was also broken in.

The room had no windows and so was shrouded in darkness.

That's where I found the first body.

Actually, I stumbled on his leg as I looked for a light switch on the wall. I almost fell. Then I waved my hand above my head and found the chain for an overhead lamp. When the light snapped on, I was looking into one of Glen Thorn's bright gray eyes. His other eye had been destroyed by the ice pick that was lodged in his brain.

I looked quickly around the small room. It had pine floors with no carpet and a pair of small brown stuffed chairs. Between the chairs stood a round table with a whiskey glass set upon it. Below the table, taking up most of the floor space, was the body that had once housed Glen Thorn. He wasn't wearing a uniform now, just black trousers, a red-and-black checkered shirt, and tennis shoes like the kids wore.

There was a pistol in his left hand.

The only neat thing about him, I now knew, was his appearance. I'd seen his filthy house and the literature he devoured. I saluted him because he had fooled me with his appearance. Glen Thorn had taught me something, and that was worth a last good-bye.

It was a shotgun house with a cottage facade. I went through the next door and found another body. This was the second MP who had accompanied the man who called himself Captain Clarence Miles. This corpse had been strangled, by hand. I could make out the finger marks along his throat and neck. Whereas Glen had no real expression on his face, this man's eyes and mouth were strained with fear. I would have been scared too if I had been looking into the murderous visage of Christmas Black while he was throttling the life from me.

This room was a kitchen, the body it contained a conundrum. How could Christmas Black, no matter how proficient he was, kill two trained soldiers in two different rooms? There was nowhere to hide in the room where Glen Thorn had died. There wasn't enough time for Christmas to jump out of some window and come back around. And even if he had used that trick, why leave a perfectly good weapon in the eye of his first victim when there might have been another assassin in the house?

I entered the next room with mounting trepidation. I expected to see Captain Miles, or whoever he was, on the floor with an arrow in his chest.

But the small bedroom was empty. There was just a mattress on the floor and a lamp. The bed was made in flawless military style. There was a window, but it was locked and barred. I looked around for the clues but found none.

Back in the living room, I noticed that one of the legs of the round table had a folded piece of paper underneath it. The table had been rocking, no doubt, something Christmas wouldn't have stood for.

I expected the wedge to be a take-out menu or a matchbook, but it was a brochure from Beachland Savings in Santa Monica. It promised a free electric fan to anyone who opened a checking account with one hundred dollars or more.

I pocketed the pamphlet and reimagined the murder scene. I tried my best to imagine the second MP coming into the kitchen and being overwhelmed by Black. Even a Green Beret would make some noise killing a man with his bare hands. Where was Thorn when this was happening? Why not kill the first MP with the ice pick and then take the other one out with his hands? Why not use a gun?

The only answer was that there were two men in the first room when the MPs broke in. One of those men, probably Christmas, feigned running into the kitchen while his cohort stood pressed into a corner, as I had done in Tomas Hight's hallway. Christmas grabbed his pursuer in the kitchen, or maybe he turned and then dragged the unsuspecting MP after him. The other man, Christmas's cohort, then blindsided Glen Thorn, who must have been concentrating on the fleeing Black. Glen got an ice pick in the eye while his friend was being strangled in the kitchen.

None of that helped me. The only lesson to be learned was to stay out of the way of this juggernaut of death. But I wasn't a willing student that day.

★   ★   ★

On my way out, I looked both ways down the street and sighed, relieved that I was in Los Angeles, where there was never anyone on the street to witness anything, not even a black man coming out of a broken door behind which was more mayhem than most honest Angelenos would see in a lifetime.

# CHAPTER 21

Saul Lynx often said that he thought of me as the unwilling detective. When I asked him what he meant, he said, 'It's not a profession for you. You're out there to help people because you hate what's happened. But really you'd rather be reading a book.'

'Wouldn't everybody rather be rich than workin'?' I asked.

'They tell you that, but most people in a job like ours are driven to be here, peeking through keyholes and mixing with scum.'

Well, I was no longer an unwilling detective. I was voluntarily moving toward a destination even though I had no idea where or what that was.

For some time, Mouse had had a sidetrack girl-friend named Lynne Hua, a Chinese beauty who had appeared in various films and TV shows. She never had more than a line or two, sometimes not even that, but she was gorgeous and worked pretty steadily. She didn't want to get married or live with anyone, so she was the perfect girlfriend for Mouse, who had the perennial problem of his temporary lovers' wanting to displace EttaMae to become Mrs Mouse.

Jesus's common-law wife, Benita, had been one of these. When she wanted more of Mouse's attention, he dropped her and she swallowed forty-seven sleeping pills. After taking her to the hospital to pump out the chemicals and restart her heart, I brought her home, where Jesus took care of her like he did all the strays I took in.

I was on my way from downtown LA to Santa Monica when I thought of Lynne. I got off the freeway at La Brea and rode north to Olympic, where Lynne lived on the third floor of a mission-style apartment building.

I had been to Lynne's before with Ray. I'd drink a glass of club soda with them before they left for some fancy Hollywood party. Lynne couldn't be a star, but neither did she have to worry about people in the movie business being nonplussed by her being with a black man. No one but her Chinese aunts would be concerned about her dating Ray.

The stairway was rust colored and external, leading upward in a tight spiral. When I got to her door, I stopped and wondered what I'd say if Mouse was there. He wouldn't like it that I was trying to find him for Etta. No, that wouldn't be the approach. I needed help because of Christmas, that's what I would say.

Lynne answered wearing a short red silk kimono with nothing underneath. Her face was made up, and there was a martini glass in her hand. For a moment I thought I had found my wayward friend.

Her lips said, 'Hi, Easy,' but the tone in her voice and the way she smiled said, 'I wondered when you'd come by alone.'

'Hey, Lynne,' I said, addressing her words, and then added, 'Lookin' for Mouse' to reply to her insinuation.

'He's not here. But why don't you come in? I hate drinking alone.'

The centerpiece of Lynne's apartment was her living room, a large octagonal space with a big, almost wall-size window looking toward the Hollywood Hills. There were bookcases on every wall and a perfectly round yellow sofa, eight feet in diameter, set deliciously off center.

'Watermelon juice and vodka?' she offered.

'Not drinking these days,' I said, but I sure wanted to.

'Come sit.'

She lay on the sofa enticingly, and I sat next to her, a schoolboy with an obvious itch.

'I haven't seen Raymond in a week,' Lynne said, pouting a little.

'You know where he's been?'

'No. He said it was serious business. That meant he didn't want me to ask where he was going or when he was coming back.'

'Was he worried?'

'Ray never worries. He's never scared of

anything. But I know better than to fall in love with a man like that.' She was on her back, looking up into my eyes. I could see her left breast clearly, and she could see me looking.

'Has your girlfriend come back?' she asked, sitting up. Her black hair fell down around the sides of her face.

'She's getting married.'

A combination of mischief and sadness formed itself on Lynne's perfect face.

'I'm so sorry,' she said. 'Can I do anything for you?'

She touched my left forearm with her fingertips.

'Yeah. Yeah, you could.'

'What?' she asked through a knowing smile.

'Go put on something so I don't lose my mind and get us both killed.'

This brought about a series of changes in the actress. First her face straightened out, then she stood and nodded. As she walked from the room, I wondered if I understood anything about women . . . or men.

I went over to the bookshelf and pondered the titles, which were eclectic. There was a physics textbook and *Moby Dick*, books in French, Chinese, and Spanish, a guide to knitting. After seeing all the different titles and languages, I thought that the books were just a designer's decoration, a counterbalance for the erotic charge of the room, but then I realized that they were placed in alphabetical order, by title.

While I was pondering Lynne Hua's library, she returned. Now she was wearing a schoolgirl's green-and-white plaid skirt and a white blouse buttoned up to her throat. She even wore black shoes and white ankle socks.

Her smile seemed to be suppressing a sneer.

She sat and I did too.

'I'm sorry,' she said. 'I haven't been working, and Raymond is gone for I don't know how long. And . . . and sometimes I drink too much.'

I had all the information I needed from her, but I couldn't just walk out after making her get dressed.

'You haven't been working?' I asked.

'I've been waiting for a job to start.'

'What's that?'

The hidden sneer receded.

'There's a new TV show called *My Dad the Bachelor* that's supposed to air in the fall. I have a recurring role.'

'What is it?'

'You're a funny man, Mr Rawlins. I a Chinee girl speakee funny, lookee like ugly duck next to beautiful white swan.' She mimed the last part for me, and I smiled in condolence.

'Oh.'

'They pay okay,' she said. 'The bachelor dad has a Chinese houseboy who takes care of the kids. The houseboy, Ralph, has a girlfriend who's always yelling at him and cursing in Chinese. That's all she does. He tells her something and then she

145

screams. Once every three weeks I'll go in to do that and they'll pay my rent.'

'But why would they make a woman as beautiful as you into an ugly woman?' I asked.

'You think I'm ugly,' she said.

'You know that's not true, girl. You look so good to me I have to cross my legs to keep decent. It's just that Ray's my friend and, as you said, he's serious.'

The smile she showed at the hint of death was everything I needed to know about Lynne Hua.

'Blow jobs,' she said.

'Say what?'

'I give great blow jobs. There's one guy casts for commercials, acts like he's my agent because he knows that if I get a job he does too.'

She was trying to shock me and succeeding. It's not that I was surprised what a man would do to get a woman down on her knees in front of him, but I was amazed that she would admit it so blithely.

'Have I scandalized you, Mr Rawlins?'

'No . . . I mean, yes.'

'You don't think a woman has to do these things to get by?'

'Oh, no, yes, yes, of course they do. It's not that,' I said. 'It's you telling me about it.'

'You think I should tell Raymond what I do to get work?'

'No. I'm just wondering why tell me?'

'I have to tell somebody.' Her face was

completely straight and honest looking. The words she spoke, I was sure, were the absolute truth.

'But why me?'

'Because,' Lynne said, 'Raymond says that you are the most trustworthy man he had ever known. He says that you can tell Easy anything. He says that it's like dropping a killing gun in the deepest part of the ocean.'

Watermelon juice and vodka were the prescription for her moments alone. I had just happened along when she was under the sway of her medicine.

'That's why I wanted to make love to you,' she said.

'Because why?'

'I thought afterward I could tell you what I did and you would forgive me and I would keep our secret. But I didn't even have to do that, did I?'

I held out a hand to her, and she wrapped her arms around me. We stood there a moment in that embrace. I kissed the top of her head and squeezed her shoulder.

When we let go, I asked, 'How would you go about finding Mouse if you had to, Lynne?'

'Mama Jo.'

Of course.

# CHAPTER 22

Leaving Lynne's neighborhood, I took Olympic down to Santa Monica. On the way I tried to resolve the differences between people like the Chinese actress and Tomas Hight. Lynne lived an exciting life that was split between black gangsters and glittering Hollywood parties. She was well educated, I believed, and bright as a cloudless day in the Palm Springs desert. Tomas, on the other hand, didn't have much – maybe didn't understand very much. All he had was a job working construction and one room to live in. The difference was that Tomas could be president of the United States one day, and all Lynne could hope for would be to give the president a blow job.

This reality had nothing to do with my being black, Negro, or colored, bearing the inheritance of slavery. Lynne came from a culture that remembered itself all the way back before America's colonizers could even speculate.

While having these idle thoughts, I was driving past palm trees, coral trees, eucalyptus trees . . . a whole arboretum of trees of every species. That was Los Angeles too. We were a desert with all the water we needed, a breeding ground for the contradiction of nature. Any seed or insect or lizard or mammal that found itself in LA had to believe that there was a chance to thrive. Living in Southern California was like waking up in a children's book titled *Would Be If I Could Be.*

But the desert was waiting for all of us. One day the water would stop flowing, and then the masters of that land would reclaim their domain.

I parked on Lincoln Boulevard a block north of Olympic. Strolling a block east brought me to Beachland Savings. The building was shaped like a slice of pie, crust side out, placed on the corner. The front was a wide arc of glass revealing the comings and goings of everyday people tending their checking accounts and Christmas clubs.

I walked in happy about the fact that I would not be likely to find a dead military man in that building, happy just to be moving forward.

I was still in my gray suit, still looking presentable, but this was Santa Monica, and all the business in that bank was being conducted by white people. In 1964, I would have been an anomaly walking in there, obviously far from home, looking around at the faces of employees and customers alike. But in 1967, two years after the Watts riots, I was no longer a mere abnormality but a threat.

'Excuse me, sir,' a uniformed guard said as he walked up to me.

'Yes?'

'Can I help you?'

He was shorter than I, red faced and pale eyed. There was a stolid certainty in his stare. His body was telling me that I couldn't move forward before answering his question, so I considered the different routes to my goal.

After a moment went by, I asked: 'You still got them new fans in here? It's hotter than a oven down at my place. My girlfriend wants me to get a air conditioner, but you know it's not just what the unit cost but all that electricity it suck down.'

'You have to start a checking account with a hundred-dollar minimum in order to get a fan.'

I took out one of my two remaining hundred-dollar bills and held it out to him as if he were an usher who needed to read my ticket in order to guide me to my seat.

He almost reached for the bill, but then he remembered who he was and where we were. Resentment replaced the indifference in his gaze. His nostrils flared a bit. He waited as long as he could and then gestured to the left, where an old lady and a man in a checkered suit were sitting on a long marble bench.

'You're third in line,' the guard said, as if reminding me of my place in the grand design of things.

I thanked him with a smile and an exaggerated

nod, then went to sit, where the lady and the man ignored me.

Across from us was a paper-thin, waist-high, red-stained pine wall. Beyond this wall two bank officers manned twin oaken desks; a bird-boned man who wore thick-lensed, green-rimmed glasses side by side with a vivacious Hollywood blonde who might have been playing a loan officer on a movie screen.

Both bankers were in earnest conversation with the men sitting before them. I watched the dramas unfold. The bank officer with the green glasses was processing a new account, but he acted as if it were all very official. He checked identification and studied the information his client, a long-haired man in cutoffs and a T-shirt, had written on his form.

The other officer had a sorry look on her face. The businessman she was speaking to had asked for a loan and was in the process of being denied. He was aggressive, kept pointing at her and at other parts of the bank. She made a gesture of helplessness and managed to frown and smile at the same time.

I was taken by her empathy for this rude customer. I could hear his angry voice though not the words. He was arguing with her authority, but she didn't take offense.

I guess I was staring at her when she began to notice me.

At first it was just a glance, but after a while she

was completely distracted. No one else would have noticed. She was still patient with the businessman, she still sat posed and perfect for the camera. But I caught her trying to see me.

This wasn't an unusual situation for me to be in. I often made white women upset by noticing them. Sometimes I could see them concocting responses to the raw pickup lines they knew I would utter if I got the chance. I thought I had her figured out, but then the woman looked up and right at me, deeply into my eyes. There was frank interest in me, my being there, and I understood what was going on.

She turned her head to the businessman and said something blunt. She was no longer smiling, no longer understanding. The man moved his head as if he had been slapped. He sat up straight while deciding how to respond. There was a momentary face-off, but then the man stood and walked through the red-stained pine gate and left the bank, consciously avoiding eye contact with anyone else.

I watched him leave, noticing that the blue suit he wore was threadbare and that his shoes were so old they had almost completely molded to the shape of his feet.

'Sir?'

The blond officer was standing over me. She had one of those figures that made you look away in modesty. Just her close proximity made my hands hot.

'We were first,' the man in the checkered suit said. He had a mustache and a tic in his right eyelid. I hadn't looked at his face before, so I didn't know if the tic was due to the bank officer's coming up to me or not.

'We'll be with you as soon as we can,' the curvaceous officer said. And then to me, 'Come with me, sir.'

I took the place of the down-at-heel businessman, noticing the officer's nameplate – FAITH MOREL.

'Thank you, Miss Morel,' I said, 'but that gentleman was before me.'

'Mr Treeman comes in every other day to argue about the rounding of the decimal on his interest,' she said in a pleasant, unhurried voice. 'We tell him that it is bank policy to round point five and below down a penny, but he wants to argue. If his time is that worthless to him, he might as well wait till last.

'What can I do for you, Mr . . .'

'Rawlins. Ezekiel Rawlins.'

I watched her eyes to see if she knew the name, but she didn't seem to.

'What can I do for you, Mr Rawlins?'

'This electric fan,' I said, taking out the brochure and pointing. 'My girlfriend says she wants a air conditioner, but . . .'

I stopped because I could see the desperation in Faith's expression. She had seen something in me, and now I became something else. Maybe

153

I was a threat or some fool looking for a free lunch.

She didn't break down, but the breakdown was straight ahead.

I placed my hand on hers, and she grabbed on to it.

'I'm sorry,' I said. 'I didn't mean to play with you.'

I pulled my hand away and took out my wallet. I opened it to a photograph of Easter Dawn Black that the child had given me five months before, at Thanksgiving. Christmas took Easter to a photographer every three months to have his memory of her documented.

'Do you know this child?' I asked.

She nodded, not crying.

'Her father left her at my house two days ago. I've been looking for him since then.'

'How did you find me?'

'I went to two houses Christmas had been staying at. In the second one there was a brochure for this bank; in the first there was a picture of you standing on a yacht named *New Pair of Shoes*.'

'Oh.' Faith looked up at the clock and then down at her hands.

Faith Morel was disintegrating right there in front of me. Any moment she would break down completely.

'Why don't we get out of here and go to that diner across the street?' I suggested. 'You can tell the boss you need to take a break.'

She nodded and I rose. She watched me as if I were a soaring redwood – a tree that lived on fog, a tree that could not thrive in a desert even if that desert was flooded and lined with the sweet rot of corruption.

# CHAPTER 23

The diner could have been designed by the same company that built the bank. Glass and chrome and red linoleum and vinyl were all it had to show. There was a counter with fourteen high stools and six booths along the glass wall. I sat in the corner stall farthest from the door. A red-eyed, red-faced, red-haired waitress of thirty and then some came up to me and said, 'Sorry, honey, but the booths are for two or more.'

Her name tag read RILLA.

'My friend is coming over from the bank in just a minute,' I said. 'She wants strawberry shortcake and coffee. I'll have the same without the strawberry shortcake.'

This made the hard-living waitress smile. She showed me her stubby yellow teeth and said, 'I had a boyfriend like you down in San Diego one time. The things he did with words kept me laughin' so much that even when he stole my money and my car I still thought he was almost worth it.'

'You never saw it comin',' I said, 'and he don't know what he left behind.'

Her grin widened, and she shook her head as a sort of agreement.

I looked at Rilla, thinking about the thousands of species of trees that proliferated under the Southern California sun. You couldn't count them because new ones were coming in every day. There were more kinds of people than there were types of trees in LA. Rilla in her blue-and-white checkered uniform and I in my charcoal suit were kindred seeds blown in from far away. Just thinking that lightened my spirit.

The waitress would have stayed awhile to see what other gems I might put down, but Faith Morel came in then. I looked up and Rilla turned.

'Right here, miss,' the red-on-red-on-red woman said. 'He's a laugh a minute.'

Faith tried to smile but only managed an aspect of wan nausea. Rilla looked at her and shook her head again.

'You take care of her now, Groucho,' the waitress told me.

It seemed to me like an annunciation, a pronouncement from the deity I imagined who only appeared now and then to advise us and then watch us fail.

Rilla left, and Faith moved in across from me.

She was devastated. This wasn't a state of mind that had just come upon her, I could see its history in the lines around her eyes and the slump of her shoulders.

'What happened?' I asked.

She tried to speak but could not bring out the words. I admired her ability to work so amiably while carrying this weight.

'I'm sorry,' I said. 'I know it must be bad news that brought you here. I mean, to get Christmas to let go of Easter Dawn is pretty serious all by itself.'

There was something ethereal about Morel. Her mind seemed to be pressing into mine as she stared at me, wondering if I could even understand her pain. I was drawn to her like a beast that smells water and is dimly reminded of its distant infancy, romping with snuffling brother and sister pups many seasons gone.

That diner was a defining moment for me. . . . Maybe not that, not a seminal event but a time when I got to see what I had become. While Faith examined me for strength and fealty, I watched her, thinking about Bonnie Shay. Faith had that aura about her, the same as Bonnie did. Sitting there feeling what had been gone from my life for so long, I understood that I could not live without Bonnie. It did not matter that she'd been with another man; it did not matter about my masculinity or my rage. Either I was going to be back with her or, one way or another, I was going to die.

'Here you go,' Rilla said, putting two coffees and an obscenely large portion of strawberry short-cake on the table.

'I didn't order this,' Faith said.

'Funny man here did,' Rilla informed her.

Faith turned to me as Rilla went away. A barrier was removed from the bank officer's blue eyes and she smiled. Something about me ordering her something sweet to make her feel better. It's funny the way we make up the truth about people.

'Have you ever heard of the Sisters of Salvation?' she asked me.

'No sisters, just the army.'

'We were . . . we are a group of lapsed nuns of different denominations and religions that got together to help women all over the world. We have a mission in Vietnam. I worked there for three and a half years. I ran an orphanage on the outskirts of Saigon.'

'That's more than a job,' I said.

'Christmas brought Easter to me after he'd massacred seventeen civilians near the DMZ. He came to visit her every chance he got and he confessed to me what he had become, what the military had turned him into.

'He was in pain, trying to figure out if he should join forces with Ho Chi Minh or kill himself to pay for his crimes. After a few months I convinced him to adopt Easter Dawn. I told him that they could save each other, and I guess they have . . . at least so far.'

Most beauty fades upon closer examination. Coarse features, unnoticed awkwardness, false teeth, scars, alcoholism, or just plain dumb; there is an abundance of possible flaws that we might miss on first sight. These blemishes are what we come to love in time. We are drawn to the illusion and stay for the reality that makes up the woman. But Faith did not suffer under the light of earnest scrutiny. Her skin and eyes, the way she moved even under the weight of her fears, were just so . . . flawless.

'But Christmas isn't the problem now, is he?'

'No,' she said.

I waited for more, but it was not forthcoming.

'I see that you were wearing a wedding band not too long ago,' I said.

She covered the light spot on her ring finger with her right hand as the coffee cooled and the ice cream melted.

'Craig,' she said. 'He was a navy-trained pharmacist. He worked on an aircraft carrier preparing medicines. I met him and . . . convinced him to donate some pills and drugs for the children I cared for.'

'Where is Craig now?'

There was something wrong with time itself as we sat there. There was something wrong with me. I was that beast smelling a far-off lake. Rilla and I were the pups that once played together heedless of the dangers that we were to face. And Faith was the being that had looked over us. I was hungry for her. I leaned a few inches across the table. The minutes were not passing by but pooling around, waiting for a sign to continue on their mindless way.

'I was offered the chance to bring all of my children back to the States to look for parents to adopt them. Craig had asked me to marry him.' Faith locked her eyes with mine. 'He was a weak man, Mr Rawlins. He wanted everybody to like him and to respect him. He boasted and blustered, but he wasn't a bad man.'

*Wasn't.*

'So you came back to America and brought your orphans,' I said, 'and your new husband. Was his name Morel?'

'No. My married name is Laneer. Morel was my mother's maiden name,' she said, and then continued with the story she was telling. 'We found homes for my kids, and then, and then Craig bought us a big house in Bel-Air.'

'Whoa,' I said. 'Weak but rich.'

'He and some other men had made a deal with a warlord in Cambodia. They were smuggling heroin out of Vietnam into Los Angeles and other cities. When I realized that he was selling drugs. I told Craig that I wouldn't have it. I told him that he had to stop. When he said that he needed time to work it out, I left him.'

She was looking into my face but seeing the images of her husband and her choice.

'I went to stay with a friend in Culver City. I told Craig where I'd be. The next morning I was reading the newspaper and saw a picture of him on page three. It said that he had been tortured and murdered and that I couldn't be found. I stood up from the table, and the dining-room window shattered. Someone had tried to shoot me.

'I ran out of there and kept on going for two days. I was out of my mind . . .'

'Did you call the police?'

'No.'

'Why not?'

'The article made it seem as if I was to blame. Our neighbors talked about us arguing and, and I was worried because the men who killed him were in the army. I thought I'd be arrested and killed. You know that happened all the time in Saigon.'

I took her hand then. It just seemed like the right thing to do.

'I stayed in a motel for three days,' she continued, 'until I thought of Christmas. I had his number in my mind because I called him every other week to say hello and find out how Easter was coming along. She's such a special child. He came and got me. After that he set me up in an apartment in Venice.'

'I want to believe this,' I said, 'but I don't get the thing about Easter. She saw you in the car with Chris, but she didn't recognize you.'

'She was a baby when he took her. She doesn't remember me, and because of the circumstances of her parents' death we decided not to tell her too much. She wouldn't have remembered me before I went out to their house in Riverside.'

'Do you know who it was that tried to kill you?' I asked.

'Not exactly. I knew some of the men that Craig was involved with, though. There was a marine lieutenant named Drake Bishop and a guy they called Lodai. And then there was that grinning idiot, Sammy Sansoam.'

'Black guy?' I asked. 'About five ten?'

'Yes. Craig told me that they made hundreds of thousands of dollars. I guess they tried to shoot me because I'm the only one who knows anything about them. They killed Craig because I tried to make him quit.'

The guilt in her was so powerful that I felt it. For a while there, her feeling superseded my broken heart.

'It's them that's the killers, not you,' I said, taking both of her hands now.

'I know,' she said.

She was gripping my fingers hard enough to cause pain. I was happy to give her the outlet.

'You guys want anything else?' Rilla asked. Neither one of us had seen her coming.

'No,' I said, realizing that my voice was heavy with emotion. 'That's all, Rilla. Thank you.'

Rilla, my long-lost pup sister, looked at me with real empathy. She put the flimsy yellow check on the red tabletop, saying, 'You can just leave it here.'

When the waitress had gone, I asked Faith, 'Do you know how I can get in touch with Christmas?'

'No.'

'Can I do anything for you?'

'You could give me a ride to my apartment.'

'Aren't you going back to work?'

'I told the manager that I was going to meet you, and he told me that I had to stay at my desk. So I quit. I would have done it soon anyway. It's just too hard trying to pretend that everything's fine.'

Faith had a beachside courtyard apartment down in Venice. I walked her to the secluded entrance. She turned to me. It seemed that the easiest thing in the world at that moment would have been to throw that door open wide, carry her across the threshold, and make love until the sun set and then rose again. These thoughts seemed to be in both our minds as we stood there.

'Christmas didn't tell you anything to do in case of emergency?' I asked.

'He gave me a number to call,' she said, and then she recited it.

'That's my phone,' I said.

'Easy,' she said in mild surprise. 'Short for Ezekiel.'

Damn.

'Will you call me?' she asked.

'Yes.'

'Will you come visit?'

'Definitely.'

# CHAPTER 24

I drove a long way with nothing but the notion of the Blonde Faith in my mind. She'd been blindsided by the power of her own commitment to life. Not only did she know what was right, she did something about it. And now her charity had betrayed her; her own husband had given her up to assassins.

I understood at last why Christmas had brought Easter to me. He also believed that the military men could get at Faith despite police protection. He was going after the men on his own, and judging by the body count, he was doing a good job.

I had solved the mystery. I knew the players, their reasons, and the danger they posed. The right choice now was to go home and be with my family. But the idea of home was like a coffin to me. Jesus and Benita would take care of the children, and I'd continue my investigations for no good reason except that it kept up my momentum.

But even at that fevered point in my life, I wasn't so foolish as to believe that I could continue on my way without backup.

So I found myself driving to Watts and through Watts on the way to Compton, an ever-growing Negro enclave.

I kept going until I hit a street named Tucker and took that until a dead-end stand of overgrown avocados stopped me.

I parked half on asphalt and half on hard soil, got out, and pressed my way through dense leaves and thorny bushes until I came to a door that seemed more like a portal to another world than an entrance to a house. You couldn't even see the home behind it, just trees and leaves, the dirt beneath your feet, and the hint of sky above.

*Mama Jo*, Lynne Hua had said.

It was like the house that Mama Jo had lived in in the swamplands outside of Pariah, Texas. I never knew how she found such a place in Southern California. It seemed as if she had conjured it out of her own knotty desires.

I was about to knock when the door came open. Tall and black-skinned, ageless, handsome, and bristling with power, Mama Jo smiled upon me. I suspected that she had some kind of alarm system like Christmas Black employed, but it could have been that she really was a witch who could sense when those she loved or danger approached.

'I been waitin' for ya, Easy,' she said.

I wondered as to her meaning. Waiting for what of me?

We had made love once, more than two decades

before, when I was nineteen and she was around forty. She was maybe an inch shorter; that and a few gray hairs were all that marked the passage of years.

'Jo.'

She put an arm around my shoulders and pulled me into her witch's den. The floor was swept earth. The walls were shelves lined with glass and crockery containing herbs and dried animal parts. The fireplace was actually a hearth where a small pig was roasting on a spit. Above the fireplace was a shelf that held the skulls of twelve armadillos, six on either side of a human skull, the keepsake that Jo kept of her son's father – both named Domaque.

'How's Dom?' I asked as I sat on the wooden bench at her big ebony wood table.

'On a commune up north.'

'A commune?'

'Uh-huh. City of the Sun, they calls it,' Jo said as she poured me some of the tea that was always abrew at the side of the fire. 'He met this little girl at a picnic in Griffith Park, and she asked him to go live with her there up near Big Sur. Nice place. The kids there tryin' to get all the craziness outta their bones.' Jo shook her head and smiled at the thought of such an impossible task.

'How long did he know this girl?' I tasted the dark brew. Mama Jo's teas were medicinal and strong. Almost immediately I could feel my muscles releasing.

167

'No more than a day, but I believe that she asked him to come with her even before she bedded him.'

'That's kinda quick, ain't it, Jo?' I said, relishing the flush of the herbs raging through my system.

'Love don't work on the clock, baby,' she said, looking into my eyes.

I turned my head away and took a deep draft.

Jo sat beside me on the bench. Her breath wafted across my forearms, and I regretted having come.

Jo might have been a witch; I didn't know. She was certainly a botanist and a physician and possessed of deep insight into human nature, my nature.

Ever since asking Bonnie to leave, I had avoided Jo. I knew that she saw right through the pain brought on by my own stupidity.

'Have you seen her?' Jo asked.

'No. She called, though. She's marrying that prince of hers.'

'The man you drove her to.'

'Yeah . . . right.'

Jo was looking at me while I stared at the hard yellow earth she walked upon. Her feet were bare and the flames from the fireplace threw odd-colored waves of light around the room.

'You know you got to go to her, baby,' Jo said after many long minutes of silence.

'Yeah,' I said again. 'I know.'

'Man cain't be a man without a woman and chirren to love him,' she said. 'You got to take her up or let her go.'

A loud screech tore through the room. I leaped to my feet, and Blackie, Jo's pet raven, spread his wings in alarm. The ebony bird had been so still in his dark corner I hadn't noticed him.

My heart was beating fast, and I was tired, very tired.

'Do you ever make love potions, Jo?' I asked the witch.

'You don't need a love charm, Easy. You got more love than you know how to handle now.'

I slumped down on the bench, placing my elbows on my knees. Jo put her hand to the back of my neck the way she had when we made love so long ago.

'It's like wakin' up in a shallow grave, baby,' she whispered. 'There's dirt in your mouth, and you so cold that you cain't even feel it. You wanna go back to sleep, but you know that can only bring death.'

'What should I do?' I asked.

'What you doin', child.'

I laughed. 'What I'm doin' is runnin' full throttle without sense or worry,' I said.

'You always know what's right, Easy,' she said softly. 'Always. If you runnin', then there's a reason for it, even if you don't know what that reason is.'

A sweet, frightening shock went through my mind like a live wire cut loose from its stem. Suddenly I had my bearings. I knew where I was – and I wasn't at all happy to be there.

'I'm lookin' for Ray, Jo,' I said, no longer sad or heartbroken or unsure.

'You two always lookin' for each other,' she said sagely. 'I don't know where he's at right now. He come by a couple'a weeks ago sayin' that he was gonna be gone awhile – on business.'

We both knew what that meant: Somewhere some bank or armored car or payroll was going to be robbed, or maybe there was a soul destined to die.

'If he gets in touch with you, call me,' I said, standing up and feeling strong.

Jo rose with me and kissed me gently on the lips. This made me smile, grin even.

'You mostly see the truth,' she said. 'But sometimes you like a man stranded on a island, lookin' across a wide stretch'a ocean at a faraway shore.'

# CHAPTER 25

I could see the truth, all right. It was like swimming in a peaceful lake and suddenly seeing the beady eyes of a crocodile bearing down upon me.

I didn't speed on the ride back to my house because I didn't want to be stopped by the police and therefore lose time. Going to see Mama Jo was always a revelation. That's why people shied away from her. Who wants to see the truth? Not the condemned man, the dying woman, the child who will be orphaned.

I decided somewhere in a corner of my mind to let go of Bonnie and move on. I would not go to the wedding. I would not grieve for my loss. The world did not revolve around me or my pain.

I went through a whole list of decisions that I had put on hold for the past year, mainly so that I wouldn't think about what might have happened while I was wallowing around like a pig in its sty.

Sammy Sansoam, otherwise known as Captain Clarence Miles, knew my name and office address. And even though I was unlisted, it wouldn't take much time for him to find my house. If he suspected for any reason that I was a friend of Christmas Black, then he might come for me. Jesus would die protecting Easter, so might Feather and Benita.

Fighting the men that killed Faith's husband was like fighting organized crime or the FBI. They had limitless resources and were ruthless.

I pulled to the curb and jumped out of the car with my pistol in my hand. I ran to the front door, and burst in.

Jesus's body looked like fresh kill spread out on the couch, with the fingers of one hand grazing the floor and the other hand over his forehead. His eyes were closed and in shadow.

'Juice!'

The dead boy opened his eyes and sat up with a quizzical look on his face.

'What's wrong, Dad?' he asked.

Feather came running in with Easter and Benita right behind her. My heart thudded against its cage and the room shimmied. I lurched over to the couch and sat as Jesus moved his legs. I would have fallen otherwise.

Sitting there, I tried to control my breathing but could not. My heart was going so fast that I believed I was going to die right then. If there had been whiskey in the house, I would have drunk it. If there had been opium in the house, I would have swallowed it.

'What's wrong, Daddy?' Feather asked.

She sat down beside me and wrapped her arms

around my head while Easter sat on Jesus's lap and put her hands on my thigh.

My heart thundered through all of that. My ears were hot, and I wanted to kill Clarence Miles.

*All men are fools.* The words came into my head, but I could not remember where I had heard them. The source did not matter, because the content was true. All men were fools and me most of all.

My children could have died while I was out acting like a child.

I stood up. Jesus did too, taking hold of my right arm. I put the gun in my pocket and said, 'Pack up everything you need for a trip.'

'Where are we going?' Feather asked.

'Away for a while. There's some bad men out there and they might come here.'

'But why?' Benita asked.

Jesus took his common-law wife by the hand and led her into the back room. Feather needed no direction. She packed her things in a small blue suitcase and put Frenchie in a bag made for the transportation of small dogs. Easter started to gather her things with military precision.

I took in a deep breath. I was a fool, but I was lucky too. Just that thought made me laugh. I lit a cigarette while Benita and Jesus argued and the girls packed. Fifteen minutes later, we were all crowded in the car, headed west.

We arrived at a doorway half a block from the Pacific Ocean on a street named Ozone. I knocked and

173

rang and knocked again. Jewelle came to the door, wearing a yellow dress that perfectly accented her dark brown skin. As the years had passed, the plain-Jane girl had been supplanted by a subtly beautiful maiden. She had been the lover of my property manager Mofass until he died heroically and now she was with Jackson Blue, who was both the smartest and the most cowardly man I knew.

'Easy,' Jewelle said, looking at the brood that surrounded me. 'What's goin' on?'

'I need help, baby. I need it bad.'

Jewelle smiled, and I remembered that she loved me in a way that she felt for no other man. She wasn't sexually attracted to me, but she felt a connection like a daughter feels for her dad.

'Come on in.'

The doorway led to a long set of stairs that went down two floors to the apartment below. The ceilings were twenty feet at least, and the walls sported bookshelves from top to bottom.

Jackson Blue had read every book on those shelves at least twice. He kept only books that he intended to read again, and again. Jewelle had been working her way through Jackson's library, having long discussions with him about the meanings and ramifications of the texts. Jackson was the first man she met who proved that he was smarter than she, and she loved him for it.

'Hey, easy, what's happenin'?' Jackson asked when we got to the main room at the bottom of

174

the long stairway. He was wearing a dark red silk robe that was tied carelessly about his slender waist. He was yawning even though it was late afternoon.

'I wake you up?' I asked.

'I been workin' day and night for the past three days at Proxy Nine,' he said. 'They was puttin' in this special line to pass information over the phone, but the technicians didn't have it right. You know I had to roll up my sleeves, baby.'

'You installed a computer line all the way from France?' I asked.

'Oh, yeah.' Jackson sighed. He was lazy in everything but his mind. Physical labor was an abomination to him, but Immanuel Kant was a piece of cake.

'You don't have any training in that,' I said, not because I believed it but to pull him out of his stupor so that I could ask for his help.

'Ain't so hard, Easy,' he said. 'The thing that gave me the most trouble was learnin' French so that I could talk with the technicians overseas.'

'You speak French?' my daughter asked.

'Oui, mademoiselle. Et tu?'

'Un peu,' she replied modestly.

'Jewelle, can you take the kids out on the patio for a while?' I asked. 'I need to talk to Jackson here.'

Feather, Jesus, Easter, and Benita with Essie followed the lady real-estate genius outside into her garden at the bottom of a well-like yard.

When they were gone, I told Jackson what had been happening.

'Damn, Easy,' he said when I was through. 'Why don't you get into somethin' sensible? Shit. You think that they woulda really killed the kids?'

'I'm sure they would, man. Will you keep 'em for me?'

'Okay. No problem. I mean, it'a mostly be Jewelle takin' care of them. I'm workin' at the office, but she do most of her work over the phone.'

'How's it goin' with her?'

'She's a silent partner in that new Icon International hotel goin' up downtown,' he said proudly. 'If it fly, she be so rich that we could live in downtown Rome, and I don't mean Rome, New York.'

'I might need to call on you again, Jackson,' I said.

This request caused fear to rise in the small man's face. He didn't want to have anything to do with me. He had a good job and made more money than anyone we knew, except Jewelle. He wanted to kick me out of his house, but even a coward like Jackson knew when his debts had come due.

'I hope not, Easy,' he said. 'But I'll be there.'

I went outside and explained to my extended family that they were to stay away from their friends and neighborhoods, their homes and schools. They shouldn't make phone calls or answer them or tell anyone where they were.

'What if my mama wanna talk to me?' Benita asked.

'Tell her that Juice is taking you to Frisco for a few days, by boat. Tell her that, and she'll wait for you to come back.'

'Are these men really all that bad?' Benita asked.

'They make Mouse look like Juice,' I said, and she didn't ask any more questions.

# CHAPTER 26

Once I was in my car again. I felt a moment of exhilaration. My children were safe, my family protected from the assassins of Christmas Black's world.

Also, I was shocked out of the melancholy that had settled in on me. I remembered what it was to be a man living in the cracks: a slave, nigger, jigaboo, coon, spade, spear-chucker, darky, boy. Walking down the streets of white gentility, I was always a target. And a target couldn't afford roots or a broken heart. A target couldn't fire back on the men who used him for sport.

All a man like me could do was to wait for the sun to go down, move through darkness, and hope.

The validity of this litany of the past was fading, but it had not gone away. It was true – I was an American citizen too; a citizen who had to watch his step, a citizen who had to distrust the police and the government, public opinion, and even the history taught in schools.

It was odd that such negative thoughts would invigorate me. But knowing the truth, no matter how bad it was, gave you some chance, a little bit of an edge. And if that truth was an old friend and the common basis for all your people all the way back to your origins, then at least you found yourself on familiar ground; at least you couldn't be blindsided, ambushed, or fooled. They could try and kill me, but I'd see them coming. They might see me too, but I would see them first.

I wasn't even thinking about Faith Laneer, but there I was parked in front of her courtyard apartment complex. It was logical that I came to her. She was the closest link to Christmas and the men he had somehow fooled into thinking that they were stalking him.

The sun was just a red glow on the horizon, and I sat in my car with no particular thoughts in mind. Bonnie would pass through now and then, but I had left her in the light of day, where people made lives like marble statues that couldn't be moved.

I was a shadow and the sun was going down. In this transition I remembered a book that Gara, Jackson Blue, and I had read passages from some while before, *Phenomenology of Spirit* by Georg Hegel, a German philosopher who had no respect for Africa. Gara and I had found the dense prose hard going, but Jackson took to it like a vulture clawing through the guts of a dead elephant. He explained how Hegel saw a thing and its opposite as connected and that this connection was what caused progress.

'It's like turnin' into a skid, Easy,' Jackson Blue had said. 'You slidin' right and turn in the same direction. Logic tell ya that you gonna go even farther over, but the truth is, you straighten right out.'

The darkness was my negative freedom. While everyone else feared and avoided night, I saw it as my liberation. I lived a life opposite from Hegel's bright light of truth, and so, I realized, he, my enemy, and I agreed on the path that set us at each other's throats.

She opened the door without asking who it was. The charcoal-colored dress was shapeless, but her figure would not be denied.

'Mr Rawlins,' she said, the catch in her voice telling me that she had been alone for too many days and needed the company of a man who would buy her strawberry shortcake to sweeten her bitter lot. 'Come in.'

The living room was small, but the window faced the vastness of the Pacific.

'All I have is water,' she told me.

'Want me to take you shopping?' I offered.

'Let's sit for a while,' she said.

The small sofa was coral colored, built for two and a half people. She sat at one end and I at the other, but we were still close.

'Have you found Chris?' she asked.

'No. I got worried about my family, though, and moved them out of my house.'

'You're married?'

'No. I adopted some kids. One'a them has a girl-friend, and now they have a kid. And then there's Easter Dawn.'

'You're like me, Mr Rawlins,' Faith said.

'How's that?'

'You have a little orphanage that you care for and love.'

I held out my hand, palm upward, and she took it with both of hers.

'I had a girlfriend,' I said. 'But she was torn. There was a man, an African prince she saw now and again. I left her.'

'Did she love him?'

'Yeah. But, but not like she loved me and our little family.'

'Then why leave her?'

Her question grabbed me like a pair of pliers working on a rusty lug nut. At first I resisted her, but then I gave way.

'Did you ever feel like there was something you wanted?' I asked Blonde Faith. 'A way you wanted someone to make love to you? A way you wanted to be touched?'

Faith breathed in deeply. I could feel the grip on my hands tighten ever so slightly.

'Yes,' she whispered.

'That was me and Bonnie. The way we came together was everything I had wished for but never known. In a way, she created my desire and then satisfied it.'

One of Faith's hands moved up to my wrist. It tickled, but I didn't want to laugh.

'And then I found out about him and everything was tainted. And even though I loved her more than I ever did anyone else, the fact that she wasn't all there meant that I was always gonna be unhappy when I looked at her and thought about him . . . And then I met you.'

'Me?' Faith moved closer, an effect of gravity as much as anything else.

'Yeah,' I said, thinking about shadows negating the darkness in my life. 'You gave your love to a man despite his flaws. You gave him a chance and then he betrayed you, but you didn't, not even one time, say something bad about him. You listened to that man who wanted the loan while he bad-mouthed you and shouted, and you still smiled; you even felt for him.

'That's what Bonnie taught me. She taught me that you can care for somebody and it isn't the end of the world. That's why I loved her.'

'How did you know that Mr Schwartz was looking for a loan?' Faith asked.

'You were just talking,' I said. 'The other guy, the one with the glasses—'

'Mr Ronin.'

'Yeah. He was looking over forms and stuff and giving his guy a passbook and a checkbook. You were saying no.'

I suppose that insight was reason enough for Faith to kiss me. Her mouth was the texture of a ripe fruit that begged to be eaten. I tried to put my arms around her, but she held them away.

'Craig was always so, so brutal,' she said as she pushed me down on the sofa, kissing me and unbuttoning my shirt.

'You want me to just lie here?' I asked.

'Yes,' she said. I felt her tug at my zipper and then reach inside.

I realized I was getting older, not because I didn't respond to her caress but because for the first time in a long time I had the erection of a teenager.

Smelling the sweet peach-scented shampoo in her hair, I said, 'I need to take a shower.'

Holding on to my manhood, she guided me to the shower in the bathroom. I reached to take off her clothes, but she shook her head. I understood. She took off the gray dress, revealing one of those bodies you see only in magazines and on movie screens. Her nipples were the size of apricots; she was beyond gravity's reach.

We didn't talk for a long time. I stood in the small shower while she hunkered down, washing me with a soft sponge. My erection got harder and harder, but I didn't feel urgent at all.

'Do you want me to powder you?' she asked after we were dry.

'Can I touch your face?'

I let my fingers travel from her temples to her breasts. She shuddered and wavered.

'Let's just go to bed,' I suggested.

*　　*　　*

183

I lay beneath her while Faith moved up and down slowly, holding my face so that I would be looking up at her. Every time I got excited, she'd say, 'Not yet, Easy. Not yet, baby.'

I don't even remember the orgasm, just her looking into my eyes, asking me to wait for her.

# CHAPTER 27

We held hands walking along the beach under a crescent moon. No one could see us clearly, but we were there. Faith Laneer's concerned observations made me feel safe. There she was under the protection of Christmas Black but at the same time sheltering me.

We had been talking about Jackson Blue for quite a while. Actually, I did most of the talking. I liked telling stories about the cowardly whiz kid, about how most of his life he had done everything wrong.

'He's a genius, but he's twisted,' I was saying. 'Like if he was a caveman, he'd invent the wheel and then use it to escape from the head Cro-Magnon because he'd been sleepin' with the boss man's wife.'

'Is he a good friend?' Faith asked.

'I didn't used to think so. He's a liar and a coward, but one day I was telling a story about him and I realized that I cared about him enough to laugh at his faults. That made him a friend.'

Faith hugged my arm, bumping into my side as she did so.

'I like the way your skin smells,' she said. 'I want to rub my face against it and breathe you into me.'

As we stood there kissing under the sliver moon, I felt a howl in my soul. There I was, a black man kissing the epitome of northern European beauty, with a gun in one pocket and a short fuse in the other. There was no sex in the world better than that.

We didn't make love again. I walked her home and stood with her in the doorway, talking about any number of events in our lives. I liked to cook. She used to be a painter before becoming a nun. I'd seen the northern lights over Germany while a cannon battle raged. She married a homosexual named Norman after giving up her vows.

'That way I thought I could maintain my celibacy,' she told me. 'But I found myself wanting him in the night. I would come to his door and listen to him and his lovers . . .'

After more than an hour, she brushed her lips against mine and went in. I stumbled away in a kind of daze.

I was completely enveloped in darkness now. My family was hidden. I knew the identities of my enemies. Faith had shown me without trying to that there was love for me somewhere if I wanted to take it. My stupor was akin to the feeling you have when waking up from a night of jumbled dreams. At first you wonder if all that nonsense really happened. Was I arrested and sentenced to death? Did I come upon two brutally murdered men in a house that wore a disguise?

I got home at midnight and found the front door of my house broken in. Even though I knew the kids weren't there, I rushed inside and turned on the lights.

Nothing had been touched or stolen. The contents of my dresser drawers were orderly; my mail was unopened. All Sansoam's men wanted was blood.

I tried to remember the moon and Faith's lips on mine. I tried to dismiss the break-in and what it meant. For a while I worked on the door, re-attaching the hinges and clearing away the shattered portions of the jamb.

I sat down in my favorite chair and turned on the TV. From the outside, everything would have looked normal, except for the door sitting crookedly in its frame and the .38 in my hand.

There was a Western on. John Wayne was blustering his way through a story I'd seen a thousand times.

I was thinking that nothing had changed, that Christmas and his henchman would kill the men who had broken in on me. I told myself that all I had to do was go to ground and wait until it was over or the right moment came. But my heart would not listen to my mind. I felt the way I had in World War II when we were preparing to engage the enemy. Death, my death, was a foregone conclusion. I couldn't think about survival. All I could comprehend was the promise to rain down wrack and ruin upon my enemy.

I wanted a drink. The biting scent of sour mash whiskey seemed to waft into my nostrils. I looked around, thinking that maybe there was a bottle nearby. It was too late for a liquor store to be open, and I didn't want to go to a bar.

I wanted a drink to settle my raging mind. It would have been like balm against the murders I was contemplating. But then I decided, with my heart, not to go after alcohol. I didn't want to become calm or numbed. What I wanted was to kill Sammy Sansoam before Christmas got the pleasure.

I was already drunk.

Just the idea that those men, whoever they all were, would break into a house that my children called home shattered every covenant the civilized world lived by.

This thought made me laugh at myself, thinking that I lived in a civilized world where lynchings, segregation based on race, and all the men who died for freedom's lie were somehow under the umbrella of enlightened concern.

I staggered and laughed my way out to the car. I had rarely been so intoxicated. I had never been that evil.

# CHAPTER 28

Someone shouted out a desperate plea, but I didn't understand the question. The words were clear, but I couldn't make sense of them. I wanted to understand what was being said and who was speaking, but not enough to open my eyes. The shelter of sleep was too delicious.

The mattress under me was ponderous and heavy, like thick mud under a thin layer of straw.

Someone screamed and then laughed.

I opened my eyes in the shadowy room. I could make out a desk piled with papers and a bookshelf that held everything from a Bible to a set of wrenches.

There came more screams and laughter, the thudding of running feet and the smell of something frying. On the other side of that closed door was a whole house full of children about their morning business. Yellow green shades were pulled down to cover the windows, but there were small holes in the fabric and a strong sun on the other side. Tiny wires of light were suspended above my head, attended by dancing motes of dust.

This was a man's room, I could tell from the

sour smell. And the child's question had been phrased in Spanish, a language I loved listening to but did not understand.

I thought about sitting up. The various governing bodies in my mind all agreed that this would be a good thing, but there were disputes over the timetable.

Two boys started shouting, and I was reminded of Mouse and Pericles Tarr. Pericles went to a bar every night with Mouse to get away from his noisy household, but Primo, the master of this house, only went out drinking one night a week. Primo loved being with his children, even though he seemed to ignore them most of the time, and at this late date, most of his charges were not sons and daughters but grandchildren, nieces, nephews, and wandering waifs plucked from the street.

That room and the whole house belonged to me. It was the first piece of property that I had ever owned. I hadn't lived there for nearly twenty years, but I couldn't bear to let it go. Primo, his wife, Flower, and an endless flow of children they raised lived there rent free because that lot was more my dream than it was real estate.

Pericles Tarr. I wondered why I was thinking about him; this brought to mind Faith Laneer. Making love to her had, at least momentarily, dislodged my depression over Bonnie. Bonnie was still there in my mind. She and I had visited Primo and the Panamanian Flower a dozen times. She, Bonnie, was still the love of my life, but the pall of her leaving, even her upcoming marriage, had blown away.

I remembered being enraged over Sammy Sansoam's breaking into my house. This also helped to dislocate the sadness.

Finding Mouse meant finding Pericles Tarr.

I sat up with all the ruling bodies of my mind in harmony. I was wearing a pair of cotton trousers and a white T-shirt that had seen better days.

In the hallway I encountered two small children, a girl and a boy. They looked to be five and distantly related. They were picking at each other's hand-me-down pajamas when the door to Primo's office opened. The boy's eyes widened when he saw me. The girl grabbed his top and dragged him toward the kitchen, shouting something frightened in that beautiful tongue.

I followed them into the large kitchen that had once been my domain.

With my permission, Primo had expanded the kitchen to accommodate an oak table that could seat sixteen. The shortish brown emperor of that table was sitting there among the knights and ladies from two to sixteen, eating beans and tortillas with eggs, chorizos, and crumbly white cheese.

'Easy,' Primo said, and the din at breakfast subsided. When the master had a guest, the children knew to keep it down.

'Hey, Primo. Thanks for lettin' me in last night, man.'

'You looked like you were going to kill somebody, my friend.'

I didn't respond to his insight. Instead I turned my gaze to the sink, where the scared kids who had seen me come from their guardian's inviolate den had run to hide behind Flower's bright blue skirt.

I went to the black-skinned Panamanian and kissed both her cheeks.

A few of the middle children ooed.

Primo leaped from his chair, knocking it to the floor, and said, 'What? You are kissing my wife right in front of me?'

He ran at me, and for a moment I shared the fear of his big extended family. But then Primo put his arms around me and hugged me tightly.

I could tell how ragged my feelings were, because the embrace brought air to a gasping emptiness somewhere in me.

The children cheered, and we all ate breakfast together.

Flower never sat down. She made tortillas, wheat and corn, from scratch and kept frying the beans and sausages and eggs while the children downed plate after plate.

I ate heartily and shared jokes with my old friends.

I was in no hurry. It was early, and my new plans needed time to ripen in the desert heat.

After Flower had hurried the school-age kids off, Primo and I went out on the front porch to sit.

It was then that he had his first beer of the day. He offered me one even though he knew I didn't drink. I would have accepted his offer if I wasn't afraid of losing the edge of my rage.

'How's Peter Rhone doin' at your garage?' I asked my friend.

'I like him there because Mouse comes by now and then with this wonderful tequila he gets from a man he does business with. It's the best tequila I ever had in my life.'

Raymond had his fingers in many pies by 1967. One thing he did was smuggle goods and people back and forth over the border from time to time. He liked Primo because Primo liked to laugh.

'At first I told Pete,' Primo continued, 'that he should move away from that house. I told him that Raymond was a bad hombre and that sometimes he killed people for no reason. But you know, the riots changed everything for good and bad.'

'What do you mean?'

'Pete works hard and he makes good money for the job, but he gives it all to EttaMae and he lives on the porch. I ask him why he does this to himself.'

'And what does he say?' I asked.

'He says that he's making up for all the bad things his people have done. I told him that he was loco, that he didn't owe me or Mouse or Etta anything.'

'Yeah? And what he say to that?'

'That he did owe us because nobody ever made him do what he was doing. He said that because it was his choice to serve her family, that proved he was guilty.'

I had rarely talked to Rhone since clearing him of the murder of his black lover Nola Payne. But hearing his claim, I understood that he wasn't just another crazy white man. He was nuts, no doubt about that, but the madness was brought about by his sensitivity to sin. I might have spent some hours discussing this oddity with Primo or Gara or even Jackson Blue, but I had other problems to solve.

I told Primo the story about Mouse and Pericles, including a description of the Tarr household, which so reflected his own.

'It's funny, Easy,' Primo said. 'For a man like me, children are a treasure. You raise them like crops and they pay off or die. You love them as Christ loves them, and they love you like God. I feel like this because I am from another country, where my people have a place. Maybe we're poor, but we are part of the earth.

'But your man Pericles is not like me. Every new child makes him afraid of what will happen. I see it in my own children. In the United States, we are not of the earth but the street. Pericles has known this, but his wife is fertile and he is just a man.'

'You know Perry?' I asked.

'Oh, yes. Mouse and him bought a dark blue Pontiac from me three weeks ago.'

'Together?'

'They came together.'

'Really?'

A whole new train of thought opened for me. I would have left that very moment if Primo had not put his hand on my arm.

'I am moving from your house, my friend.'

'Back to Mexico for a while?'

'East LA, where the Mexicans live.'

'You lonely for your amigos?'

'The boys fight all the time with black children now. Especially our grandchildren who look Mexican. It's the riots. Now all the peoples hate each other.'

Pericles flitted out of my mind as if I had never heard his name. My home was passing from me. I felt that loss deeply.

'You know my lawyer, Tina Monroe?' I asked.

'Yes.'

'Go to her next week. I'll sign a paper selling you this house for a hundred dollars. Sell it and buy you a place wherever you goin'.'

We stared at each other awhile. I could tell that it meant a lot to him, my gift.

'It's just 'cause I need a place to go now and again,' I added. 'I look at it like rent for the future.'

# CHAPTER 29

I kept a suit in the closet in Primo's den. That was Flower's idea.

'You come in the middle of the night, beat up or sweating hard,' she'd said. 'Keep some clothes here.'

'I don't want to be an imposition on your household, Flow,' I'd said at the time.

We were holding hands while Primo sat in a chair in the middle of the lawn, drinking beer.

'It is God's house,' she said.

As I donned my light brown two-piece, I thought about what she had said. I wasn't a believer. I didn't go to church or get chills when the Gospel was quoted. But I did believe that that house was beyond anyone's control. It was to me a piece of history, a memory to be thankful for.

It was in that grateful state of mind that I arrived at Portman's Department Store, about nine-fifteen. Pericles Tarr must have left some shred of his trail at his last place of employment.

They called themselves a department store, but

all they sold was furniture. There was a ground floor that displayed cheap goods and a basement filled with junk. The merchandise on the first floor consisted of two maple dining tables with somewhat matching chairs, a red sofa, a dusty reclining chair, and various stools made for the recreation room that everyone wanted but no one built.

Nobody was buying tables and chairs at that time of morning, so the manager was sitting behind his desk at the back of the sparsely stocked room.

This desk was the nicest piece on display. It was dark hardwood with hints of maroon and blond at various places: signs of life under the oppression, or protection of night.

The Negro salesman was made from loose fat held together by skin the color of yellow cream fresh from the cow. His face was flabby; it had once been happy in his twenties and early thirties, but now, midway into the fourth decade, his smile expressed mild discontent.

The plastic nameplate at the edge of his desk told me to call him Larry.

Larry did not stand to greet me. I suppose I didn't look like a good prospect.

'How much for the desk?' I asked.

'Not for sale,' he replied, giving me his slightly nauseated smirk.

'Pericles here?' I inquired, looking around and wondering when was the last time anyone had swept.

197

'Who?'

'Pericles Tarr. He sold me a dinette set that I'm not happy wit'.' I contracted the last word to let him know that I was a fool.

Larry stuck out his generous lower lip and barely shook his big, close-cropped head.

'No. He sound like somebody from Mother Goose or somethin'. I'd remember a name like that.'

That was all Larry had to give. If I wanted more I had to ante up.

'You know the other salesmen?'

'Only me. Eight-forty-five a.m. to seven-fifteen p.m., Monday through Saturday except Easter week and Christmas.'

'And how long have you worked here?'

After looking at his watch he said, 'Three weeks, two days, and thirty-seven minutes.'

I gave him a weak smile measured to equal his and nodded.

He nodded back, and we parted company forever.


Most of the children at the Tarr household had gone off to school when I got there a little after ten. Leafa answered the door. Seeing her made me happy. I suppose that showed in my face, because she smiled brightly and held her arms up to me. It seemed like the most natural thing in the world to hold her in the crook of my arm.

'Shouldn't you be in school?' I asked.

'Mama's sad,' she replied. There was no need for further explanation.

I walked into the house, holding Leafa. The child and I had bonded. I loved her, had become her protector. There was no sense to this feeling between us, just trying to be human in a world that idolized the kingdom of the ants.

Her head against my chest, Leafa pointed to a door in the right corner of the jumbled living room. Through there I found Meredith sitting in a straight-back chair, her head buried in her hands, flanked by two cribs and three toddlers.

With the subtlest shift of weight, Leafa told me that she needed to get down on the floor to make sure her ugly little brothers and sisters didn't do something terrible. I put her down and kissed her check.

'Mrs Tarr,' I said, still squatting.

When she lifted her head, I could see that she'd aged a good six months since our last meet two days ago.

'Yes?'

'I'm so sorry, ma'am, but if you can bear it, I'd like to ask you some questions.'

She stared at me, not comprehending simple English. Beyond her, Leafa was herding the giggling tots into a corner.

I reached out my hand, and Meredith took it. I led her out of the baby room, through the devastation of the living room, and into the kitchen, where I cleared debris from two red chairs and bade her sit. I made instant coffee while she gazed at the floor.

It occurred to me that Meredith probably hadn't asked Leafa to stay home. The child just saw her responsibility and took it the way Feather had done with Easter Dawn.

'You take milk and sugar in your coffee?' I asked.

'Milk.'

There were only a few drops left at the bottom of the half-gallon carton.

I gave her the coffee and sat facing her.

'I've found out a lot about Alexander and your husband in the past couple days,' I said. 'I know that they were seen at a bar together and that they picked up a car at a garage in South LA.'

'The police was here,' she said.

'What they say?'

'If I had heard anything from Ray Alexander.'

'He's back in town?' I asked.

'I guess he is. They thought he might'a called me on account'a I called the police. They said he was a dangerous man and I should move somewhere where he don't know where I am 'cause he might want revenge. But how can I move all these kids? Where could I take them?'

It was a good question. I found it hard to imagine one woman giving birth ten times.

'How can he hurt me worse than he already has?' she wailed.

I took her hands. The skin was rough and callused, ashen and tight with muscle.

'I need to talk to Perry's friends,' I said softly. 'Do you know any of them?'

'His friends?' she asked.

I nodded and squeezed her hands.

'What good is friends when you ain't got nuthin' and they never call?'

'They might know something, Mrs Tarr. He might have said something about where he was hanging out.'

'They put a eviction notice on my door,' she said. 'Where Perry's friends gonna be when I'm out on the street with twelve kids? Where the police gonna be when I'm diggin' through trash cans tryin' t'feed my babies?' She looked at me then. 'Where you gonna be when that's happenin'? I'll tell you where, asleep in your bed while we livin' with the rats.'

Being poor and being black were not the same things in America, not exactly. But there were many truths that all black people and poor persons of every color had in common. One of the most important particulars in our lives was the understanding of the parable of the Gordian knot. You had to be able to cut through that which bound you. Maybe that was leaving a woman behind or breaking into a bank under cover of darkness; maybe it was bowing your head and saying 'Yessir' when a man had just called your wife a whore and your children dogs. Maybe you spent your whole life like some John Henry banging away at a boulder that would never give.

I took a hundred-dollar bill from my wallet and pressed it into Meredith's hand. I could have cajoled her, called a social worker, talked until I was blue in the face. But the knot was the rent and the sword was that hundred-dollar bill.

'What's this?' she asked, lucid at last.

'It's what you need, right?'

Leafa was standing in the doorway behind her mother. I was happy that she had witnessed our exchange.

'Mama?' Leafa said.

'Is somebody hurt?' Meredith asked, still watching me.

'No.'

'Can you take care of it?'

'Yeah, I guess.'

'Then go away, baby. I'll be there in a few minutes.'

Leafa backed out of the room as Meredith sat up straight.

'Why you givin' this to me?' she asked suspiciously.

'My client is paying,' I said truthfully. 'I need to know who Perry's friends are, and you need the rent. I'll put you down in my books as an informant.'

It was a logic that she had never encountered before. Nothing in her life had ever had monetary value, just cost or sweat.

'I give you the names of three worthless niggahs and I can keep this here money?'

'The money is yours,' I said. 'I just gave it to you. Now I'm asking for those names.'

Leafa appeared again at the doorway. This time she remained silent.

'That don't make no sense,' Meredith said. She was angry.

'You're right,' I said. 'It's what they call irrational. But you see, Mrs Tarr, we, all human beings, just think we're rational when really we never do anything that makes sense. What sense does it make to throw a poor woman and her kids into the street? What sense does it make for a man to hate me for my accent or my skin color? What sense war or TV shows, guns or Pericles' dying?'

I got to her with that. Her life, my life, President Johnson's life in the White House, none of it made any sense. We were all crazy, pretending that our lives were sane.

# CHAPTER 30

There was a small park down in the center of Watts next to a giant sculpture called the Watts Towers. The gaudy towers were built by a man named Rodia over a period of thirty-three years. He built them from refuse and simple material. It was a whimsical place in a very grim part of town.

The park had a few trees and picnic tables on grass worn thin by hundreds of children's tramping feet. Meredith Tarr had told me that Timor Reed and Blix Redford were there almost every day, 'Drinkin' gin and wastin' time.' Pericles would go to visit Tim and Blix once a week or so to share their rotgut and play checkers.

I got there just before noon. There was loud music coming from one house across the street, two teenage lovers playing hooky in order to study the facts of life, and two men of uncertain age sitting across from each other at a redwood picnic table, leaning over a folding paper checkerboard. The board was held together by once clear, now yellowing adhesive tape. About half of the pieces were light-colored stones with crayon X's, either red or black, scrawled on top.

Looking at those men and that board, I felt as if I were witnessing the devolution of a culture. The decrepit park, the shabby clothes Blix and Timor wore, even Otis Redding moaning about the dock of the bay on tinny but loud speakers, spoke of a world that was grinding to a halt.

'Mr Reed. Mr Redford.' I said to the men.

They looked up at me like two soldiers from vastly disparate battlefields who had died simultaneously and were now sitting in Limbo awaiting the verdict of Valhalla.

One man was fat and wore a gray-and-black hat with tiny ventilation eyes sewn in along the side and an old gray trench coat. From Meredith's description, I knew this was Blix Redford. He smiled expectantly and stood up, saying, 'Yes, sir, do I know you?'

At the same time the smaller Timor leaned back and scowled. He wore boys' jeans, a threadbare T-shirt, and said nothing. Judging from the look of desperation on his face, I thought he might have been considering making a run for his life.

'My name is Easy Rawlins,' I said to Blix. 'I just came from Perry Tarr's house. I told Meredith I was looking for her husband, and she send me here to you.'

Timor calmed down a bit, and Blix's smile evaporated.

'Didn't she tell you that Pericles done passed on?' Blix asked.

'No,' I said, shocked at this intelligence. I took the opportunity to sit down next to Timor. The little man turned to face me warily. I could see that his left foot was encased in a filthy plaster cast.

'Oh, yeah,' Blix assured me. He sat down too. 'Yeah. Raymond Alexander done slaughtered him and put him in the ground somewhere down around San Diego, I hear.'

'Really?' I said. 'Is this Raymand in jail now?'

'Where you from, man?' Timor asked me; the sneer on his face was a hatred older than the mouth that carried it. 'Everybody in Los Angeles know about Mouse.'

'Who?'

'Ray Alexander, fool,' he said. 'The man that killed Perry Tarr.'

I turned my palms to the sky and shook my head. I was a stranger from another country. Local folklore was a mystery to me.

'You're telling me that this, this Mouse done killed my friend Perry and the cops won't even put him in jail?' There was a threat in my voice.

'Keep it down, man,' Blix said. 'You don't play with Ray. That's what they say around here. Maybe back in Arkansas or Tennessee or wherevah you from they don't know that. But around here he's the Grim Reaper.'

'You know where I can find this man, this Raymond Alexander?' I asked.

'Didn't you hear what I said, brother?' Blix asked. 'This man's a killer. He'll crush you like a bug.'

'Shit,' I said, approximating the tone of many a fool I'd listened to. 'He gotta gun; I gotta gun too.'

'Come on, BB,' Timor said to his friend. 'Let's play checkers an' let this fool go. We told him. That's all we can do.'

Timor turned his gaze down upon the board. Blix kept watching me.

'We don't know where he's at, man,' the friendlier friend said.

'Well, how can I find him?' I pressed.

'Just jump off the top'a city hall, brother,' Timor said, not looking up. 'You be just as dead, only a hair quicker.'

That was all I was going to get there. I stood up, still acting as if I were angry, about to go out looking for the man who killed my friend. Then I paused.

'Tell me sumpin', man,' I said to Timor.

'What?' He still wouldn't look at me.

'If this mothahfuckah so bad, how come you safe?'

That got his attention.

'What you talkin' 'bout, niggah?'

'You.'

'Me? You don't know me.'

'I know you just sat there on yo broke-leg ass and accused Raymond "Mouse" Alexander of murder. I know you said that he killed Pericles Tarr and buried him in San Diego.'

'Blix said that!' Timor yelled. 'You cain't put that on me!'

He pushed himself up from the table and hobbled off on his broken foot. Blix called to him, but Timor raced away as fast as his lame gaint would carry him.

Blix sat at the checkerboard laughing to himself.

'That was a good one, man,' he said. 'You give me somethin' to needle him with for the next five years.'

# CHAPTER 31

There was a big fish market on Hoover. It was just a series of stalls set in a square on a vacant lot. All day long a man named Dodo picked up ice and dry ice and delivered it to those stalls in order to keep the mackerels, perch, eels, halibuts, sand dabs, crabs, sharks, and swordfish moist and fresh. Small trucks brought the fish in in the early, early morning after the fishing boats arrived all up and down the California coastline.

People from every part of LA came to that nameless fish market. Japanese, Chinese, Italians, and Mexicans. Every culture in LA liked their fishes.

The owner of the open-air market was a big Irishman called Lineman. I don't know if that was his first or last name or maybe just a handle he'd gotten from playing football as a youth.

Lineman was a big guy whose character was fit for the black part of town. He was loud and familiar with anyone he met. He cursed, told risqué jokes, and judged people solely by how they responded to him in business and in life. He didn't fit in in the white world very well. Maybe if he had been a silent worker in the back of some shop he would have gotten along okay, but Lineman was a good businessman, and whites got mad when he showed up at a fancy ball with some dark-skinned senorita or when he invited someone like me to the country club on the west side of town.

The wealthier white circles of Los Angeles found Lineman intolerant of their intolerance, and so the seafood entrepreneur slowly adjusted his life to work within the black and brown communities. He lived in Cheviot Hills, a mostly Jewish enclave, and worked in Watts serving all men as they served him.

'Hey, Lineman,' I said, slapping his wide-shouldered back.

'Easy Rawlins,' he hailed. 'How you doin'?'

'They barred me from the complaint desk, so I guess everything must be fine.'

Lineman liked to laugh.

We were standing at the northeast corner of the block of sixteen stalls. Every one of the fish stands was an independent dealer. They rented the stalls for a hundred dollars plus expenses a week apiece. Lineman kept the ice flowing and made deals all over Southern California, selling fresh fish to everyone from restaurants to school cafeterias.

'What can I do for you, Easy?' Lineman asked.

I told him about Pericles Tarr and how I got Jeff Porter's name from his wife.

We were walking around the perimeter of the block as we talked. Lineman never stood still. He was always doing something, going somewhere, just getting back or preparing to leave.

He'd once been arrested for the kidnap and murder of a black girl, Chandisse Lund. She was fourteen and had worked for the fish market a couple of years. The last anyone had seen of her, she was getting into Lineman's brand-new cherry red Cadillac. He made bail and came to my office, telling a story about a child who had been molested by her own father and who wanted to escape to her older sister's house. The only problem was that the sisters had disappeared and no one could find a witness to say the two were together.

'How could I say no?' he asked me. 'Child comes up to me and says her father's doing that to her, I had to do what she asked.'

'You could have gone to the cops,' I suggested.

'I could have spit in her face too,' Lineman said. 'You know the cops aren't gonna worry about some black girl in Watts.'

'They might.'

'Would you take that kind of chance with your children?'

That convinced me of Lineman's character and his innocence. I went out looking and found out that the sister, Lena, had a boyfriend named Lester. Lester had gone missing too, but he kept in touch with his uncle Bob, and so I located them in Richmond up in the Bay Area.

I brought Chandisse down to the Seventy-sixth Street Precinct, where she and her sister's minister pressed charges against her father and at the same time cleared Lineman of any wrongdoing.

Two weeks later Lineman came to my office again.

'You haven't sent me a bill, Mr Rawlins,' he said. 'I like to pay my debts.'

'You know, down where I come from we trade favors,' I told him. 'So I was thinking that maybe every month or so I could drop by and get a couple of sand dabs for frying or some blue crabs for a gumbo.'

We'd been close since then.

'I need to talk to Jeff Porter,' I told Lineman as we walked down the row.

He stopped, turned around military-style, and walked me back three stalls.

'Hey, Jeff,' Lineman said to a big black man who resembled a walrus in size, shape, and skin color. He even had a drooping salt-and-pepper mustache.

'Hey, Lineman,' Jeff replied. 'What's up?'

'This here is Easy Rawlins,' Lineman said. 'He's a very special friend of mine. He saved my life. And he's a good man, somebody to trust.'

Porter nodded in a dignified manner.

'He wants to know some things,' Lineman continued. 'It would be a favor to me if you obliged.'

Lineman patted me on the back and moved off like a shark that would suffocate if it didn't keep going forward. At the same time, Jeff Porter put out a hand for me to shake. That was an odd experience. Porter's hand was both powerful and blubbery. It seemed to me at that moment that the whole block was turning into some kind of fabulous underwater paradise.

'What can I do for you, Mr Rawlins?' the big man asked.

I wanted to reply, but I was distracted by the blood and entrails that festooned his broad white apron. The thousands of deaths represented by that haphazard map of destruction oppressed me.

Was Pericles Tarr slaughtered in San Diego like Blix had said? I wasn't sure if I had the heart to find out.

'It's gonna be a nice day, huh?' I said.

'Sun's not good for a fish man, Mr Rawlins. We like shade and cool breezes, otherwise the product might go bad.'

'Pericles Tarr,' I said.

'They say he's dead,' Porter said in answer to my implied question.

'I'd like to prove that.'

'That's a dangerous piece of business, isn't it?'

I knew what he was talking about.

'I was raised as a youngster in Houston,' I said. 'One of my best friends was a skinny boy with a big mouth named Raymond Alexander.'

It's hard for a walrus to look surprised, but Porter managed it.

'I'm a private detective, Jeff,' I said. 'I'm one of

Ray's closest friends, but I'm looking for Perry because his daughter Leafa told me that she doesn't think her daddy is dead.'

'Leafa's a child.'

'She's the clearest mind I've met in the Tarr household,' I said.

Jeff laughed and then nodded.

'You might be right about that,' he said. 'And who knows, maybe the girl makes some sense.'

'Why you say that?'

'You know Perry was not happy in that house full'a ugly, unruly kids. He used to go ovah my place to take a nap because he said that every time he heard footsteps in his house he'd start to shakin'. Meredith wasn't nuthin' but a dishrag up in the bed, an' Perry was workin' harder than three slaves in master's cotton field. I don't know if Mouse killed him or not, but you know if he did it woulda been a blessin', not a crime.'

'He ever say that he wanted to run?' I asked.

'Not too much. Only every day for five years.'

'You say Meredith wasn't satisfying him. He have some other woman for that?'

'Perry's my friend, man. You know that's not how you talk about your friends.'

'Every man and woman I talked to so far has said Perry is dead. How's tellin' me how I might find out why gonna hurt?'

The walrus scratched his mustachios and pondered. Finally he shrugged and said, 'Pretty Smart.'

'What is?'

'That's her name. Her mama named her that.'

'You know where she lives?'

'I don't even know what she looks like. All I know is that Perry would call her from my house sometimes. Maybe she come by there and took a nap with him if I wasn't home.'

# CHAPTER 32

Driving away from the fish market, I had the feeling that I'd done something right. More than that, I felt good about my life . . . for a passing moment. I liked Lineman and the men and women who worked the fish trade, but I didn't want my life to be like that: to go every day to the same place, do the same things, and say the same words to the same people.

My dalliance with Faith Laneer had put Bonnie in a box in a corner of my mind. She wasn't gone, but she wasn't in plain sight either. This was, I believed, the first step out of the sadness that had enveloped me.

I got to my office and went straight to the phone book. There was only one Pretty Smart listed in the Negro neighborhood; actually in any neighborhood.

I leaned back in my swivel chair and took the time to breathe deeply and enjoy the leisure that the moment provided. I even considered picking up a book I'd gotten at the Aquarian Bookshop. *The System of Dante's Hell* by a young writer named LeRoi Jones. It was a difficult tome, but something

216

about the certainty of the author's tone made me think about freedom.

I didn't pick up the book, but at least I thought about it. This was another milestone in my recovery. I lit a cigarette and gazed at my white ceiling. There were no faux bumblebees or even a water mark to betoken the poverty of my neighborhood. I was all right, on the road to a better tomorrow, free, or almost so, the best the scion of slaves could hope for.

Someone knocked at my door.

All that comfort and hope drained out at my feet. The cold reality of murder and grim retribution filled me more quickly than I could gauge the change. It was as if there had been no change at all; I had always been desperate and frightened, vengeful and ready to run.

I patted my right pocket to make sure my gun was there.

I went over to the far right corner away from the door and shouted, 'Who is it?'

'Colonel Timothy Bunting,' a young man said in a practiced commanding tone.

I took a step to my left just in case the man decided to fire in the direction of my voice. All the regular questions went through my mind. Was he alone? Had he come to kill me? How many drug smugglers were there? It did not occur to me immediately to question whether he really was a military man come to see me for some valid purpose. Why would I think that? All I had met so far were victims and killers, and the killers were all in uniform – or at least once were.

'Mr Rawlins?' the man called.

For a moment I considered shooting him through the door. After all, wasn't he there to kill me? That's when I knew that my bout with insanity was not yet over. I was prepared to murder a man I had never even seen. I had become those white men chasing me up the stairs in Bellflower – that was just not acceptable, not at all.

I went to the door and pulled it open, the gun in my pocket and my hands not in fists.

A natty young man in a colonel's uniform stood there in front of me. He wore no medals and had his officer's cap under his left arm. His face would not grow into manhood for at least another decade. He was tall, slender of shoulder in spite of exercise, and his skin was olive colored, not from the sun.

'Mr Rawlins?' the thirty-something officer asked.

'Show me some ID.'

'Excuse me, sir, don't you see the uniform?'

'Show me some ID now,' I said.

'I represent the United States government, Mr Rawlins . . .'

He stopped talking because I pulled out my .38 and pointed it at his left eyeball. The young officer knew enough to see when he was in a no-win situation, so he carefully took his wallet from his back pocket and opened it to show his military identification card.

This displayed his name, rank, and photograph.

I put the gun in my pocket and a smile on my lips.

'Come on in, Colonel,' I said. 'It's been quite a while since a man in uniform has told me the truth.'

I took the seat behind my desk and the young officer sat before me. We experienced a few seconds that dragged on into a minute of uncomfortable silence. I had pulled a gun on a man who was used to treating the smallest exhibition of insubordination with harsh retaliation. But here he had to swallow my defiance and continue as if nothing had happened.

'What did you mean?' the colonel asked.

'Come again.'

'What did you mean when you said that men in uniform were, uh, lying to you?'

I considered being cagey, putting out a few feelers to see how much Bunting knew. But I wasn't in the frame of mind to tiptoe around. Bunting was either with Sansoam or against him; either way we were going to have to put our cards on the table. So I told him what I knew about Clarence Miles.

'I'll have this Miles looked into,' he said officiously.

'Don't bother, Tim,' I said. 'There is no black Clarence Miles in your army, at least not no captain.'

'How do you know that?'

'I know things that would amaze you, Tim. Just take my word on it. Clarence Miles's real name is Sammy Sansoam.'

Bunting knew the name. He might have been an officer, but he'd never be a cardsharp.

'You should refer to me as Colonel, Mr Rawlins.'

'If you don't like what I say, then get your ass outta here . . . Tim. I been jerked all around this city by everyone from security guards to colonels. I refuse to respect you because you don't give a shit about me. So if you need somebody to kiss your ass, you can just move on down the hall.'

Again the young man needed a moment to collect himself. He was a soldier, and our country was at war. I should have been falling over myself to help him – that's what he thought.

'Samuel Sansoam was an officer,' Bunting said at last. 'We suspect him of having been involved with criminal activities in the army and even now after his discharge.'

'What crimes?' I asked.

'I'm not at liberty to say.'

'Drug smuggling for a warlord in Cambodia, maybe?' I said, trying to look like an innocent.

Bunting was injudicious in his silence. He should never have been made colonel, but he'd probably end up with five stars.

'What other information do you have, Rawlins?' he asked in a hard-as-nails voice that he must have practiced at night.

'Mr Rawlins,' I said.

220

This time a look of hurt went across Bunting's face. If I could call him Tim, then why couldn't he use my last name?

*Life is not fair.* These were some of the few words of advice I had left to remind me of my father. What he meant was that a black man had to swallow his pride, his pain, and his humiliation on a daily basis when it came to dealing with white folks. It felt good to turn the tables on that adage. And I felt no remorse for doing so with the self-important boy-officer.

'Do you have any other information . . . Mr Rawlins?'

'First you tell me how you got to my door.'

'I'm not here to answer your questions, sir.'

'You're not here at all, son. You are a soldier and I am a civilian. I'm not answerable to you, and you hold no jurisdiction over me. So if you want to play nice, I will consider answering your questions. Otherwise we can go on playing this silly game.'

'I'm looking for Major Christmas Black,' Bunting said. 'He was once a member of our special forces, but he left the army.'

'And you think that he is a part of your drug smugglers' cabal?' I could tell that Bunting didn't understand the last word, but he covered it up pretty well.

'No. We had a letter from a former soldier, a pharmacist named Craig Laneer. He told us that he'd been part of this smuggling ring and that he wanted to turn over the organization. Laneer was subsequently murdered. His wife, a woman named Faith Laneer, disappeared. We found out from her Vietnamese charity that she had been friends with Black. The LAPD told us that Black and a criminal named Raymond Alexander were friends and that you and this Alexander were very close.'

'I'm here to find out if you can help me find Black.'

By the end of this explanation, I was fairly certain that Colonel Bunting was who he said he was and that he was looking for the same people I was.

'I know Christmas,' I said. 'He has a house up in Riverside.'

'We've been there. He's gone.'

'Did the police tell you that Raymond has disappeared and is wanted for questioning in the disappearance of a man named Pericles Tarr?'

'No.'

'Maybe the cops want you to do their work for them,' I suggested.

Bunting frowned, remembering something that he did not share.

'They were right about me and Ray bein' friends, though,' I added. 'I've been tryin' to run him down myself. So if you want to leave me a number or something, I'll be glad to call you if I get a line on Christmas.'

'You would?' He was really surprised.

'I don't have anything against you, Colonel,' I

said. 'I just need you to respect me as much as you respect the flag.'

The soldier looked at me in a way that said this encounter would stay with him for the rest of his life. He might forget my name and the circumstances of our meeting, but the changes wrought in him would be indelible on his understanding of power, its distribution, and its use.

He wrote down his numbers on a piece of paper that I provided.

'It's time,' I said.

'Time for what?'

'For you to get out of here and follow your nose.'

# CHAPTER 33

Out of habit I put the pistol into the top drawer of the desk. I had places to go, but even after the colonel was gone I did not rise from the chair. I felt tired, not sleepy but dragged down by life.

Many a time I had visited clinics and hospitals, bedrooms in homes and apartments where dying men and women lay. They had watery eyes and wan expressions, tacky skin and nothing to say. They reclined under sweat-soaked sheets as if they'd just run a mile, but the rest never worked. They could barely whisper or lift a hand.

I'd say *Hey, Ricky* or *Mary* or *Jeness*, repressing the question *How you doin'?* And they'd smile and mouth my name, try to remember something that we both knew well.

'Hey, Easy,' John Van once said to me, as if he were shouting into a pillow, 'you remembah that night Marciano knocked Joe Louis out?'

I nodded ruefully.

'I won twenty dollahs off'a you. I told ya: you don't play a horse a'cause of its color.'

There was a chair next to the bed and a clock

somewhere in the room. There were usually children playing on the floor or in the hall. They rolled around because that's all they knew, the only way they could bring happiness to a waiting room for death.

I often wondered how those dying people felt when there was no one there to distract them from their passage. What did they think about when sleep came on or the sun went down? Was there a sudden fear when they nodded off or just a malaise like I experienced after talking to that fool colonel?

I felt as if I might fall asleep, that if I fell I might not get up again. I wondered what difference it would make. After all, Oswald shot Kennedy, and hours later LBJ was being sworn in as president.

No one was indispensable.

Feather would go to Bonnie or Jesus, and Easter Dawn had a whole army to look after her. Frenchie would piss on my grave, and I had no close relatives except a daughter somewhere who probably didn't even know my name. I could just close my eyes and never open them again. That would be it.

'Don't move a muscle!' a loud voice commanded.

I jumped to my feet, or at least I tried to. My left foot got traction, but the right heel slipped out from under me. I dropped back down in the chair, reached for the pistol in my top drawer, grabbed it, and held it up at an awkward angle. It wasn't until then that I saw the slovenly, overweight white man in the bad suit looking down on me.

225

'You gonna shoot me with a stapler, Easy?' Sergeant Melvin Suggs of the LAPD asked.

I used to keep a pistol in a wire mesh net underneath my desk, but as time went on I worried that I might kill someone without looking or that somebody might break into the office and steal my piece. That's when I moved it to the top drawer with my scissors, stapler, Scotch tape, and paper clips.

Dumb luck is better than no luck at all.

There I sat, stapler in hand, too upset to be humiliated and too scared to put my fake weapon down.

'What's wrong, Easy?' the white man asked.

'Bonnie's marrying another man and all I can do is sit here.'

Melvin was of middle height and a little less sure of himself every day. He'd started out with the regular white American's arrogance and so he was still more certain than I ever would be, but his eyes were opened after the Watts riots and the horror we uncovered together.

It wasn't fair to call Suggs's eyes brown. They were taupe colored, like a fawn or a forest mushroom, given to him to make up for the sloth of his life.

He squinted and I sighed, half a mind in my office and the other still in the waiting room for the dying.

I regretted my rash confession to the lawman.

'I'm here about Alexander,' Suggs said, deciding to ignore my words.

226

That's why I smiled. 'And how are you, Mel?'

He pushed my client's chair and fell back into it. I could hear the joints strain.

'I'm okay. Met a girl, met her boyfriend, showed him my pistol, and made a small investment in the Johnnie Walker Corporation. You?'

I smiled wider. 'I forgot how many blackbirds go in a pie.'

He smiled.

'Alexander,' Suggs said to show me that he could stay on the scent.

'He didn't kill Pericles Tarr,' I said in a voice not my own. I say not my own because the tone belonged to those men that dropped napalm on Asian men wielding bamboo sticks, whose forefathers preached equality only not for women or niggers or crackers without a pot, who made decisions in their hearts without any consideration for their souls.

Maybe it was my voice.

'Where is he?' Suggs asked.

'I don't know,' I said, myself again. 'I've looked everywhere. But listen, Mel. Mouse is not a loan shark, neither is he the kind of man who shoots and runs. We both know what he is and what he isn't. Mouse did not kill that man.'

'Since when did they make you a judge?'

'The same night they ordained you and yours as executioners,' I said, wondering who spoke through me now.

Suggs paused at that charge. He smiled again.

'I won't lie to you, Easy,' he said. 'They want him this time, his head on a sharpened stick.'

Suggs's suit was tan and his shirt was either white or light green. Both were soiled, wrinkled, worn to the edge of their threads' ability to hold on.

'Who?' I asked him.

'Captain Rauchford.' Suggs said, 'Seventy-sixth Precinct.'

I turned my face to the wall, taking in this information. Rauchford had rousted me a few times before I was given a PI's license by the deputy commissioner. He was both an ugly and a prissy man. Every hair in place and the girls still shunned him; every T crossed and he was still passed over for promotion. And like all white men who couldn't bear the weight of injustice visited upon them, he regurgitated his rage onto others; men like me.

When I turned back, Suggs was rising from his chair, Benedict Arnold to the men in blue. He'd drink a whole bottle that night, hoping maybe he'd find forgiveness on the other side.

# CHAPTER 34

The drive over to Champion Avenue was pleasant. Suggs's visit, though not actually restoring my faith in mankind, had at least given human nature a positive wrinkle. He wanted me to know that there was a semi-official plan in motion to murder my friend.

Suggs was a good cop. He solved the crime. That was his downfall. Most Americans (and maybe everybody else around the world, for all I knew) didn't look directly at the problem. If you heard shots, the first thing you did was duck and then run. After that, most people hid. Suggs's way of hiding was to think.

He didn't know if Mouse was guilty, but he did know that killing a man you cannot arrest legally is wrong. He couldn't go against Rauchford and he had no idea what Mouse or I would do, but he had to tell me.

I spent the rest of the brief drive thinking about Colonel Bunting. In my mind I called him Bumbles. He was like so many young black men who wrapped themselves in the latest styles and thought that made them invulnerable. Bunting

229

believed that his uniform made him superior; my brothers in the street thought it was ruffled shirts and unborn-calf-skin shoes. Manhood and childishness blended together in both Bumbles and my slave-descended kin. The only difference was that the newspapers and television agreed with Bumbles. No one laughed at a puffed-up, preening white fool in uniform.

The Supremes were singing 'Baby Love,' much too loudly, behind the pink door. I pressed the buzzer repeatedly, breaking now and then to work the brass knocker.

It was a nice house, small and set farther back on the lot than the other homes around it. The lawn was cut and well trimmed, and the rosebushes along the sidewalk were clipped and blossoming. Big flowers with red, white, and orange petals hung heavy on the thorny branches, and a profusion of violet dahlias flourished along the side of the house. The light on the lawn was so strong that I felt I might reach down and pick it up in my hands.

The song was coming to an end, and I was just beginning to understand how powerful my emotions were. The idea that I could hold sunlight in my hands sent a shiver through my bones. I might have come to some deep revelation had it not been for the sudden silence.

I pressed the buzzer and pounded on the door at the same time.

The next song didn't come. Instead a woman asked in an insulted tone, 'Somebody there?'

'Easy Rawlins, ma'am,' I said to the pink door.

The sunlight was behind me now, but the insanity still thrummed at my forehead. Sex and murder felt like possibilities. Given the chance, I would have taken Prometheus's fire and laid waste to the California coastline from San Diego all the way to Mount Shasta.

But then the door opened.

She wore red. You could have called it a dress, but it was much more like a wrapper. Her figure could not have been more obvious if she were naked and oiled. The medium-brown face and thighs, arms, and neck were ignited by eyes dark enough to be called black. Pretty Smart was short, built to populate the countryside, and lovely in a way that Christians interpreted as sin.

All that I saw she could see in me.

My attention dawdled on her sandals. They were black, with red ribbon straps between the second and third toes of each foot. The ribbons then ascended, twining sinuously around her ankles to hold the shoes in place.

'Yes?' she asked, not nearly so put off by my arrival as she had been before opening the door.

'Those are wonderful sandals,' I said.

Pretty had big lips to begin with, but when she smiled they seemed to swell.

I thought again about the sunlight. It seemed to me that Pretty's tawdry and ethereal beauty was

231

like that: touchable and untouchable, an artifact wedged in my mind like hunger and fear.

'I got 'em on sale at Gump's in Frisco,' she said. 'What's your name again?'

'Easy Rawlins.'

'Do I know you, Easy Rawlins?' It was a suggestion as well as a question.

'No. But you know a friend of mine.'

'Your friend send you here?' she speculated.

'No man in his right mind would send another man to you, Miss Smart.'

Her teeth were white and, I noticed, her nails were long, healthy, and clean.

'What man, then?'

'Mouse.'

The woman-child's terra-cotta face froze as if it were really made of ceramic. She had to think, to wonder what danger I posed. Her power meant nothing next to Mouse's threat.

'Is that a man's name?' she asked lamely.

I smiled and shook my head slowly. 'There are ten thousand men of every race and age in this city alone,' I said, 'who would leave their wives after just seeing your photograph. You know that and I do too.'

The young woman frowned, trying to resist the compliments she craved.

'And,' I continued, 'you also know Raymond Alexander just as well.'

'Oh . . . Ray . . . Yes, I know Ray Alexander. I don't have no nickname for him, though.'

I smiled again.

'What do you want, Mr Rawlins?'

Her voice had turned cold.

'I'm looking for Ray, and a man I met sent me here to you.'

'What man?'

'It doesn't matter what man, honey,' I said. 'What matters is that he told me that Ray been seen with a man named Pericles Tarr and that Pericles and you were close.'

It's always a sadness to see a beautiful woman's eyes turn sour while gazing at you. Even though I wanted to see what she felt, I still lamented the lost opportunity . . . at least a little.

'You'll have to excuse me, Mr Rawlins,' she said. 'I got to go.'

She backed away from the door, preparing to close it.

'Miss Smart.'

'What?'

'Do you know where Raymond is?'

She closed the door and I allowed myself a chuckle.

I went to the sidewalk and strolled all the way to the corner, where I turned to the left and waited for three minutes. If Pretty had watched me go, she would have returned to the house by then.

'Mister?' a voice asked.

I turned to see an older black man wearing clothes that were once colorful but now had devolved into browns and sad, tinted grays.

'Yeah?'

'Can you help a veteran out?' he asked me.

'What war?'

'The big one back in nineteen sixteen.'

'You kill anybody back then?' I asked him, I don't know why.

He grinned at me and I noticed he only had three teeth; each one looked as strong and brown as an old oak stump.

A giant cockroach ran a jagged line on the sidewalk between us. The store behind him was closed and boarded up.

I took a twenty-dollar bill from my wallet and gave it to the man. When he saw the denomination, he was shocked.

'Thank you, mister,' he said with emphasis.

'No problem at all, brother,' I said.

He held out a dirty hand, and I shook it. This contact had a cleansing effect upon me.

'I'm'onna take this money and try and do sumpin' with it, my friend,' the old man said. 'I'm'a try and get myself situated, get a job and put down the wine.'

He was looking me in the eye and I knew he meant every word. What difference would it make if he failed? We all failed in the end.

# CHAPTER 35

I left the veteran and went back to my car down the street from Perry Tarr's girlfriend's house. For the first five minutes, I sat there trying to figure out how I could read and watch her driveway at the same time. It was a problem I always thought about when on a stakeout. But the answer was ever the same: I could not read and watch at the same time. Whenever I came to this understanding, it left me feeling a little sour.

I sat there in my resentful contemplation, hoping that someone would come to or leave the pretty girl's house soon. Unable to distract myself with reading and not wanting to hear any more music, I started thinking about the woman I'd just met.

Pretty Smart was not Bonnie or Faith or EttaMae Harris. She wasn't the kind of woman that could move me to put my life on the line. But, I thought, wouldn't life be better with a woman like Pretty? Wouldn't it be fine to be with a woman who made your blood run like a teenager's but who didn't make you feel like you might die when she was gone?

This line of thinking was an appealing distraction. The idea of beauty without consequence and love that was purely physical allowed my heart a brief span of elation. I didn't imagine making love with her. It was enough just to have a brief conversation and to see her smile.

While I was having these thoughts, a navy blue Volkswagen backed out of Pretty's driveway. She was an excellent driver. She backed into the street in a tight arc and drove past my car on some mission that my visit no doubt precipitated. I turned my head as she drove past, but it probably wasn't necessary. Nobody looks at faces in Los Angeles. In LA people are too busy making hay because the sun never seems to go down.

I could have tried to follow the dark blue automobile, but in my experience a vehicular tail rarely works. Traffic lights turn against you; bad, sloppy, and drunk drivers cut you off; and even though people don't look at faces in LA, they certainly keep a sharp eye on their rearview mirrors. You need at least two cars for an adequate tail. With one man, you're much better off trying B and E while the subject is off in her car.

I knocked at her door again. There was no loud music and no answer.

I went around the back. The windows were all shut. The white paint on the back door was cracking and growing a thin veneer of olive-hued lichen. The blades of grass were long and bright.

A bushy pine hid the backyard from view. All of this along with the silence boded well for my kind of business. But the best sign was that Pretty Smart's back door was unlocked and ajar. If I were dealing with Christmas Black, I would have suspected a trap, but I knew that Miss Smart paid too much attention to her own beauty to be distracted by locks and burglars. After all, her wealth was her beauty, and she carried it around with her.

The back porch was fitted with a washer and dryer, but the kitchen that led from there didn't even have a pot to warm her leftover takeout meals. The tiny living room was furnished with a very large white sofa that had deep cushions and a high back. There were a dozen or more pillows of various pastel hues on the couch. Before the bed-size divan sat a big walnut coffee table that supported a pink portable TV and a brand-new hi-fi system. The carpet was white shag. Three huge abstract paintings hung from as many walls. The furnishings and decorations were made for a much larger room. It felt as if a giant had moved his furnishings into a room made for a pygmy.

Pretty's bedroom was surprisingly spartan. A single bed with a metal filing cabinet instead of a dresser or chest of drawers. There were shelves in her closet that held her hose and bras, garters and silk panties. There were five dresses hanging from a rod; three of these still had price tags on them.

The filing cabinet had three deep drawers and

a Polaroid camera sitting on top. The back door had not been locked, but the filing cabinet was. I found a screwdriver under the sink in the bathroom and twisted the keyhole until the lock snapped off.

There were seven hanging files in the top drawer, the first of which was labeled MEN. Inside this folder was an eight-by-eleven photo album, maybe forty pages long. Each page held six Polaroids of men's erections. Black men, white men, men who were neither black nor white. Some were young, others old, a few were so fat that they had to hold their bellies up off their hard cocks. More than a couple were slick and wet, and one was in the middle of an ejaculation.

It was no surprise that Pretty had locked her files away. I wondered how she got the men to pose for her. Probably she said that she wanted to remember their manhood, their night of loving.

'If you're not here, I wanna remembah you inside me,' she might have said.

The other files kept her finances, her modeling résumé, her secretarial résumé, her high school transcripts, her date calendar, and, finally, her phone diary.

Perry Tarr's home address and phone number had been crossed out and replaced with a new address on Ogden between Eighteenth Street and Airdrome.

I wrote the address on a blank piece of paper that I carried around in my wallet for just that purpose. After that I snapped off the next two locks on the filing cabinet and rummaged around her jewelry, cash cache, checkbook, bankbooks, and savings bonds. I took the cash, about one hundred and eighty dollars, her checkbook, and two rings that looked to be valuable. Then I took the creation album and put it on her bed, gaping open.

I did all that to make it seem as if I were some teenage burglar instead of a man on the trail of Perry Tarr. She might still guess at the identity of her robber, but that was all I could do after breaking the lock on the first drawer.

I was about to leave when I noticed the one girly part of her austere sleeping quarters. It was a pink princess phone on the floor next to the head of her bed.

I should have left, but instead I picked up the receiver and dialed a number.

'Marvel's Used Cars,' she said.

'Can we have dinner tonight?'

'Easy?'

'Uh-huh.'

'I can't tonight, Easy,' Tourmaline said. 'I have a date. Maybe this weekend?'

'That would be just as good,' I said, thinking my tone was light and airy.

'What's wrong?' she asked.

'Nothing. Why? Do I sound like something's wrong?'

'You sound like it looks when a girl is turning her head away.'

'A girl?'

'Where are you right now, Easy Rawlins?' Tourmaline Goss asked.

It was a crack in the dam, a fissure I felt all the way down to my childhood. Tourmaline was that perpetual Black Woman and I was the forever child. Her tone paralyzed me there on the party girl's military-style bed. I could see the bushy pine out Pretty's small window. For all I knew, Pretty had gone to the pharmacy to get aspirin for the headache I had given her. She might have been on the way back at that very moment.

'I just broke into this house,' I said. 'Somebody said that a friend'a mine killed somebody, but I knew this woman could prove that the man who's supposed to be dead is still alive . . .'

For the next hour and a half I told Tourmaline most of the important moments of my life. I told her about Mouse, whom she'd heard about, and Jackson and Etta and Bonnie. I told her all that I had been through up to the moment I threw Bonnie out of my house. I didn't mention any killings or murders outside the one Mouse was blamed for. That would have been unfair to an innocent university student.

Tourmaline listened to me patiently even though she was at work. People interrupted her now and then, but she always got back on the line and said, 'Go on.'

I had hoped the confession would relieve me, but instead it brought on a sense of emptiness.

Laying my life out like that made me see that I had wasted my potential on misguided pride and rage at strangers.

'I should go,' I said at last, 'before the young woman comes home.'

'What time are you going to pick me up?' Tourmaline asked.

# CHAPTER 36

I had planned to leave when I got off the phone with Tourmaline, but after all that confessing I didn't have the strength to stand up. She had wanted to hear about me, my life. Most of the men she'd met had been either silent or braggarts. It was rare for her to hear a man talk about his life the way he felt about it. But I hadn't been completely honest. What I had said was true, but what I had done was fool my heart into believing that I was talking to Bonnie, confessing to Bonnie, working my way back into her heart.

The lie didn't hurt Tourmaline, but it tore me up. Everything I thought I had accomplished in the past days faded, and I was once again at odds with myself.

It was very quiet in the unadorned bedroom. When the phone jangled I leaped from the bed. It rang ten times. At the start of each ring I decided to leave the house, but by the time the interval of silence returned I had lost my resolve.

I was afraid to leave Pretty Smart's crazy, shallow

242

home. Her life was so simple and straightforward. It was almost as if she were living in a movie set rather than a real home. There was solace in that simplicity.

There was danger outside.

I picked up the hunched pink receiver and dialed another number.

'Proxy Nine,' a woman answered.

'Jackson Blue,' I said.

'And your name is?'

'Ezekiel Porterhouse Rawlins.'

'What company do you represent, Mr Rawlins?'

'No company. I'm a one-man operation.'

'And what is the purpose of your call?'

'Purpose? I want to speak to my friend.'

'Does he know you?'

The woman wasn't stupid, I knew that. What I was experiencing was just another example of the world changing while I sat sulking in place.

'Very well,' I said. 'We've been friends since before the war.'

'Oh.'

I could almost hear her trying to think of some other way to more closely identify me before passing the call on to Jackson. It was her job to protect the uppity-ups at Proxy Nine, the French insurer of international insurance companies and banks, and Jackson was as uppity as you could get. He was the vice president in charge of data processing.

'One moment, please,' the operator said.

243

There was a series of clicks and then a ring. 'Jackson Blue's office,' another woman said.

'Easy Rawlins for him.'

'What company do you represent, Mr Rawlins?'

It was at that moment that Jackson changed in my mind. He had *two* secretaries protecting him from outside calls. From now on our relationship would be at the whim of his largesse. Somehow the cowardly genius had managed to circumvent the machinations of racism. He had more power and access, protection and esteem, than most white men.

'Hello,' he said into my ear.

'Hey, Jackson,' I said. 'I need to come by.'

'Kinda busy, blood,' he said with barely a stammer.

'Listen, Jackson. I'm sittin' here on a bed in a woman's house. I broke in here and now I'm afraid to leave. It's like if I went outside there'd be an ambush just waiting.'

This was not a continuation of my confessional with Tourmaline. Jackson and I had had one foot on the criminal side of things since we were kids. Admitting to a break-in was no big thing. And fear was Jackson's native tongue.

'Okay, brah,' he said. 'All right. Come on by.'

Jackson's words were like an incantation that served to break the spell Pretty Smart's house had cast over me. I walked out the front door, closing it carefully as I left. I walked to my car and headed for the Proxy Nine building down-town.

The officers of the company were all on the thirty-first floor. I remembered that because Jackson had called me when he found out where his desk would be situated.

'I asked 'em t'change it, Ease,' he told me at Cox Bar on a Sunday afternoon, 'but they said that I gotta be there 'cause Jean-Paul wants me close at hand.'

'Jean-Paul?'

'Jean-Paul Villard. He's the president'a the company,' Jackson said, as if he were talking about a distant cousin rather than the master of a multibillion-dollar operation. 'So I'm thinkin' I should quit.'

'Quit? Why you gonna quit over somethin' like that?'

'Thirty-one, man,' he screeched. 'Thirty-one. That's thirteen backwards.'

It took me and Jewelle and Jewelle's minister to keep Jackson from resigning. It was amazing to me. Jackson was the only man I knew personally who understood Einstein's theory of relativity, and he was still more superstitious than a room full of four-year-olds.

After three phone calls and four receptionists, I finally got to Jackson's oaken door. The woman who brought me there had a French accent, brown hair, and a parsley-colored dress that clung tightly to her Jayne Mansfield – like figure. She tapped on the door, listened for something, heard a sound that I did not hear, and then stuck her head in.

When her head came out from the crack of Jackson's door, the young woman had an impressed look on her face.

'He wants you to go right in,' she said, not believing her own words.

'Is that a surprise?' I asked.

'Why, yes,' she said. 'Monsieur Villard is in there with him.'

Jean-Paul Villard was an olive-skinned man with dark eyes and a dark finely trimmed mustache. His hair was black. He was wiry but not skinny, tall, wearing black trousers and a herringbone jacket over an iridescent apple green shirt, which was open at the collar. He was lounging on one of the two yellow sofas that faced each other in front of Jackson's huge ebony desk.

I hadn't visited Jackson's work since before the move. The size of his office was monumental. Fifteen-foot ceilings above a room that was at least twenty feet wide and thirty long. His picture window looked out at the mountains north of the city. On the walls were original oil paintings of famous jazz musicians.

Jackson and his boss rose to meet me.

'Jean-Paul,' Jackson said, 'this here is Easy Rawlins.'

The Frenchman smirked at me and shook my hand.

'I have heard many things about you, Monsieur Rawlins.'

'Oh? Like what?'

'Jackson tells me that you are the most dangerous man he knows.'

'More dangerous than Mouse?'

Villard's eyebrows rose at the mention of the diminutive killer. I supposed that Jackson had told him so many stories laced with what had to be hyperbole that he probably thought that Mouse, and the danger he represented, had to be mostly myth.

'He said that Monsieur Mouse was . . . how do you call it? The most deadly, oui, yes, the most deadly man he knows.'

'He's right about Mouse,' I said, releasing the surprisingly strong handshake. 'But I don't see how I could be more dangerous than that.'

'Raymond just take your life,' Jackson said with a deadly grin on his dark face. 'Easy take your soul.'

There was an aspect of pronouncement to Jackson's words. After a moment of semiprofound silence we sat down. I perched on a cushion next to Jackson, and Jean-Paul squatted down on the edge of the couch across from us.

On the low marble coffee table between us there was a bottle of red wine and two glasses.

'Let me get you a glass,' the French businessman offered.

'Don't bother, man,' Jackson said. 'Easy don't imbibe.'

*Man.*

'Thanks anyway,' I said. Then I looked around the room. 'Nice paintings.'

'My lover painted them,' Jean-Paul said with pride. 'When she met Jackson she made him take them for his office.'

'Nobody had to make me,' Jackson said. 'You know, Easy, Satchmo hisself sat for Bibi to do that one there. She did a whole bunch'a writers too. Richard Wright, Ralph Ellison, Chester Himes . . .'

This was another new experience for me. Jackson was a coward, but he wasn't a kiss-ass. He really liked Jean-Paul and the strangely foreign paintings of American musicians. He belonged in that room.

For a while we exchanged pleasantries. The white man poured himself a glass of wine and sat back on the yellow cushions. It became apparent that he had no intention of leaving.

We had just come to the end of a brief discussion about Vietnam and how no white men, American or French, belonged there.

'So what you need, Easy?' Jackson asked.

Jackson and the Frenchman might have been friends, but he and I went way back. We hadn't been true friends for all that time, but we could read each other in the dark. With those five words he told a whole story. Jean-Paul was fascinated by Jackson and the tales he told. He was hungry to see an America that was not broadcast on TV and the radio. He wanted to experience the Black Life that had given birth to jazz and the blues, gospel and the Watts riots. Jackson was his first real taste of what there might be under the sanguine white-American facade.

Jackson looked up to this man, wanted to impress him, and so he was asking me to allow the president of Proxy Nine some insight into how our lives went. He trusted that if I had killed somebody or found myself in serious difficulty, I'd just roll out some neutral story and come back to the real details later on when Jean-Paul had had his fill.

Every day in the late sixties was like a new day. From hippies to a war America couldn't win. There were black people rioting for their rights and getting somewhere with it; Playboy clubs and good jobs; black sports heroes and French millionaires hobnobbing with the likes of me and Jackson Blue.

'EttaMae called me,' I said, deciding to kill two birds with one throw.

When Jackson heard Etta's name his friendly smile paled, but I kept on talking.

'She said that the cops were looking for Mouse. They think he murdered a man named Pericles Tarr—'

'An' you want me to go speak with ole Etta?' Jackson asked, hoping to end our conversation.

'No, no, no, no,' I said. 'Hear me out, brother. Like I said, the cops think Mouse murdered this man and laid him in a shallow grave down in, uh, San Diego—'

'Did they find the body?' That was Jean-Paul. He was all the way into my story.

'That's just it, J.P.,' I said. 'No. They haven't found a body, and the murdered man's wife says that Mouse was playin' loan shark and did her husband in because he couldn't pay the note.'

'What's this "loan shark"?' Villard asked.

Jackson rattled off an explanation in amazingly fluent French. Even while I was teaching him a lesson, he was showing me that being in his company was sharing the presence of brilliance.

'Oh, yes, quite right,' Jean-Paul said in English learned from an Englishman.

'So you know that this Pericles isn't dead?' Jackson asked hopefully.

'Right . . .'

I laid out the story, then explained, without admitting to burglary, that I'd gotten information from the girlfriend.

'I'm bettin' that Perry's the kinda man slip out the back window when trouble comes to the door,' I said. 'So I need you to ring the bell while I wait at the back.'

'You are going to catch him by the nose,' Villard speculated.

'And twist a little,' I added.

250

'May I come with you, Mr Danger Man?' the president asked.

'Sure,' I said. 'Nothing spells trouble like a white man knocking at a black man's door.'

# CHAPTER 37

'So what did you do during the war, J.P.?' I asked on the way over to Ogden.

'My family is very rich,' he said. 'They went to Switzerland and South America. A few went to our plantations in Mali and Congo.'

'And you?'

'I wanted to fight the Nazis. I was young and I wanted to kill the people who were raping my homeland.'

'Is that what you did?'

Jean-Paul was sitting shotgun, and Jackson was in the back-seat. The Frenchman's dark eyes flashed at me and he wondered. I was wondering too. Here I was speaking to a man whose family was old and rich. They owned plantations in Africa, so they had probably been slavers at one time; they might still be today . . .

'I worked in a small apartment, making radio codes for the Resistance,' he said. 'Our little station was across the street from the Gestapo. I never left my post. For three years I went outside only two times. Once when there was a fire in our building and we feared that the transmitter would be found, and once . . . once down in an alley where a German officer would go to have sex with little girls of twelve and thirteen.'

'What you do down there?' I asked, because I didn't want the son of slavers to think I couldn't handle his experience.

'I cut his throat and then I cut off his prick and put it in his mouth.'

I glanced up at Jackson in the rearview mirror. I don't know what he was thinking, but I remembered a conversation we'd had many years before. I had asked him if he thought that a black man and a white man could ever be friends.

'Hell, yeah,' he'd answered. 'Sure can. But you know a white man got to go through sumpin' 'fore he could call a black man friend. White man got to see the shit an' smell it too before he could really know a black friend.'

Jean-Paul had smelled the shit.

The Ogden house was a small stucco hutlike structure the color of mottled blood orange. It was perched on a raised lawn at the center of the block.

After a few minutes of deliberation, I decided to walk up the driveway as Jackson and Jean-Paul went toward the front.

They were to ring the bell while I made my way toward the back door on light and fast feet.

There might have been barriers to impede me, a locked gate or a guard dog, for instance, but I took the chance.

The backyard was small and barren. It was a paved patio under the dubious shade of a dying pomegranate tree. There were two rusting poles standing across from each other supporting a clothesline that held two shirts and about half a dozen socks.

I stood to the right of the door with my .38 in my hand. It might seem to the layman that a pistol out and at the ready would have been overkill for a situation like that. But when you enter into the occupation of ambush, you have got to go all the way or you will, sooner or later, regret it.

I didn't have to wait long. Within sixty seconds the back door opened, allowing a short and stealthy man to step outside.

He was the color of a well-used two-year-old Lincoln penny, stubby in his build, with small, strong hands and a green cap. His pants were black and his short-sleeved shirt was brown.

'Hold it, Perry,' I said, 'or I'll shoot you dead.'

I expected to scare him, to keep him still. He went me one better by falling on his knees and putting his hands up above his head. I went around my prisoner with the gun in evidence. His head was bowed.

'Look up at me, man,' I commanded.

His face and body were a hodgepodge of the true Afro-American experience. There were northern European features to his bulbous nose and cheeks, Slavic influence in his Asiatic eyes, serflike economy to his compact bone structure and wide hands. His hair was kinky and his lips

254

full. He was the jambalaya of the New World, a dozen or more European and African races competing for a piece of his body's geography.

'Who you?' the frightened man whispered.

'Easy Rawlins.'

'What trouble you got wit' me, man?'

'They say that Raymond Alexander killed you.'

'No, brother. No. I ain't dead.'

'But the cops think you are,' I argued. 'They after Ray.'

'Mouse know where I am, man. He got me this place.'

'You a lyin' mothahfuckah,' I said, digging deep into the language of the street.

'I could prove it.'

I waited maybe thirty seconds before speaking. I wanted Pericles Tarr as frightened as possible so that I could get down to the truth quickly and switch back onto the track of Christmas Black.

'Get up.'

Inside, Jackson Blue, Pretty Smart, and Jean-Paul Villard were sitting in the sunken living room, gabbing like old friends. Pretty was leaning forward in her chair, asking J.P. a question.

She was wearing a blue wrapper now, with sandals that had yellow ribbons to hold them in place. When she saw me, she stood up and said, 'You,' with a kind of emphasis that implied I was in trouble. But then she saw the pistol in my hand and decided it was time to sit down.

'Hey, Easy,' Jackson said, 'come on in. Pretty was just tellin' us how she live in this cute li'l house all by herself.'

I was wondering how my accomplices had insinuated themselves into the mercenary young woman's good graces, but I didn't have time to consider that for long.

'Yeah,' I said. 'She's been known to stretch the truth in my brief experience with her. She also said she don't know Mouse.'

'I said I didn't know that nickname for him,' Pretty said.

'Uh-huh. Listen up. You people stay out here and continue on with your chat. Me and Perry gonna go in the bedroom and figure a few things out.'

Perry glanced at Pretty, looking for some kind of support or help, but she turned her head away.

'Come on,' I said to the dead man.

Down the hall on the right side was a bedroom with two single beds. The one on the right was tousled. I sat on the made bed and gestured with the pistol to the one that Pretty and Perry had used for sex.

Perry sat down, clasping his hands. He slapped the palms together and rubbed them like an anxious fly.

'So?' I said.

'What you worried 'bout, man?' he whined. 'I ain't dead, so they cain't hang Ray.'

'They can if they don't find you,' I said.

'I wouldn't let 'em take Ray down.'

'Don't look like that to me.' I was speaking a street dialect that was filled with unspoken threats. This was a language that black people all over the nation knew.

'I give you my word,' Pericles pleaded.

'An' what you give to Leafa?'

'Leafa?'

'I'm a detective, Pericles. Your wife borrowed three hunnert dollars for me to hunt you down. She told me about when you got ambushed in the war, about how you smeared the blood of your dead friends on your own face to keep from gettin' killed. She said that she knew you weren't dead.'

My claim was so shocking that it knocked the fear right off Perry's face. He was trying to understand how his ploy had failed.

'Who gonna lend Meredith three hunnert dollahs?'

'EttaMac Harris, that's who. Meredith went to EttaMac and told her that she didn't believe Ray killed you. She said that she would hire me if Etta lent her the money.'

'What? She borrowed three hunnert dollahs just in case I was alive? She some kinda fool?'

'She's desperate, man.' I said as if I were an enemy pretending he was a friend. 'She ain't got nuthin'. You gone. They wanna kick her outta that rented house.'

'I got money for her,' Pericles said, squaring his shoulders at the insult to his manhood.

'You do?'

'Thirty thousand dollars.'

My mind went blank for a moment. There wasn't one Negro out of a thousand that I ever knew who could say that they had held thirty thousand dollars in their hands. As for the ones who could make such a claim, they were all gamblers or criminals.

Mouse.

'Armored car or payroll?' I asked Pericles.

'Say what?'

'You heard me, niggah,' I said, lifting the .38 three inches.

'Payroll.'

'What state?'

'Washington.'

'Are you a fool. Mr Tarr?'

'What you mean? What you tryin' to do, man?'

'Lemme tell you,' I said. 'You went up there in a blue Pontiac you and Ray bought from Primo. You had regular plates up to Washington, but then you put on stolen ones when you got near the job. Early in the mornin' you walked into the shop where guards were movin' the money, two hunnert fifty thousand or more. The guards let you hit 'em in the head, and you and Ray moved all that money into the trunk, went to a motel, put it in boxes, and shipped it down here to this house.'

'Who the fuck are you, man?'

258

'Have you told Pretty where you got the money?'

He shook his head.

'Because if you do,' I continued, 'Ray will kill both'a ya'll.'

'I ain't said a word.'

'You told me.'

'You got a gun and you already knew most of it.'

'If you tell anybody, you'll be dead.'

'I just told Pretty that I won twelve thousand on the trifecta. That's all I said. I bought her some dresses an' said I'd take her to New York in style.'

'Gimme the money for Meredith and the kids,' I said.

Perry didn't even stall. He went to the closet, turned an iron plate in the floor, and pulled out a pillowcase filled with stacks of twenty-dollar bills held together by rubber bands.

'Thirty thousand,' he said. 'There's a letter in there already sealed and addressed to her. I was gonna drop it off when they were asleep tonight.'

'When you leavin' for New York?' I asked him.

'Monday. We flyin' first class. We gonna live in Brooklyn. After I get a divorce, we be married.'

I doubted that the nuptials would ever take place, but that was okay. Perry would be better off without Pretty Smart.

'One more question,' I said.

'What?'

'Where's Raymond?'

He blinked four times.

'No, man,' he said. 'I cain't tell ya that. Ray kill me wherever I was if I told you about that.'

I put the pistol in my pocket and sighed.

'Okay,' I said. 'All right. I can see that you really mean it.'

'I cain't tell ya,' Perry said again.

'I know. So you won't mind when me and my friends hog-tie you and drag you back to Meredith and all them kids.'

Pericles Tarr was a man of decision despite his weaknesses. He was more afraid of his family's love than he was of the deadliest man in Los Angeles. He gave me the address in Compton without another word of hesitation.

# CHAPTER 38

When Perry and I came back into the living room, Jean-Paul was talking to Pretty. She was grinning and ducking her head coyly. I had the pillowcase in one hand and the .38 in the other. I'd taken the gun out again to dissuade the young bombshell from asking questions.

When Jackson saw us he got to his feet. Reluctantly, Villard followed suit.

Perry went with his woman to stand by the front door. They watched us file out. There were no words of good-bye or good luck.

'How'd you get that girl to let you in the house?' I asked Jackson as we were driving away.

I had put Meredith's nest egg in the trunk.

'Jean-Paul's shoes what did it,' Jackson said with a grin.

'Shoes?'

'Martin Lane,' Jean-Paul added.

'Who?'

'These shoes cost twelve hundred dollars,' the insurance kingpin informed me.

'So?'

'Pretty asked me if I was wearing Martin Lanes,' he said. 'It seems that she keeps up with the fashion.'

'That was the icebreaker, Easy,' Jackson bragged. 'She was fallin' all ovah herself to get us in there an' figure out why my man here got them shoes. She and him goin' out on his yacht for dinner tomorrow night.'

'Perry told me that they were flyin' to New York on Monday,' I countered.

'She didn't tell us nuthin' about that. I guess she gonna be spendin' Sunday night packin' or sumpin',' Jackson said. 'You know Perry don't know Martin Lane from John Henry.'

At least I broke into her house, I thought. At least she will feel some discomfort.

I was angry at Pretty for being like me. She was showing her man the door because she couldn't control her compulsions. She wanted to be near real wealth and was willing to give up whatever it was Perry had to offer for a ride on a yacht.

I was upset by her betrayal, but wasn't Pericles the same? He'd run from a wife and a house full of children. He was just getting what he deserved. None of us were innocent. Why shouldn't Pretty go for the brass ring?

Jean-Paul and Jackson were talking about how sexy Pretty was when I started considering Mouse.

I knew his address, but still I had to tread

cautiously. He'd done the robbery already; that job was over. So why was he still so scarce? The only answer was that he'd gotten into some other business upon his return. And whatever that business was, it was probably dangerous. I was Raymond's best friend, but he didn't want me sticking my nose in his affairs.

'. . . right, Easy?' Jackson was asking.

'What?'

'Ain't it true what I said to Jean-Paul? That most white men in America don't know how beautiful a black woman is.'

I could almost see Mouse turning toward me in anger. I felt the thrill of fear right there in the car.

'That's right,' I agreed.

'Why is that, Easy?' Villard asked.

I resented him using my name without knowing why. He was a nice enough guy. He was a philanderer and a murderer and maybe a trafficker in slaves, but none of that had anything to do with me.

'Because they know what would happen if they let themselves love our women,' I said from some unconscious, resentful, frightened place.

'What do you mean?'

'If they loved our women, then they would become our men,' I said. 'And once that happened, they'd lose their advantage. Their children would be dark skinned. Their history would be our history, and their crimes would be shown for what they are.'

Jean-Paul frowned, truly contemplative for the first time since I'd met him. I gazed up in the rearview mirror and saw that Jackson was looking at my reflection in a rare show of intellectual respect.

I drifted back into thinking about my problems.

How was I going to give the money to Meredith Tarr? She didn't look all that stable from where I sat. She might, given the right (or maybe wrong) circumstances, start blaming me for killing her husband. She wouldn't have to look too deeply to find out that Ray and I were friends. Maybe I was part of a plot to pay her off.

I decided that I'd have to read the letter.

There's never a scarcity of problems for people like me. As soon as I'd come to a conclusion about Meredith's money, I started thinking about Bonnie's wedding. It came up in my mind stealthily, as if I had already allowed it into my consciousness without any resistance.

I had spent the night with Faith. I was on my way to a relationship with Tourmaline. The kids had accepted Bonnie's marriage.

'You ever been in love?' I asked the gabbling men.

'You know I love Jewelle more than my whole family,' Jackson said. 'You know that.'

'What if you found out that she was seein' another man on the side?'

'She wouldn't do that,' Jackson averred.

'Course she would, man,' I said. 'When she was

livin' with Mofass she got you that house on Ozone. She was out there with you two nights a week.'

'That was different.'

'I don't see how,' I claimed. 'She loved Mofass more than a baby love her mama. And he died for her.'

We were in my roomy Ford, but it felt as if I were alone, communicating with men in other worlds. Jackson was in my mirror like an image on a small TV. I could see him responding to my statements. I could tell by his distant gaze that Jackson had not considered the depth of Mofass's love. It was possible, very possible that the old man had loved Jewelle more deeply than Jackson ever could.

Jean-Paul was sitting next to me, wondering about the gravity of the conversation. He was right there, but to me he was no more than a cartoon. He lived in a world that I could never fit into. I lived in a world where he didn't belong no matter what kind of shoes he wore.

'But,' Villard said, 'if a man can love more than one woman, why cannot women love more than one man?'

'You really believe that?' I asked the cartoon.

'I do not want to smell him,' Jean-Paul said. 'I do not want him fathering my children. But love, it is like the weather. It is wonderful or it is terrible and then it changes. But you can never change it.'

I was in a vulnerable emotional state at that time. That's the only reason Jean-Paul's words seemed so deep. He was telling me something that I already knew but that I never really believed.

'You tryin' to say sumpin' 'bout Jewelle?' Jackson asked.

'Naw, man,' I said. 'Bonnie's marrying Joguye Cham.'

'The prince?' Jean-Paul asked.

'Yeah. You know him?'

'Oh, yes, very well. We have conducted business with him over the years. Investments and some insurance.'

'What's he like?'

'He comes from a long line of headmen of his people. He was educated at Oxford and was active in revolutionary movements. He's a . . . what you say . . . a good guy.'

A good guy. He was more than that. He saved my daughter's life and then took my lover in payment.

# CHAPTER 39

I rented a room at a motel called Ariba on Centinela. I didn't know if the military men had enough grunts left to stake out my house, but safe was definitely better than sorry. Not that sorry had left me unscathed. I lamented almost everything, even those things that I hadn't and couldn't have done.

I lay down on the bed with the pillowcase containing thirty thousand dollars at my side. I never once thought of keeping the money. It wasn't mine, and I would have paid for that theft. One day I'd meet Leafa after she'd lived in the street for ten years. I'd see the pain in her eyes, and whatever money I'd stolen would be gone.

After thirty minutes of trying to sleep, I reached into the bag and pulled out Pericles' letter. The envelope was made from cheap gray paper. It had been sealed and also taped. I used my razor-sharp pocketknife to sever the seam. The Dear Meredith letter was written on white paper of a higher quality than the envelope.

Dear Meredith:

I'm so sorry honey to tell you like this but I just couldn't face you now. I'm going away. I can't take it any more. I sit up in the house every night listening to them kids making sounds like wild animals and you in the bed next to me like Sonny Liston done knocked you dead.

It was the last straw when Hanley threw up on my newspaper and then Lola cried because she couldn't read the funnies. Ten minutes later they were both laughing and I wanted to kill them. Then you says that I needed to get a new job to pay for all that. It came into my head right then like God talking to Moses. I needed something new all right. And I'm doing that.

Don't get me wrong baby – this hurts. I came by the house just two days ago. I watched you guys from the alley across the street. I saw Leafa out there in a nice new green raincoat. She helping Lana learn how to ride a two-wheeler, and you were sitting there watching them. I almost went to you but then the whole brood came out of that house like pestilence and I ran away.

I am giving you this money. This $30,000.00. You can pay rent and feed the kids for a few years with that, maybe more. I will send more money when I can get it.

I am sorry baby.


Pericles Tarr


I read the letter three times, wondering what Meredith would think when she read it. It was the truth, but how could she know that? Pericles' leaving her had nothing to do with Pretty Smart. He just couldn't take it anymore. It was a house filled with noise and ugliness that only a mother could love. It's a wonder that she didn't understand what her man was going through. But then I thought, what would understanding have done for her? He would still have left. She would still have been set adrift with a dozen kids in a paper boat.

But none of that was my concern. I'd bring Meredith her money, and she would make it into their life preserver.

We all just make up life as we go along. At some point Pericles must have loved Meredith. He wanted a big family, or at least he wanted what she wanted and believed that she understood the consequences. And when the life he'd made turned out not to be the life he was making, Perry made up Pretty, robbed a payroll in Washington state, and bought two tickets for New York.

It was all make-believe, their lives and mine.

⋆    ⋆    ⋆

I pulled up in front of the Tarr home a little after four-thirty. The front door was open, and there were children ripping and running in and out of the house. There were more than twenty kids crying out loud and going crazy. The Tarr children had friends whose parents would never let them run wild like that.

I stepped over two wrestling eight-year-old boys to get past the threshold. In the kitchen I found Leafa making peanut-butter-and-jelly sandwiches for smaller kids who needed fuel for their disasters.

When the perfect child saw me, she smiled. She had her father's nose.

'She's in the back room, Mr Rawlins,' Leafa shouted, pointing with the jelly knife.

I went past the line of preschoolers to a closed door that I opened without knocking.

Meredith was there in a straight-back chair, sitting at an odd, distinctly unfeminine angle and staring at the wall.

'Mrs Tarr.'

No response.

'Mrs Tarr,' I said again, moving closer to her corner.

She turned her frozen gaze to me and frowned slightly.

'Have you fount his body?' she asked.

I handed her the pillowcase and the page Pericles had penned. She put the bag on her lap and unfolded the note.

Either she was a slow reader or Meredith Tarr read Perry's last words to her many times over. I stood there because there was no other chair in that malleable room. After a long time, Meredith took up the pillowcase and looked inside. After that she turned her attention to me.

'What does this mean?'

'I found Perry in a house in Compton,' I said. 'He was leaving for New York and said that he was going to send you this money. I told him you were just about to get evicted and offered to deliver it.'

'Did you read his letter?' she asked, ignoring my subtle lies.

'No.'

'It says he don't love me no mo'.'

I had no reply.

'Was he with a woman, Mr Rawlins?'

'Not that I could see. There was a woman in the house, but she was very definitely with another man.'

'What am I supposed to do now?'

I had been thinking about that question on the ride over.

'First I need to know something,' I said.

'What's that?'

'Do you believe that Perry wrote this note?'

'Yes.'

'Why don't you think that I wrote it and that I brought you this money to hush you up?'

'Because Leafa just got that raincoat from the

Anders across the street four days ago, but that ain't all.'

'What else?'

'Hanley didn't vomit on that newspaper, Henry did.' She smiled. 'Perry was always confusin' Hanley with Henry. He had to be alive to write this note. And it sounds just like him and this is his writin'.

'Why didn't you just steal this money, Mr Rawlins?'

'Because of Leafa,' I said.

'Leafa?'

'She's a special child, Mrs Tarr. She deserves better than she has.'

'She does.' Tears rolled down Meredith Tarr's face, but she didn't sob or moan.

'Mrs Tarr.'

'Yes, Mr Rawlins?'

'I'm going to give you some advice. So please listen.'

Meredith Tarr's destroyed eyes became clear and focused.

'Do you have a good friend or a sister somewhere?'

'Melinda. She my half sister from Arkansas.'

'Call her. Have her come and live with you to help with these kids. If not her then someone else. Take the money and get a safe-deposit box. Don't let anybody know you got this money, not even your half sister. I'm gonna have a friend call you, a woman named Jewelle. She will help you buy a house for ten thousand dollars or less. Buy the house and use the money you got left to pay for your sister and these kids. Rest up for a while and then get you a job. Perry told me that he'll get in touch and send you more money when you need it.

'Are you listening to me?'

She nodded in a sentient manner.

'Where'd he get this money, Mr Rawlins?'

'I don't know and I didn't ask.'

Meredith nodded again, this time sternly.

We went over my advice four or five times. I drilled it into her and I believe that she listened. When I was sure that she at least understood the way to go about taking care of all that cash, I headed for the door. I was half the way out of the back room when Meredith shouted, 'Bastard!'

I turned to see if she was talking to me, but Meredith was staring at the wall again. Her healing had finally begun.

# CHAPTER 40

By the time I'd made it back to the Ariba, Meredith and Pericles Tarr were out of my mind. I turned on the news and lit up a cigarette, kicked off my shoes, and sat there while Jerry Dunphy lectured me on a wide range of unconnected stories. A boy had been kidnapped and then released for a quarter million in ransom. The confessions of two captured American pilots shown on a North Vietnames film release were denied by American lip-readers. The Oscars might be postponed due to a strike. And Governor Ronald Reagan was slashing jobs in California's mental-health system. There were no black people in the news that night; no Mexicans or Indians or Africans either. But eleven students in Germany were arrested for a plot to assassinate Hubert H. Humphrey.

None of what I saw meant anything to me. I didn't believe or disbelieve. Watching the news was just a way to pass the time. If I were a child, I would have been watching cartoons.

After a while I turned down the volume on the TV, picked up the phone, and dialed.

'Hello?' Peter Rhone said in his sad and cultured tenor.

'Hey, Pete,' I said.

'Mr Rawlins. You want EttaMae?'

'Yeah. But first tell me somethin'.'

'What's that?'

'Did you tell Etta about that blue Pontiac that Raymond and Pericles bought from Primo?'

'No. No, I did not.'

'Why?'

'Because Ray asked me not to, and I usually do what he asks.'

I couldn't argue with that.

'Just a minute, Mr Rawlins, I'll get EttaMae.'

I sat there watching Jerry Dunphy's boyish face. He was smiling now, giving out good news, I guess.

'Hello,' Etta said in my ear.

'Pericles Tarr is alive,' I said. 'I can go to the police with that, and his wife will back it up.'

Etta gave me twenty or so seconds of silence. The kind of quiet a woman gives when she wants you to know you've gotten to her.

'Thank you, Easy. Thank you, baby,' she said. 'I don't know what I would'a did if they took him from me again.'

'We both know that nobody's ever gonna take Ray again,' I said. 'Anyway, I did what I did because he's my friend.'

'Where is he?'

'That's another question, Etta. I don't know yet.'

When people have known each other as long as

we had, they speak in silences and unspoken questions. Etta knew that I could intrude only so far into Raymond's life. The same was true for her. We'd saved him from a murder rap. She'd have to console herself with that and wait for his return.

'I'll call you later, Etta,' I said. 'When I get on top of a few things here.'

'Sumpin' wrong, Easy?' she asked.

'No, baby, not at all. Why you ask?'

'You sound funny. Like a man drivin' his usual way home and he comes up to a dead end.'

I wondered what daytime TV show had given her those words. Etta had never read a book, but she studied the TV like it was the Library of Congress.

'Light's just red,' I told her. 'Bye.'

I hung up too quickly, or maybe I meant for her to understand that she was right. Communication gets sophisticated when you grow older. Sometimes it's impossible even to know what you're saying.

I picked up Tourmaline a block away from where she worked. She wanted to keep her bookkeeping job through the summer, and Brad Knowles certainly would have fired her if he ever saw us together.

From Compton we went to a club on the south side of downtown LA. It was called Bradlee's and it was a place to dance. The building was a unique structure, a great octagonal edifice housing a single room that was one hundred feet across. In the middle of that room was a raised dais where a big band of black men, with one black woman vocalist, performed. From swing to rock and roll, they played music that made you want to move your feet.

I was not a dancer, never had been, never would be, but Tourmaline had enough rhythm for both of us that night. All I had to do was look at her or feel her move and listen to the music. I wasn't Fred Astaire, but my missteps only served to make my date laugh.

She was wearing a black skirt that was short and tight and a blouse covered with silvery plastic scales. Her eyes were aglitter and her body moved sinuously, insinuating all those things that young boys suspect.

At ten I bought her a beer so she'd give my forty-seven-year-old feet and hips a break.

'You could be a good dancer if you worked at it a little,' she told me.

'I could be a physicist if I went to college for eight years too.'

'But physics isn't as fun as the boogaloo.'

'I don't know about that. I think of a pirouette when I look up at the stars. You know the universe is a ballet that never stops.'

'I like you, Porterhouse,' Tourmaline said. She put a hand on my arm and leaned over to kiss me. Her mouth was cold and wet from the beer, but her tongue was warm.

I closed my eyes like a schoolgirl, and when I opened them she was still there, still smiling.

The dance was wonderful and frightening. There were hundreds of people of all colors and ages around us. They were twirling and hopping, dipping down low and moving their shoulders in deft interpretation. I was there with them, but at the same time I felt that I was capering toward a precipice, about to fall off into the darkness. The only way I could stay alive was to keep on dancing. I worried that my legs would give out and my feet would stumble . . .

When I walked Tourmaline to her apartment door, she turned to me and held out a hand, palm up. It was a question to which I had an answer. I pulled the hand to me and kissed her now warm lips. She molded her body to mine as she had done on the dance floor and made a sound of deep satisfaction.

We kissed for a very long time there outside her front door. It took me five minutes to get down to her neck and another ten before I lifted her skirt so that I could hold her behind. When half an hour had gone by, Tourmaline shoved her hand down the front of my pants. It struck me that I had lost quite a bit of weight since buying that suit. When her hand gripped my erection, I went still and stiff all over.

'I got you,' she whispered.

'I need you,' I replied.

She kissed me, gave me a squeeze, and asked, 'For what?'

'Huh?'

'What you need me for?'

'For my life,' I said, and she began to stroke me softly, maddeningly.

'The next time you come over we're gonna start up right here,' she said. 'Right here where we stop tonight.'

I groaned in disappointment, which made Tourmaline grin and pull harder for a moment before taking her hand from my pants.

'Go home and take a cold shower, Mr Detective,' she said. 'When you come back to me I expect somethin' good.'

# CHAPTER 41

My heart was still beating fast half an hour later. I pulled into the parking lot of the Ariba Motel but didn't get out of the car. I just sat there thinking about all of the motels I'd stayed in while homeless, on the run, or stalking someone. I remembered the chemical-sweet odors and the stains on graying sheets, the holes in the plaster, the moans through the walls, and the continual drone of cars going by. Televisions sounded different in a cheap motel. The voices were tinny and without resonance.

After twenty minutes I turned the ignition and drove off.

For a while I toyed with the idea of going back to Tourmaline's garage apartment. She might have been expecting me. We were both hot after that exchange at her door. All I had to do was knock and take her in my arms. All I had to do was make love to her until the soldiers were all dead and Mouse was back in Etta's house and until Bonnie married and became a queen.

In those days or weeks of new love with Tourmaline, Pericles would lose Pretty, and

280

Meredith would buy a new home. Leafa would make dozens of meals for her siblings and stroke her mother's hair. My granddaughter would grow older, and Jesus and Feather and Easter Dawn would have dreams of a life in which I was no longer a factor.

I drove to Tourmaline's street and parked at the curb. I turned off the headlights and faded into darkness. I wanted to climb out of my seat, but entropy held me in place once again. There was no rising up for me. I was a paraplegic in a blackout after a bombing.

I would have sat behind the wheel of my car the whole night if not for a couple I saw walk by.

They were older lovers, late thirties or beyond. His gut hung out, and she had a big butt. They went arm in arm, fitting perfectly. Invisible in the darkness, I felt as if I were dreaming them.

They stopped not ten feet from me and started caressing. These two had experience with love. They weren't delicate or tentative. The woman made sounds of deep-throated ecstasy. Their hands moved and so did their heads and torsos. If I hadn't known what I was looking at, I'd have thought I was watching the silhouette of a predator subduing and devouring its prey.

After a few minutes they ambled on. I waited for them to get to the end of the block before I turned the ignition.

Tourmaline and I lived in completely different worlds. She was enjoying the dance of bringing a new man into her life, while I was a denizen of the old graveyard, charged with bringing the plague dead to their final rest. She wanted to dance. I was walking on a poorly marked path toward a vat of quicklime.

None of that explained why I aimed my car for Faith Laneer's apartment. It wasn't because I was frustrated with the place Tourmaline had brought me. I could have returned to my motel room and fallen asleep on the sheets with no problem. It might have been because Faith was a part of my cracked, melancholic world. She would understand my problems. Maybe I was going there just because I had promised I would.

It was too late to go to Mouse's house. Whatever he did in the dead of night, he preferred to do it alone.

I wondered, as I neared Faith's court, if I would be glued to my seat again. I took a deep breath and looked up just in time to see a car driving in the opposite direction, away from the place where Faith lived.

The car might have been some color other than gray, but we were between street lamps. When my headlights flashed on the driver, he was looking to his right, preparing to turn. He wasn't looking at me. People don't look at people in LA. They look at cars.

Sammy Sansoam would never know where he'd been fingered.

Sammy turned smoothly and drove east. I

wondered for a moment if I should follow him; if I should run him down and shoot him in the head. I could have done it. I wanted to kill him. But I had to play the long shot.

The lights were off, and she didn't answer my knock. But the door wasn't locked. I walked into the tiny home in darkness and I wanted it to stay that way. But that bumblebee from Christmas's house was humming somewhere. I waved my hand and found the chain and pulled.

He'd left her naked and bleeding. She hadn't been dead, not at first. Maybe she had feigned death. Maybe she'd lost consciousness when he stabbed her . . . again and again.

She'd crawled across the room, oozing her life into the oak floor. She was too weak to yell and so she tried for the phone. Her pale fingers were still curled in the cord. Her life gave out before she could dial.

Naked and dead, Faith Laneer was looking up at me from another, final world, where I was headed but had not yet reached. My breath was coming in short gasps, and the room was shaking ever so slightly. I knelt down next to the onetime Sister of Salvation and touched her hand. It was still warm, still supple.

That was the moment that Sammy Sansoam died.

I hated myself for not killing him back at the intersection. I knew she was dead. I knew she had no chance. The drug trafficker's purpose in life was making sure that she couldn't tell on him. *Tell on him.* We were like children. We hadn't changed since we were kids hoping that the good ones wouldn't tattle on the bad.

I went into her bedroom, trying not to think of the brief love we had had there. On her desk was a piece of paper on a green blotter. She had scribbled my name thirty or more times across that solitary sheet. Easy Rawlins, Easy Rawlins, Easy Rawlins, Easy Rawlins . . .

She'd experimented with different lettering and inks and pencils. I took the blotter and paper, turned off the house lights, and fled.

# CHAPTER 42

I staggered out of the house and headed down toward the ocean. It was the same walk I'd taken with Faith after we'd made love. I ripped up the evidence of her schoolgirl crush and dropped it in a trash can half a mile away, then I trudged through the sand while the waves hissed and shushed.

Faith Laneer had been a heroine in a world that didn't know it. She stood up for children and weak men and for what was right. And I mourned her.

Part of me sneered at this weakness. What difference did one dead white woman make? I'd seen thousands of dead, murdered, tortured souls. I saw the concentration camps in Europe and fought side by side with boys who died carrying America on their shoulders through Africa and Italy, France and the Fatherland. I'd choked, stabbed, beaten, shot, and drowned men in my day. I'd seen black men castrated, lynched, burned, and stomped to death, and all I could do was watch – or turn away. I'd seen the flu go through little hamlets like plague, killing children by the dozens. I'd seen car crashes that had strewn mothers and their babies across the highway. I had watched while men and women drank themselves to death, laughing and dancing all the way to the grave.

Faith's death was no worse, not really. She'd died afraid and helpless, but most of us go that way. She was young, but she'd known love. She was beautiful, but that would have faded . . . probably.

The problem was that this was the last straw for me. It had started when I woke up one morning and my father told me that my mother had died in the night. And it ended here, with Faith Laneer murdered while I was dancing and kissing and sitting in my car.

The air was cold and I welcomed the discomfort. There were no lights near the water and so the night embraced me.

I wasn't thinking clearly. I knew that but didn't mind it.

'Life doesn't make sense, it just make a mess of things,' Lehman Brown used to say. He lived in the room next to mine in a residence hotel in Fifth Ward, Houston, before I went off to war.

There was no right and wrong out there by the water, only my desire for revenge.

I would kill Sammy Sansoam to pay for every death that cut at me. I'd hack that shit-eating grin off his face.

'Hey, buddy,' a man hailed.

I couldn't see him at first. I looked around, but the source of the voice eluded me. Then I saw him standing off to the right. A small white man wrapped in a blanket formed of dark and light colors.

'You lost?' he asked me.

'Yes, I am.'

'Come on over to my lean-to and we'll talk about it,' he said.

I'd been staggering and stumbling, moving down the sand, gesturing like a tragic prince delivering his soliloquy near the end of a Shakespearean tragedy. This man was drawn to me like a white moth to a suicide Buddhist aflame on a street in Saigon.

I followed him to a place where he'd set up a huge three-sided cardboard box held in place by two public metal trash cans.

'Sit,' he said.

The box was big enough for two. The inside of his temporary home caught the roar of the ocean and amplified it. The chill sank into my shoulders and I began to shiver.

'Here you go,' the little man said. He was proffering a newly opened quart bottle of red wine.

I stared at my benefactor. His skin was worn by the sun and the wind. His eyes glittered, but in the weak light of the moon I could not tell their coloring. He was older than I or at least looked to be. The wine and weather may have wrinkled him some, added years to his organs and bones.

He smiled at me, and I took the bottle and drank deeply.

I did not hesitate. I wasn't worried about falling off the wagon after years of sober migration. I only smacked my lips and handed it back.

'What's your name?' I asked.

'Jones.'

'Just Jones?'

'No. Jones,' he said with a grin.

'Easy.'

'What's wrong, Easy?' Jones asked me.

I looked at the man again. There was something open and encouraging about his face. That added to the spreading warmth and goodwill of the wine almost tripped me. Faith Laneer's death wanted to come out of my mouth. It wanted to beg for her life, to represent her to some higher authority. I wanted to confess to my failure to protect her.

I wanted my mother.

'How much of that wine you got, Jones?'

'Four bottles. But I need to save 'em. I'm what they call wine rich but coin poor.'

I lay on my back in the cold sand and dug a twenty-dollar bill from my pocket. I handed the currency to him and he gave me two of his bottles.

We downed my two quarts and then started on his, drinking far into the night. I spent the time avoiding what I wanted to say, what I needed to say. I talked about Raymond without mentioning his name, and Etta and Jackson and Jesus and my mother.

Jones told me that he'd never got living the straight life right.

'Oh, I could get a job all right,' he said. 'Go to work a week, maybe two. But then I'd sleep in late one day, get chewed out by the boss, get drunk that night, and miss a whole day or two. Once I met this girl and went up with her to Portland. I was in love until one day I woke up and realized I didn't know who she was. I guess I lost track of time, 'cause when I got back home there was somebody else livin' in my apartment. I just couldn't stay straight no matter what I did. I went to church. They sent me to a psychiatrist. She gave me these drugs.'

'Did that help?' I asked, just to stay on the ride.

'I kept a job for three months, but every day I woke up and looked in the mirror wonderin' who it was in there.'

Jones just wanted to talk.

When we got near the end of the last bottle of wine, I could really feel it. My fingertips and lips were numb, and the sound of the waves managed, at least partially, to cover the memory of Faith's death mask.

When a strip of orange appeared over the city, I got down on my side and closed my eyes. I can't remember if Jones was still talking. Once he started he just kept on going, telling his whole life, skipping backward and forward. He talked about his mother in North Dakota and then his grandmother in Miami. He had a son, I seem to remember . . . Noah. But like everything else in Jones's life, the boy got lost on the way to the next tale.

# CHAPTER 43

When I woke up, the sun was bright on the box where I slept. I remembered being cold, but now I was sweating under the gaze of Sol. I sat up with the memory becoming real pain in my head.

Jones was gone. There was nothing left of him in the shelter, not even the empty wine bottles. For a moment I thought my only problem was that I'd gotten drunk for the first time in a decade. But then Faith came back to me, and her death clenched my heart. I rolled to my feet on a wave of nausea and started walking.

There were no police cars swarming around Faith Laneer's address, not yet. They wouldn't find her for days. By that time it would all be over.

I pointed my car for Compton and stepped on the gas.

Ten blocks away, I stopped at a gas station restroom to urinate, throw up, and wash my face. I stayed in that small blue room for a long while, letting the cold water run over my hands and thinking. I wanted out of that room, out of my thoughts. But there was no outside for me.

The address Pericles Tarr had given me for Mouse was on Compton. I parked right out front and tore from my car as if it were a prison and I was making a break. I stormed up to the front door, no longer worried about what Mouse would think. I needed him now. I needed him to help me kill Sammy Sansoam.

I knocked on the door loudly, muttering to myself about murder and revenge. When my knock wasn't answered, I banged louder.

I was about to knock a third time when the door opened wide.

And there he was: the man I was looking for. Six foot four with the shoulders of a giant. He had medium brown skin, unsettling light brown eyes, and a white scar on the upper portion of his left cheek.

'Easy?' he said.

'Christmas?' I was completely thrown off by the appearance of my other quarry. 'What are you doin' here?'

'Come on in,' he said, while looking around to make sure there were no other surprises.

I did as he bade me, entering a room that seemed to be a perfect, almost nude, cube. There were two metal folding chairs and a cardboard box for a table on the far corner of the bare pine floor. No paintings on the walls or shelves or even a

TV. There was a radio. Aretha Franklin was wailing away at a low volume.

'How'd you find me, Easy?' Christmas asked.

'I didn't.'

'No? Then what are you doing here?'

'Mouse,' I said.

And like magic, my friend came out of a doorway to the right. In his left hand he was holding his famous .41-caliber pistol.

'Easy,' he said.

'Raymond?'

'I thought you said you was lookin' for me,' he said, responding to the surprise in my tone.

'I'm, I'm lookin' for both'a ya'll,' I said, my language devolving all the way back to my childhood, 'but not in the same place.'

Mouse's smile broadened, while Christmas's eyes got tight. At least they were reacting according to their natures.

'You been drinkin', Easy?' Mouse asked.

'How's Easter Dawn?' Christmas wanted to know.

'She's fine,' I said. 'Down at Jackson Blue's house with Feather and Jesus and them.'

'I left her with you,' the ex-Green Beret said. In any other state of mind I would have been worried about the threat in his voice.

'Yeah. Yes, you did. You left her with me with not even a note. Not even one word to tell her why you brought her there. Here I am with a child worried about her father, and he don't have the decency to let on what he's up to or when he'll be back.'

The muscle in Black's shoulders and back was so dense that it looked like a pack he toted. This mass increased with his anger, but I didn't care.

'I told you he was gonna do sumpin', Chris,' Mouse said. 'Easy ain't no pussy-ass soldier gonna wait for your orders.'

'Are you here for Mouse or for me?' Christmas asked.

'Faith Laneer is dead,' I said, answering all questions he might have had.

'Dead how?'

'Slaughtered like a hog in her own living room by a man named Sammy Sansoam.'

I hadn't known Christmas for long, but our relationship had been consecrated in blood, my blood. So I knew him on a very intimate level. He had never shown a moment of weakness or uncertainty in the time I had known him, and I was pretty sure that he rarely radiated anything but strength.

But when he heard how Faith had died, he went to one of the chairs and sat down. It was an eloquent, soldierly sign of surrender.

'But you here for me, not him,' Mouse said.

'I was lookin' for you 'cause of Pericles Tarr,' I said. 'Etta wanted me to find you because the cops think you killed Tarr.'

'Killed him? I freed him and then made him rich. I'm his goddamned Abraham Lincoln. Forty thousand acres and a whole herd's mules.'

'Yeah. I found that out and told Etta, but then this thing with Sansoam happened and I wanted you to come help me take care of it.'

The gleam in Raymond's eye almost made me smile. He recognized the murder in my soul like a long-lost brother.

'You wanna kill the mothahfuckah,' he stated.

'Yes.'

'Okay.'

And that was it. As far as Mouse was concerned, we were ready to roll. For a man to die somewhere, all I had to do was ask.

'How you get messed up with Sansoam?' Christmas asked. His voice was low and empty.

I told him about my meeting with the soldiers at his house and about the break-in at mine. Then I related my last sighting of Sammy, driving away from Faith's home.

'How could a man do somethin' like that to that beautiful young woman?' Raymond asked.

I hadn't wondered about Raymond getting together with Christmas to take care of the soldiers on his trail. They were friends and they were remorseless killers; the combination spoke for itself. What bothered me was that question, though. Killing had taken an odd turn in Raymond's mind. Would he understand killing an ugly woman or an old one? And then I wondered . . .

'How would Sammy know where Faith was?'

Christmas looked up.

'I mean,' I continued, 'Mouse wouldn't let out a secret if you cut off his arm. He wouldn't tell anybody and neither would you, Chris. And I know you put her somewhere where nobody could have trailed her. So it had to be somethin' Sammy came upon.'

'I left a brochure under one of the table legs . . .'

'No. I found that,' I said. 'That's how I got to Faith in the first place. No one else saw it, and you killed those men came in on you.'

A crease appeared in Black's forehead. His light brown eyes shone like those of any man or animal surprised in leisure.

'She had a child,' he said. 'A boy.'

It bothered me that Faith hadn't told me about her child. I didn't know why.

'Where?' I asked.

'Child didn't tell this man Sammy where she was,' Raymond said reasonably. He wanted to get on the road to killing.

'Hope,' Christmas said. 'Hope Neverman. She lives in Pasadena.'

# CHAPTER 44

We took my car for the ride out to Pasadena. My heart was erratic; sometimes it was pounding and then it would skip a beat or two. My hands were sweating, and if you had asked me at any moment what I was thinking, I wouldn't have been able to tell you. Or I might just have given a list of names and relationships that had foundered at my feet. My mother, and Bonnie, Faith, and my first wife, who had run off with my friend Dupree.

'Easy, you know where this dude Sammy is at?' Mouse asked from the backseat.

I heard the question clearly. I had no idea where Sansoam was, but I couldn't speak.

I looked over at Christmas. He was staring out the window. I noticed then that there were rain clouds forming. They were far off, over the desert, but they'd be where we were in a few days.

'Easy?'

'Yeah, Ray?'

'You all right, man?'

'I want to drive all the way to the East Coast,' I said. 'And then when I get there, I could drive my car into the Atlantic.'

Christmas nodded solemnly, and I felt something squirm in my chest.

'I knew a dude got himself buried in his Caddy.' Mouse said jauntily. 'He weighed six hunnert pounds. There was five women cryin' at his grave too. Some men just lucky, is all.'

That's when I started to laugh. It was a good laugh, happy. Mouse lived in the world while everyone else tried to pretend that they were somewhere else. He smelled the shit that fertilized the rosebush. He accepted whatever it was that came his way and either put a good face on it or pulled out his gun.

'What color was that Caddy, Ray?' I asked.

'Pink.'

'Pink?' Christmas roared. 'Pink? That's not right. If you have to have a car for a coffin, it should be black.'

'What fo'?' Mouse asked.

'Pink is not a funerary color.'

'What color you need to be to drive into the sea?' Mouse asked.

'Dead,' I said, and we were quiet for most of the rest of the drive to Hope Neverman's home.

It was a big house the color of thin-sliced smoked Scottish salmon. It felt a little overpowering for three armed black men to converge on her front door. Christmas pressed the button, and church bells sounded in the distance.

The woman who answered was white, definitely Faith's sister. She was smaller, finer boned, a pretty version of Faith's beauty.

'Mr Black,' she said with hardly a tremor.

'I'm sorry to bother you, Hope, but my friends and I need to ask you some questions.'

'Come in. Come in.'

The house had to have been in a magazine somewhere. It was southwestern in style but very modern. To the left was a large library around on oval dining table. To the right there lay a sunken living room with a horseshoe-shaped sofa and dark highly polished wood floors. These rooms were divided by a stairway with no banisters that led up to floors two and three. The stairs rose until they stopped just under the roof.

The back wall was made of sliding glass doors. These led to the backyard and the Olympic-size pool where four children rollicked under the patient gaze of a young, dark-skinned Mexican nanny.

I couldn't help thinking about Leafa and all her brothers and sisters bunged up in that small house in South Central. It made no sense that both those homes existed in the same world.

Hope was wearing a powder blue one-piece dress made from rough cotton. Her flat shoes were the color of bone, and there was no makeup on her perfectly formed face. She wasn't yet thirty. She would never be her sister.

She led us to the library, and we all sat at one end of the dining table: an impromptu meeting of the board of some charity or corporation.

'Is something wrong, Mr Black?' the lesser sister asked.

'Faith told me that she would call me now and then to say that she was all right,' he said. 'She called me every other day until yesterday, when she should have called but didn't. I'm worried about it.'

There was sympathy in Christmas Black's mien, kindness to back up his lies.

'I don't understand,' Hope said. 'Where could she be?'

'Have you spoken to her?'

'Not since the day before yesterday.'

Black laced his powerful hands and placed them on the light ash tabletop.

'Has anybody been here asking about her?'

'Only Major Bryant.'

'Major?' Christmas said.

My heart sank like some far-off balloon dipping below the horizon line.

'Yes. He came here the day before yesterday. He said that they had received her letter and needed to speak to her about what to do about this terrible thing with Craig.'

'What did this Major Bryant look like?' I asked.

'This is Tyrell Samuels,' Christmas said by way of a belated introduction. 'He's been helping me lately.'

'Pleased to meet you, Mr Samuels.'

I nodded.

For a moment Hope was quiet, waiting for something else pleasant. When she realized that something wasn't coming, she said, 'He was young and tall, on the thin side.'

'Dark complexion?' I asked. 'Like he was from Sicily or Greece?'

'Yes. Do you know him?'

'We've met.'

'Did you tell him where Faith lived?' Christmas asked, trying his best not to lose his temper.

'She didn't tell me where she was exactly,' Hope replied. 'I only had a PO box.'

'Did you give the major her PO box?' Christmas asked.

'Of course not. I knew that Faith was in trouble. I wouldn't tell anyone.'

'Aunt Hope,' a boy shouted, 'Carmen won't let me have some ice cream.'

Even from a distance I could see that Andrew had his mother's beauty. When he grew up to be a sad man, he would be deadly handsome.

'You can't eat until after swimming,' Hope said. 'You know that.'

He came through the open door, drawn to the strangers in his aunt's home.

'Oh, yeah,' he said, staring at Christmas.

'Do you know my mama?' the three-year-old asked the ex-government killer.

'Yes,' he said. 'Very well.'

'Do you know where she is?'

'She's very sad, Andy. But pretty soon she'll be better and back with you again.'

I wondered if Christmas believed in God.

Andy didn't know how to respond to the words, the man, or his tone, and so he hunched his shoulders, ran out to the pool.

When the boy was gone, I asked, 'Do you keep a little phone diary?'

'Of course.' She was a woman of certainty.

'Is Faith's PO box in that book?'

'Yes.'

'Would you mind looking to make sure it's where you left it?' I asked.

'What are you saying?'

'Please,' Christmas said. 'Do as he asks.'

Hope didn't go far. There was a desk in the corner of the library. She opened it and took out a tiny red diary.

'See,' she said, 'it's here.'

'Look up your sister's PO box,' Christmas directed.

Hope turned the pages deftly, frowned a little, turned them again.

'I don't understand,' she said. 'The page is missing, torn out.'

She looked up at us.

'Is my sister all right?' she asked.

'I hope so,' Christmas said.

It came to me then that all great soldiers had to believe in a higher power.

# CHAPTER 45

'How we gonna hit Sammy?' Mouse asked from the back. He was sitting forward, both hands on the long seat, more like an excited child than a cold-blooded killer.

I didn't know what to say. Bunting had fooled me, his youthful bravado covering up the lies. He had pumped me for information while I dismissed him for a fool. I needed a superior officer at that moment.

'Let it go,' Christmas said.

I heard the words, understood their meaning, but I found myself trying to decipher exactly how they spelled death for Sammy Sansoam and his friends. Was Christmas planning to go it alone? Was he so enraged that he wanted to kill the whole squad the way he'd murdered everyone in Easter Dawn's little village?

'What you mean, Chris?' Mouse asked.

'I mean what I said. Let it go.'

'You mean you don't wanna kill him?' Mouse pressed.

Christmas didn't answer. Just looked ahead. He was wearing a cream-colored cowboy shirt with pocket flaps that snapped down. The flaps bore complex dark brown embroidery. His pants were brown, with sharp creases that he'd probably ironed that morning. He was a forever soldier – in uniform and under orders for life.

I glanced up into the rearview mirror to see Mouse with rare confusion on his face. He respected Christmas just as much as I did and was mystified by his refusal to seek revenge. They had killed two men together only days before. This was a war and now was the time for battle.

I wanted to understand too, but it wasn't going to be a simple equation. The tone in Black's voice, the set of his jaw, said that he wasn't going to give. This was his operation and now it was over. Mouse and I, as far as he was concerned, were short-term conscripts who had no say whatsoever.

He didn't know that Faith and I had become lovers, and my instincts told me that informing him would be a tactical error, maybe a fatal one.

*Let it go*, he'd said. Three words – the code sequence for a secret weapon or the go-ahead for an invasion. The term had a religious, even a psychological meaning for me. I could have been the acolyte of some warrior religion and Christmas my priest. I had come to him seeking balm for the rage inside me, and he had waved me away with the slightest gesture.

*Let it go*, he'd said. Bonnie and Faith and any other interruption in the war of life.

'You gonna tell me what you mean, let it go, Christmas Black?' Raymond asked.

If anything, the soldier's jaw set harder. The air in the car went still.

You could count the number of men on one hand that Mouse would allow to ignore him. Christmas took up two of those digits, one for resolve and the other for muscle. Raymond wasn't afraid of Black's prowess. He wasn't afraid of anything. But he knew that there would be no settlement without a treaty and Christmas was in no mood for a powwow.

I was driving the car, but at the same time I was a child again, running through the tall weeds of summer behind the chalky wings of cabbage butterflies. There was no greater pleasure when I was a boy than to be stealthy enough to catch the little creatures. One of the only strong memories I had of my mother was her explaining why catching them was wrong.

'Chile, when you catch 'em, you rub off the fairy dust, and they lose they magics an' dies,' she'd said in a voice whose tone I could no longer recall.

Even in the car forty-two years from that hot day, the tears welled in my eyes. My mother had been everything to me. Big, black, gentler than even the butterflies, she knew the sugars I liked and the colors I wanted; she made things better even before they went wrong.

I had been thinking about butterflies because I could tell that Christmas's three words indicated that he was in pain over the decision. His resolute silence underscored that suffering. I was thinking that I had to sneak up on him as I had on those bugs.

But my mother had used the same words.

'Look, Mama,' I had cried.

'Let it go, baby,' she had said.

It was a small step from my mother to Faith Laneer. Even though both of them would also have told me to let it go, this only served to negate the soldier's command.

'What about Faith?' I whispered.

Mouse's eyes in the mirror shifted from the passenger's side to me. He smiled.

Christmas looked at me too. It was the one question he could not ignore. That's not saying he had to answer. But the look was a capitulation in itself.

'They told me that I was going to be a general one day,' Christmas said in a thick tone. 'They said I'd be in the White House, whispering in the president's ear.'

I glanced in his direction and then back at the road.

He rolled down his window, and the stillness turned into a windstorm.

'I was trained as a soldier from the day I was born,' he continued. 'I was raised on strategy and starvation, generalship and hard labor. When I give a command, crackers and niggers jump. They don't ask me why and they don't question.'

I knew all that from the way Christmas walked, the way he stood erect.

I sniffed at the air, and he grunted in reply.

'You know why Germany lost the war?' he asked.

'Because they were fighting on two fronts,' I said.

'America was fighting on two fronts. And we had real enemies; the Japanese *and* the Germans.'

I'd never looked at it that way.

'No,' Christmas said. 'Germany lost because they fought for pride and not for logic.'

'What's that mean?' Mouse asked. He liked talking about war.

'Hitler believed in his mission above the materials and the men at hand. He didn't take into account the deficits of his own armies and therefore paid the price.'

'Hitler was crazy,' I said.

'War is crazy,' Christmas countered. 'If you're a general, you have to be insane. But that doesn't relieve you of the responsibility of your position. When you lose, you lose. That's all there is to it. If I send you and Raymond out to take a tower, but before you get there they blow the tower up, then you failed . . . we failed.'

'And Faith Laneer is the tower,' I said.

He did not reply.

'So she dies for nuthin'?'

'She died for what she believed in,' he said. 'She died being who she is.'

I knew then that they had been lovers some-where along the way. Maybe a week ago, maybe five years. For some reason this made me love her more. She had lived within the madness of Christmas Black.

'What about her son?' I asked.

'What about my daughter?' he replied.

# CHAPTER 46

We parked in an unpaved open lot on the outskirts of downtown. I switched the ignition off and pulled up the parking brake, but before opening the door I turned to address my deadly passengers.

'You men need to stay here and wait,' I said.

'What for, Ease?' Mouse asked, while Christmas just stared out the window.

'The cops want you dead, Ray.'

Reading the subtle emotional changes in my best friend's face was a lifelong study. His eyes could shift from pleasantries to murderous intent with barely a twitch. Right then a steeliness crept into his gray eyes and the corners of his mouth.

'What cops?'

'I don't know,' I lied, hoping that Mouse couldn't read me as well as I could him. 'Suggs told me about it. They think that because you murdered Perry your career should come to an end.'

'That don't mean I got to hide in no car.'

'Ray, hear me, man,' I said, softly and clear.

'I got it covered. I know what I'm doin'. Just stay in the car and do what I say for a few days and it'll blow over. You know Etta be mad if I let you get killed . . . again.'

It was the joke that clinched it.

On the day that JFK was assassinated, Raymond Alexander had agreed to accompany me on a minor errand. Things got out of control and Ray wound up shot, almost dead. Mama Jo brought him back to life with her Louisiana magics, and I promised myself that I would never again be the cause of his death.

'Okay, brah,' Mouse said. 'I'm tired anyway.'

'I'll be back in a minute.'

'Hello, Jewelle speaking.'

'Hey, honey. How's my family?' I said into the pay phone, thinking, wistfully wishing actually, that some five years before, I had married Jewelle and now I'd just be calling to say hi. That would have been a whole different life, but she'd be mine and we'd love each other and the children we'd no doubt have had. Jackson and Mofass would have been mad, but I'd be happy and Bonnie could do whatever she wanted to.

'What's wrong, Easy?' she asked.

Maybe the desire showed up in my voice.

'It's not easy bein' me,' I said.

She giggled and asked, 'Do you have a pen?'

I took out the yellow number two I used for notes and calculating bullet trajectories, and Jewelle rattled off an address on Crest King, a street that began and ended in Bel-Air.

'What's this?' I asked her.

'Our place is too small for your whole family, so I decided to put them in a house I own up there.'

'You own a house in Bel-Air?'

'Yeah. One'a Jean-Paul's friends owned it, but he needed some quick money, so I liquidated a few lots and paid him in cash. I figured that you or Mouse or Jackson would need it one day, and in the meantime I'd hold on to it 'cause you know the prices are bound to rise.'

'And what are the neighbors up there gonna think when they see a whole houseful of Mexicans, Vietnamese, and Negroes.'

'That's no problem, Mr Rawlins,' she said fetchingly. 'You'll see.'

Christmas was quiet the rest of the ride. He was a soldier in defeat. There was no revenge or retaliation that would relieve him. He'd been crushed by the enemy after having won every battle. No condemnation could be worse; no tribunal could recommend a stiffer punishment than what he already felt.

'How you find me, Easy?' Mouse asked as we cruised down Sunset Boulevard past the strip.

'I asked Pericles nicely.'

'How you find him?'

'I told his wife that I was hired by Etta to prove

312

you innocent,' I began. Ten minutes later we were at the address Jewelle had given me, and I was just finishing my tale.

Mouse was laughing about Jean-Paul and Pretty Smart, and Christmas languished in hell.

The address was on a big iron door in a great stone wall. You couldn't see over the barricade except for a few trees that towered on the other side.

I had to get out of the car to press the button on the intercom system.

''Allo?' Feather said with a put-on French accent.

'It's me, baby.'

'Daddy!' she yelled. 'Drive on up to the house.'

She must have activated some mechanism, because slowly the iron gate moved inward, revealing a curving asphalt road that wound through the arboretum used as a yard.

I got back in the car and drove. You couldn't even see the house until we'd taken three turns along the way. Then we could see the place in the distance.

One man's house is another man's mansion, I'm told. We were all the other men in my car driving up to that place. It was four stories, constructed from blond wood and thick glass. There was a stand of bushy pines around the place and a fountain in front. The fountain was a sculpture of naked women and men dancing in a circle around a gushing spout of water that could have been coming out of a great blue whale.

'Where are we?' Christmas asked.

'Hell if I know.'

The front door to the house was red with an alternating black and yellow frame. It was ten feet high at least and twice as wide as a normal door. It flew open as we were getting out of the car, and all my family and Christmas's family too came running toward us.

'Daddy!' shouted Feather and Easter Dawn.

After them came Jesus in swimming trunks and Benita with Essie in her arms. Between all those legs the little yellow dog came snarling and barking, the hair standing up on his back and his eyes actually glittering with hatred.

As I hugged my daughter, I took in my friends. Mouse shook hands with Jesus and congratulated him on his child. He tried to kiss Benita on the cheek, but she turned away. Christmas picked E.D. up over his head, almost threw her, and she laughed with hilarity that she had not shown in my presence.

'Daddy,' Feather said, leaning away, her fingers laced behind my neck, 'I'm so sorry.'

'About what?'

'About hurting you.'

I wanted to deny it. I wanted to say to her that I could not be hurt, that I was her father and beyond the pain and tears that are so important to children. I wanted to, but I could not. Because

I knew that if I tried to refute her claim, she would see the pain in my heart.

'Why don't you show me the house, baby,' I said.

# CHAPTER 47

'And this is the backyard,' Feather said with feigned nonchalance.

We had already seen what E.D. had dubbed the Big Room with its long, long table and rough-hewn, heavy oak chairs. We'd seen the library with its hundreds of books, the kitchen that had four stoves and a freestanding wood-burning oven, the roof garden, eight of the twelve bedrooms, including the master bedroom, and five or six other rooms whose purposes were not immediately apparent.

I was amazed along with my friends, but in my heart there was a war going on. I'd think of Bonnie, of walking with her from the house to the tree garden. The pain of that impossibility brought back to mind my name written thirty times by a woman who was killed as she was falling in love.

'Goddamn,' Mouse exclaimed. 'Will you look at that pool? It's like a goddamned lake.'

To accent Mouse's claim, Jesus ran forward and jumped in, followed by Feather even though she was wearing shorts and a T-shirt. The pool led to a lawn and the lawn ended at a cliff overlooking a valley. In the distance you could see the Pacific Ocean.

I wondered what kind of deal Jewelle had made to come up with a place like that. She was always looking around, buying up lots of land on the cheap in hopes of future projects. A lot that prevented the construction of a downtown skyseraper might have been worth this hidden mansion.

Easter took Christmas to her room to show him what it looked like. Benita went to the other side of the pool to watch her lover and his sister while at the same time avoiding any contact with Raymond.

'She hates me, huh, Easy?' Mouse said.

'Sure do.'

'Well . . . I guess she got good reason.'

We were sitting on a pink-and-gray marble bench that was anchored in the concrete. He was wearing a blue-and -purple Hawaiian shirt and white pants.

'You should go stay with Lynne Hua for a while, Ray.'

'Fuck that. Cops want me, they better be ready to lose a few'a they own.'

'Just two days, man,' I said.

'I thought you wanted me to help you kill this Sammy dude.'

'I do and you will.'

Ray grinned his friendliest and deadliest smile.

'You askin' me this for a favor?' he said.

'Yeah.'

'You been to see Lynne?'

The question threw me, but I didn't show it.

'Yeah. Lookin' for you.'

'That all?'

'Ray, how long you known me, man?'

He snorted and took out a cigarette.

I got up and wandered into the California dream house, looking for a phone.

'Hello,' she said quickly, expectantly on the first ring.

I froze. The paralysis started in my gut but traveled swiftly to my fingertips and tongue. I had every intention of speaking, of saying *hello* like any ordinary person would do. I wanted to say *hey*, but I couldn't even breathe.

'Hello?' Bonnie Shay asked again. 'Who's there?'

One of the reasons I couldn't speak was that my mind was ahead of my vocal cords. I was in the middle of telling her about Sammy Sansoam and poor Faith Laneer, but I had yet to open my mouth.

My heart throbbed rather than beat. It seemed to make a sound, a high-pitched chatter that reminded me of a winter's day in southern Louisiana five weeks after my mother had died.

It was after one of those rare Louisiana snowstorms in the early morning. A quarter inch of the fine powder covered the ground. A daddy longlegs spider was hobbling back and forth on a broad plain of white. As a child, I figured that he was probably looking for the summer again, that he thought he was lost and that there was solid ground and warm earth somewhere . . . if he could only find it.

My heart was that spider way back then.

'Easy?' Bonnie said softly.

I hung up.

Jesus was waiting for me outside the library. He had a keen sense about my feelings and a belief that he was the only one who could save me from myself.

'Jewelle told me to tell you that we could stay here as long as we wanted, Dad.'

'That's good,' I said. 'I need you up here for a while.'

'Did you talk to Bonnie?'

I looked at my son, proud of his talents and his gentle ways.

'No,' I said. 'Uh-uh. I was about to make a call to the police about somethin', but then I thought that maybe it wasn't such a good idea.'

When Christmas told Easter Dawn that it was time to go, she broke down crying. She didn't want to leave her new room or her sister, Feather. I told the disgraced soldier that we had the house for as long as we wanted and that I'd like him to stay around to make sure that my family and his were safe.

'You don't have a house now anyway, do ya?' I asked him.

'No,' he said, his head bowed down.

'Then stay, man. I got E.D. enrolled in a school. She needs other kids. She needs a life.'

The sour twist of Black's lips was the taste of bile and blood, I'm sure. He was thinking about breaking my neck. I knew this from my own impression and also because Mouse raised his head to regard us.

Easter Dawn was all that Christmas had left. He wanted to take her and crawl into a hole somewhere to heal. And there I was, the first-ever impediment between him and his daughter. My life, my home, my children called to her. Christmas wanted to silence that song.

But he was a good man beneath all the insanity. He loved his daughter and wanted what was right for her. In the car he had dismissed me as a subordinate, but that was over now. I was an equal in an unfair world.

After a few long good-byes I drove Ray to Lynne Hua's apartment. He slapped my shoulder and winked at me before getting out.

'You got to take it easy, Easy,' he told me. 'You gettin' all worked up, man. I mean, I got people out there plannin' to kill me an' I ain't as upset as you.'

'I got it covered, Ray. Just a few more steps and I'm home free.'

I stopped on La Brea in the early evening, went into a phone booth, and dropped two nickels.

320

I dialed a number I knew by heart and wrapped a handkerchief around the mouthpiece.

'Seventy-sixth Street Precinct,' a woman told me.

'Captain Rauchford,' I said in a deep voice with a growl inside it.

Without reply, she plugged me into the switchboard. A phone rang one time before a man answered, 'Rauchford.'

'I hear you lookin' for Ray Alexander.'

'Who is this?'

'Don't you worry about who this is, just listen up,' I said in a voice I heard in my mind sometimes. 'Mouse outta town right now, but he be back with his boys in a day or two.'

'Where?'

'I don't know yet, but I will know because that mothahfuckah fuckin' my woman,' I said with real feeling, too much feeling. 'She gonna run to him the minute he's in town.'

'Tell me your name,' the white man commanded.

'My name ain't got nuthin' to do with it.'

'This call has been traced. I know where you live.'

Just about then an ambulance raced by, its siren crying.

'I'll call you tomorrow, late morning or noon, and give you the knowledge.'

# CHAPTER 48

'Hello,' Jewelle said, answering her home phone.

'Hey, honey.'

'Oh, hi, Easy. How'd you like the house?'

'House? Oh, you mean Buckingham Palace?'

Jewelle giggled. 'It's nice, huh?'

'Yeah, it's nice. I won't even ask you how you got it.'

'You and your family can stay there as long as you want, Easy.'

'You don't have to do all that, baby. A month or so do us fine.'

'A month, a year, five years,' she said. 'As long as you want it.'

I realized then why Jewelle and I could never have been lovers. The majority of our relationship was a dialogue that occurred between the lines. She was thanking me for helping her when she was in trouble and in love, for not judging her when she fell for Jackson but stayed with Mofass. Jewelle and I were like the symbiotic creatures I sometimes read about in nature magazines, like the hippopotamus and the birds that picked its teeth, or the ants that herded aphids in the South American rain forest. We were not the same species, but our fates were entwined all the way down to the instinct.

'That house over on Hooper and Sixty-fourth still vacant?' I asked.

'Uh-huh. Why?'

'You gonna build there, right?'

'Lot's so big they tell me we could put in sixteen units. Why?'

'I'll talk to you later, baby. Shout at Jackson for me, will ya?'

Jewelle didn't question me any more than a heron questions the wind.

I hung up the phone and turned on the motel TV. The Million-Dollar Movie was playing on channel nine. That night they were featuring *The Seventh Seal*. At first I just had it on, but after a few minutes the stark black-and-white film entranced me. Death walked as a man among men, and we fell like leaves, like dust, around him. The Knight struggled against the Specter, each one winning even as he lost. I was deeply moved by the severe performances and the truths they told. When the film was over, I realized that I had a sour taste in my mouth. This reminded me that I had fallen off the wagon not twenty-four hours before. But I didn't want a drink; I didn't need one. I laughed to myself: all those years I'd avoided alcohol when I could have used moderation.

I was a fool.

★   ★   ★

In the morning I shaved, showered, and ironed my clothes before dressing. Across the street on Centinela there was a coffee shop that served freshly made doughnuts. I drank and smoked, read the paper, and flirted with the young waitress from seven to nine.

Her name was Belinda and she was nineteen years old.

'So what you do for a livin', Mr Rawlins?' she asked after half an hour of my asking questions about her life.

'Just about what you see me doin' right now,' I said.

Belinda had a big butt and a plain face, but when she smiled I couldn't help but join her.

'You mean you drink coffee for a livin'? Sign me up for that job.'

'I'm a detective,' I said, handing her my business card. 'Most of my investigations have me sitting in restaurants, cars, and motel rooms, watchin' people and tryin' to hear through walls.'

'You the only one in here, Mr Rawlins,' Belinda said to me. 'Everybody else jes' buy they coffee and go on. Are you investigatin' me?'

'I sure am lookin' at you,' I said. 'And you look good too. But right now I'm doin' the biggest job that a detective has.'

'What's that?' she asked, leaning across the counter, peering into my eyes.

'Waiting for all the pieces to fall into place.'

'What pieces?'

'On a chessboard, they call 'em men.'

It was an innocuous enough statement, but Belinda caught the hint of evil that it gave off. She frowned a moment but did not move away. The trouble I represented was just what she was looking for. Her mouth opened ever so slightly, saying without words that she was willing to jump over that counter and run off with me, that even though I was an old man, I had the leisure to sit with her and the goodwill to tell her that she was lovely. It doesn't take much when you're nineteen and it doesn't take long. The trouble is that it doesn't last long either.

'Why don't you write down your phone number for me, girl?'

'Why I wanna do that?' she said, not wanting to seem easy.

'You don't want it.' I said. 'I do. You must have every young man in the neighborhood ringin' your bell. I just like talkin' to you.'

Her brows knitted as she tried to find some insult or trap in my words. When nothing came to mind, she shrugged and wrote her number on the back of my check and handed it to me.

'You can pay for the coffee some other time,' she said, and the balance of power between us shifted. I had been flirting before, but now she had a hold on me. I wanted to call her, to see her, to show her the valley behind my Bel-Air home.

Our fingers touched as she handed me the

check. I took her hand and kissed those fingers twice.

I left with no intention of ever speaking to Belinda again.

# CHAPTER 49

I drove down to the Sears, Roebuck and Company department store in East LA and bought a high-powered $CO_2$ BB gun with three cartridges and a tube full of 6 mm shot. Then I drove down to Hooper and Sixty-fourth Street. Toward the corner of Sixty-fourth was a house that had gone vacant after the riots. It was a very small house on a huge lot. Maybe that's why the windows weren't broken, because you'd have to stand out in plain sight to lob a rock through the panes.

It had once been a bright yellow home, but the paint had worn away to gray mostly. There were only patches of color here and there. The lawn was both overgrown and dead.

There was a padlock on the front door. I pried that off and went inside. The house was empty, stripped bare. There wasn't a stick of furniture or any carpeting, not one painting or even any lightbulbs. No one had been living there for some time.

The backyard was just as dead and empty as the front. There had been a garage in the far corner of the property, but it had collapsed on itself and was now just a jagged pile of timbers.

It was the perfect domicile for my purposes.

Across the street was another abandoned structure. This was a three-story tenement that had been condemned by the city. The opposite of the house I'd just visited, this building took up the whole lot. Behind it I found a dark concrete lane that led to an alley.

After all that research, I parked my car in the alley, made my way to the back door of the tenement, broke in, and climbed up to the tar-paper roof. It was dirty up there, littered with beer cans and empty condom foils. This was a nighttime recreation area for girls who shared a bedroom in their parents' houses and young newlyweds off with their spouses' friends because they realized too late that they had made a mistake.

I went to the front ledge of the building that looked down upon Jewelle's real-estate investment. There I assembled my air gun and loaded in a $CO_2$ cartridge. I shot a tin vent with a large lead bead. The concussion knocked the metal cylinder out of its moorings.

I put the air gun back in its case, pulled up the tar paper at the ledge, and placed the case underneath, there to wait for things to fall into place.

Half a block away, I stopped at a phone booth. I had three dimes in my pocket and I promised myself that before the day was done, I would have dropped them all.

I dialed the first number from a card in my wallet.

'Hello,' a man's voice answered.

Curses rose to my lips, but I kept them down. Spite and hate and rage bubbled in my gut, but my voice was even. I wanted to use that calm tone to tell him what he was, but instead I said, 'Colonel?'

'Who is this?'

'Easy Rawlins.'

'Mr Rawlins. What can I do for you?'

'Colonel, I wasn't completely honest with you when we met at my office.'

'No? What else do you know?'

'I, uh, I met with a woman named Laneer. She was married to Craig Laneer.'

'Yes?'

'Faith gave me a copy of the letter you say that Craig sent to you, only this letter here gives the proof that Sammy Sansoam and them were smuggling drugs.'

The silence on Bunting's side of the line was delicious.

'I need to see that letter, Mr Rawlins.'

'Oh, yeah,' I said. 'I know you do.'

'Can you bring it to me?'

'No. No, sir. I'm scared. I've been tryin' to call Faith, but she doesn't answer. You know I think somethin' might'a happened to her.'

'I need that information, Mr Rawlins.'

'I could send it to you,' I said.

'No. Bring it to me today. We have to move on this quickly. There's no time to wait for the post office.'

It was my turn to be silent.

'Mr Rawlins,' Bunting said.

'Is there some kinda reward for this if I give it to you?'

'If the letter leads to an indictment, we can pay maybe five hundred,' he said.

'Dollars?'

'Yeah.'

'I know this house over near Sixty-fourth and Hooper.' I gave him the address while checking my watch for the time. It was 11:17 in the morning. 'Meet me there at four. I can get there by then.'

He made sure of the address and then told me to be there or he'd have the police put out a warrant for my arrest.

'I'll be there,' I said. 'I sure will.'

I went back to my roof perch after that. While waiting, I thought about Bonnie in a distant, almost nostalgic way. So much had happened that I could hardly feel the broken heart. Bonnie would have understood what I was doing. She didn't believe in sitting still when a crime had been committed. In some ways she was like Christmas.

At 12:11, Sammy Sansoam and Timothy Bunting pulled up in front of the abandoned house.

Sammy slipped through the gate and went around the back while Tim loitered on the sidewalk for a minute or two. Then the colonel, or ex-colonel or whatever he was, wandered toward the front door. By the time he'd gotten there, Sammy appeared. They looked around and then disappeared into the house.

'Melvin Suggs.' He answered on the first ring.
   'Hey.'
   'Easy? What you got for me?'
   'I got it on very good sources that somebody saw Pericles Tarr in the flesh. He's holed up with a girl named Pretty Smart.'
   'Where?'

'Captain Rauchford.'
   'He here. Right ovah there on Hooper an' Sixty-four,' a deep voice from somewhere inside me rumbled. 'It's the little house on the big empty lot. They's six of 'em in there. I heard my girl-friend talkin' to 'em on the line.'
   'Who is this?' Rauchford asked, and I hung up the phone in his ear.

The biggest mistakes run smooth and sure. The German army cut through Russia like a hot bayonet into a vat of butter. But they drowned in their own oily excrement.
   I was having these thoughts when the first of the police cars arrived out there in front of Jewelle's

investment. Twenty cops deployed themselves while I aimed my gun. A crowd of bystanders was forming, but none of them were in the line of fire.

I pulled the trigger. The silent shot fired over the heads of the police. I had been a marksman during the war. I was sure that I'd hit the windowpane. I shot again and again, but nothing happened.

Captain Rauchford was preparing to use a megaphone to warn Mouse and his cohorts. The policemen had their rifles at the ready.

I fired again, and the front window of the small house shattered.

That was all Rauchford's men needed. They opened fire. The bystanders reacted quickly, men ducking low and women screaming. Smoke began to rise from the phalanx of executioners. Children froze, watching while the policemen fired their weapons. They kept on shooting until the walls looked like a colander, until those same walls caved in and the roof collapsed, until the gas main was struck and flames leaped up from the ruins.

For five minutes, the policemen fired and reloaded, fired and reloaded again.

After Rauchford gave the cease-fire, I walked on my belly to the trapdoor and carried my air gun down the stairs and through the dark pathway to my car. I drove away without looking back. I wasn't happy for the deaths I'd conjured, but I wasn't feeling sad either.

When I got to my motel room, I called Lynne Hua's apartment.

'Hello.'

'It's Easy, Lynne.'

'What happened?'

'Nothing, why?'

'Your voice,' she said. 'You sound like a dead man.'

'Let me talk to Mouse.'

'Hey, Ease,' Mouse said a moment later. 'You wanna go take care'a that business now?'

'You already did,' I said.

'What?'

'Somebody told the cops you were at a house on Sixty-fourth. They findin' out right now that it was those soldiers instead. Turn on the news. You'll see.'

# CHAPTER 50

After murdering two men I went up to the farmers' market on Third and Fairfax and bought a basket of extrafancy strawberries and got three bottles of champagne and a pint of cognac from Stallion Liquors on Pico. I wasn't feeling a thing, nor was I worried, anxious, or guilt ridden. I knew what I had done, but the reality was like a dream to me.

I went to my house on Genesee after shopping and made a phone call.

'Hello,' Tourmaline Goss answered.

'Can I take you to dinner tonight?'

We ate at a little French place on Pico near Robertson, where they called chicken *poulet* and bread *pain*. Tourmaline had my full attention.

'Were you really burgling a woman's house when you were on the phone with me?' she asked.

This reminded me of Belinda, of how some women were drawn to danger.

'Yeah,' I said. 'But I don't think she'll mind.'

'Why not?'

I told her about Jean-Paul Villard and how I had

come upon Pericles Tarr looking for Mouse, and how the police were searching for Mouse when they attacked the house down in South Central.

'That was the man they were looking for in that shoot-out today?' she asked.

'Yeah.'

'You mean the police shot up that place lookin' for somebody who wasn't even there? They killed two innocent men, veterans, when they just heard that he was in a house down in South Central?'

'Yeah,' I said, the surprise in my voice half real.

'Yeah,' Tourmaline said angrily. 'Cops shoot up a house, kill two innocent men, but it's all okay because it's a colored neighborhood, and one of the men was black, so the other one shouldn't have been there anyway.'

'Can I come in awhile?' I asked as I pulled up the handle on the parking brake.

Her smile was demure, the assent implied.

I took the iced champagne and box of fruit from under a blanket in the backseat and followed her. When we arrived at her door, she put out a hand behind her and I reached out to take that hand.

I popped a cork and poured our champagne into jelly-jar glasses.

'I thought you didn't drink?' she asked after our fourth or fifth toast and kiss.

'I didn't back then.'

'Back then? It was just a couple'a days ago.'

'For you, maybe.'

335

My hands felt as if they were made for her breasts, my lips and tongue for her sex.

'I want you to do everything to me,' she said when she was naked on my lap and I was still fully dressed.

I did everything I knew how, and when I was unsure, she showed me and guided me and called out to gods who were murdered on slave ships long before our parents' parents' parents were born.

I couldn't stop myself. Sex came from me like blood from a wound. The champagne stoked the fires while Tourmaline stroked my heart. I was on top of her on the couch, listening to Otis Redding and making love like a movie star. I could feel a halo around my head while looking deeply into her eyes.

'Don't stop, baby,' she whispered. 'Don't ever stop.'

That was the moment that decided everything for the rest of my life.

I had been with Tourmaline completely. I was only with her, only wanted her, was ready to marry her and make a new family. There was nothing outside of that room.

But when she looked up at me, asking me to keep on going, I knew in my heart that I could not. It was as if I had inside me a glass ampoule that held the soul apart and separate from my body. Her words made me clench, and the glass shattered like the window in Jewelle's house. I made that same sound I had with Feather, and I rose up both erect and flaccid.

'Easy?' Tourmaline said.

I wanted to answer her, but I could not.

I had gone out that evening dressed to the nines. I had worn my dark green suit, spit-polished black leather shoes, a yellow shirt, and a burgundy, blue, and green tie made from an antique kimono.

I left out of her front door in only pants and a T-shirt. I wasn't even wearing socks or shoes.

Tourmaline called after me, but I stalked off like Frankenstein's monster.

'Easy. Easy Rawlins,' she cried.

But I didn't even recognize my name.

At Royal Crest and Olympic, I stopped at a phone booth and dialed. The phone rang a dozen times, and finally she answered.

'Hello?'

'Can I come over for a minute?'

*No* was hovering in the air as she considered.

'Where are you?'

'Around the corner.'

Her house was only half a block from the phone booth, but I drove there, right up into her driveway. She was at the door, as beautiful as ever, her dark blue nightgown more like royal robes.

'Where are your shoes, Easy?'

'Lost them on my way here.'

'Have you been drinking,' she asked after pecking my lips with hers.

'Joguye here?'

'No. He's in Paris. There was a coup. His parents were killed. He's in exile working to overthrow the junta.'

'Oh.'

'Come in, Easy. Come in.'

The living room was filled with African art of all kinds: paintings, sculptures, textiles, and even furniture. The colors were dark or bright, not synthetic pastel America at all. We sat on a wooden couch that had two long feather-filled pillows for cushions.

'It's been a long time,' Bonnie said.

'It feels like forever.'

'Why are you here, Easy?' she asked.

I began talking.

I started with Chevette Johnson and how I had almost murdered her porcine pimp. I told her about Mouse and Jackson and Jean-Paul. I told her about making love to Faith and then finding her dead, about the murders I'd committed using the police as my weapon. I told her about Tourmaline.

I didn't leave anything out. Somewhere along the way she took my hands in hers. She was there with me, feeling me.

'I know I was wrong,' I said. 'I know what happened happened and that you didn't mean to hurt me like I did you. I been a child and a fool and I ask you to forgive me.'

Tears welled in Bonnie's eyes as she nodded, granting me clemency.

'I love you, Bonnie.'

'I love you too, Easy.'

'When I tell you all this stuff been happening, that's just the husk, the skin a snake shucks off. But inside, you have been on my mind every minute. When I went up to the house in Bel-Air, I thought about you. When I found that dead man bunged up in a box, I turned away and thought about you. I'm not jealous anymore and I'm not proud. But please, baby, please . . . come back to me.'

Bonnie stared into me, seeing more than anyone, after my mother, ever had. She smiled and looked down and then up again with resolve.

'It's too late,' she whispered.

It didn't surprise me. I knew what she would say before I got there. I knew Bonnie. Even if I was the love of her life, she had made a promise to a man who never wavered in his feelings for her. She had pledged to him her love and a family, a future.

When she let my hands go, I rose like a half-filled helium balloon.

'I just needed to hear it,' I said.

'Sit down, Easy.'

'No, baby. We finished here. You know it and now I do too.'

'You shouldn't drive in your condition.'

'I fought a war in this condition.'

She stood up to me.

'Stay.'

'To some men that might sound like a proposition,' I said.

'You're not some men,' she said. 'You're Easy Rawlins.'

I smiled and cupped her chin with my left hand.

'You were the woman of my life,' I said. 'And I threw you away like a fool.'

It was easy after that to walk out barefoot and half dressed. The night air was invigorating, and I had faced my worst demon and lost with dignity.

# CHAPTER 51

I followed Pico down to the ocean, made a series of turns, and wound up traveling north on the Pacific Coast Highway. I was cruising in my car with the windows all open and a cigarette between my fingers. I didn't know what time it was exactly, but midnight was behind me and morning was far, far away. I'd cracked the pint of cognac and placed it between my legs. Now and then I'd take a hit, toasting dead men and women whom I'd known and lost over the decades.

There wasn't much traffic, so I was feeling free. At first I was going the prescribed limit, 50 MPH, but the speedometer kept advancing as I began more and more to leave the pain behind.

I had thirty-seven dollars and a hundred-dollar bill in my pocket, no shoes or proper shirt, and the radio played songs that sounded happy even when they were about a broken heart.

I didn't know where I was going. I needed shoes and a jacket of some sort. I'd need more cigarettes and another bottle before long. But right then, three-quarters down the pint and with eight cigarettes left, I was in a state of grace, making my way up the coast, rolling toward tomorrow.

It tickled me that the only reason I knew the ocean was out there to my left was because of the darkness, the primordial dark that had caused my kind to stop and reflect for millions of years. I laughed at the huge void.

Twenty miles or so past Malibu, a station wagon was taking its time on a steep rise. I swung around that automobile with pinpoint control. This made me laugh, made me feel strong.

Bunting and Sansoam were dead, but I didn't feel bad about their passing. I didn't feel guilt. The cops were in the wrong, but I wasn't. Those men had run a murdering streak from Vietnam to California and they wouldn't have stopped with Faith Laneer. They'd have come after me soon enough, not knowing what I might have against them.

I had a lot of living to make up for after a year of moping around because of Bonnie.

The scatter of stars over the lightless ocean called to me on the high rise up the side of the coastal mountain.

Bonnie had to turn me away. She had to marry Joguye. Africa and the Caribbean were closer to each other than American could ever be to either. He was a king and I was a bum. And tonight I would drive so far away that no one could find me to tell me if anything had changed.

My children were safe and living in a mansion.

I wasn't there to watch over them, but they had Jesus. Jesus – the boy who had always been the better man.

I lit a cigarette, took a hit off my cognac bottle, and made up my mind to call my little tribe at daybreak. They deserved to know where I was.

I wouldn't give them a number to call me because if they knew the number, every time the phone rang I'd wonder if they'd given it to Bonnie.

A big sixteen-wheeler was having trouble with the rise. I moved out a little to make sure there was no one coming and then hit the gas. I had just about cleared the cab when I saw the head-lights of an oncoming car.

That was no problem. There was a shoulder to the left. I widened the arc of my turn and tapped the brake to slow down. I had no idea that the shoulder would thin out and then fade away. I jammed down on the brakes, but by that time the wheels were no longer on solid ground. The engine stalled out, and the wind through the windows was a woman howling for help that would never come.

'No,' I said, remembering all the times I had almost died at the hands of others: German soldiers, American soldiers, drunkards, crooks, and women who wanted me in the grave.

The back of my car hit something hard, a boulder, no doubt. Something clenched down on my left foot, and pain lanced up my leg. I ignored this, though, realizing that in a few seconds I'd be dead.

Quickly I tried to come up with the image I needed to see before I died. My mind reached toward the top of the cliff. I was grasping for Bonnie, Faith, and my mother. But none of them was around for my last seconds.

The front of the car hit something, making a loud bang and a wrenching metal sound. Chevette Johnson rushed into my mind then. She was sleeping on my new couch, safe from an evil world.

I think I smiled, and then the world went black.